Also by Katherine Ashenburg

Fiction
Her Turn
Sofie & Cecilia

Non-Fiction
The Mourner's Dance: What We Do When People Die
The Dirt on Clean: An Unsanitized History

MARGARET'S NEW LOOK

MARGARET'S NEW LOOK

KATHERINE ASHENBURG

ALFRED A. KNOPF CANADA

PUBLISHED BY ALFRED A. KNOPF CANADA

Copyright © 2025 Katherine Ashenburg

All rights reserved. No part of this book may be reproduced, scanned, transmitted, or distributed in any form or by any electronic or mechanical means, including information storage and retrieval systems, without permission in writing from the publisher, except by a reviewer, who may quote brief passages in a review. No part of this book may be used or reproduced in any manner for the purpose of training artificial intelligence technologies or systems.

Published in 2025 by Alfred A. Knopf Canada, a division of Penguin Random House Canada Limited, Toronto.

Knopf Canada, an imprint of Penguin Random House Canada
320 Front Street West, Suite 1400
Toronto, Ontario, M5V 3B6, Canada

penguinrandomhouse.ca

Knopf Canada and colophon are registered trademarks of Penguin Random House LLC.

The authorized representative in the EU for product safety and compliance is Penguin Random House Ireland, Morrison Chambers, 32 Nassau Street, Dublin D02 YH68, Ireland. https://eu-contact.penguin.ie

Library and Archives Canada Cataloguing in Publication

Title: Margaret's new look / Katherine Ashenburg.
Names: Ashenburg, Katherine, author
Identifiers: Canadiana (print) 2024042008X | Canadiana (ebook) 20240420292 | ISBN 9781039056480 (hardcover) | ISBN 9781039056497 (EPUB)
Subjects: LCGFT: Novels.
Classification: LCC PS8601.S435 M37 2025 | DDC C813/.6—dc23

Text design: Kelly Hill
Cover design: Kelly Hill
Image credits: Cover images: (forefront figure) anastasy_helter/Adobe Stock; (background figure) CSA Images/Getty; Interior images: (Mannequin Stand) Atlas Illustrations, (Woman *Zémire*) koshkina, (Houndstooth Pattern, *Miss Dior*) Kirsty Pargeter, (Woman *Londres*) kordiush, (Woman *Audacieuse*) lynea; all Adobe Stock. (Woman *Bar*), (Woman *Pondichéry*) both CSA / Getty Images

Typeset in Dutch766 by Sean Tai
Printed in the United States of America

1st Printing

For my sisters and brothers
Buzz
Beth
Caroline
Bob

CONTENTS

ONE	A Scarf with Staffordshire Dogs	1
	Zemire	14
TWO	Red Silk for Cocktails	16
THREE	Wedding Party with Vogue Patterns	27
	Pondichéry	35
FOUR	The *Pondichéry* Jacket	37
FIVE	Doc Martens Mary Janes	50
SIX	Bat Mitzvah by Dior	66
	Londres	77

SEVEN	A Snakeskin Belt	78
	Miss Dior	88
EIGHT	Miss Dior	90
NINE	A Corsage with Stars of David	100
TEN	Eleven Bones, Fourteen Hooks and Eyes, Horsehair and Net	122
	Audacieuse	133
ELEVEN	Half a Dress	135
TWELVE	A Handful of Brass Buttons	142
THIRTEEN	Black Silk in a Bentwood Box	151
FOURTEEN	A Long White Baby Dress	166
	Bar	176
FIFTEEN	A Peplum Jacket and Miles of Pleats	178
SIXTEEN	A Deco Bar Pin	186
SEVENTEEN	Twenty-Six Steel Bones	200
EIGHTEEN	Red Silk for Cocktails Once More	214
	A Pink Hat with a Slouchy Brim	231
NINETEEN	The Killing of a Hat Maker	232
TWENTY	A Patchwork Coat	243
TWENTY-ONE	Encore: A Scarf, a Brooch, a Handkerchief, a Corsage and a Beret	257
TWENTY-TWO	Margaret's New Look	276

ONE

A Scarf with Staffordshire Dogs

Wearing latex gloves and a lab coat, Margaret Abrams unfurled a greenish-gold dress on the table in front of her. Silk and collarless, with covered buttons above the belt and a mass of unpressed pleats below, it was apparently simple and undeniably beautiful.

"This model is called *Columbine*," she told her audience, "a recent bequest. From Dior's second collection, in autumn 1947. Our job now is to make it exhibitable. For a seventy-year-old dress, it's not in bad condition—it has a few splits, as we call tears. And, no surprise, the usual case of pit-rot."

As she separated a sleeve from the body to show a greenish corrosion on the underarm, the mostly female crowd tittered, enjoyably shocked by the conjunction of something so vulgar as sweat with a sublime example of haute couture.

When it was empty, the textile storage hall in the Harkness Museum of Arts and Sciences was forbiddingly clinical. With its long banks of pale-grey drawers and cupboards, it resembled a dispensary or a place to store surgical implements. In reality, the metal drawers held knits and accessories, while ball dresses and tailored clothes hung on padded hangers in the cupboards.

Today the austere room was full of Rochester money. Margaret was giving a behind-the-scenes presentation to people who had donated more than $50,000 to the museum in the past year and shown an interest in the Fashion and Textiles department. This happened a few times a year, but today's event had a special point. The museum's collection of couture, and especially Christian Dior couture, was renowned, and Margaret was mounting an exhibition that centred on Dior's New Look collection of 1947. It was the most ambitious—and expensive—show of her tenure as Senior Curator, Fashion and Textiles, and she needed financial support.

So she played to the crowd of about twenty-five, chummy but not too chummy. In her mid-forties, she was a decade or two younger than most of her audience. She flattered them with technical or semi-technical terms like *exhibitable* and *splits*. (She wondered if *pit-rot* could be considered a technical term.) Normally Margaret did wear latex gloves when touching vintage textiles, but the lab coat was an affectation for the donors' benefit: conservators wore lab coats, not curators. Taking their questions seriously, she tried to work in a reference to the upcoming exhibition whenever possible.

A woman wearing what looked like a Dries Van Noten jacket asked, "Why did you say 'the usual' about the underarm deterioration in the silk dress?"

"It's one of the sad facts of life, isn't it, that when you're wearing your best silk, you're very likely to sweat. In the case of this particular dress, the problem springs from an unholy combination of deodorant, perspiration, the silk itself and some oxidation in the metallic threads in the fabric." (Belatedly, she hoped that no one in this close-knit crowd recognized the dress as belonging to the late Helen Steppings. She was being indiscreet.)

The woman asked, "Will you be able to fix it?"

Margaret smiled sadly, taking them into her confidence. "Probably not. We can sew up the splits in the skirt with fine hair silk, but I'm not optimistic about the pit-rot. What we can do is design a mount that won't show the underarms."

The presentation was to end at noon, and by twelve thirty the last of the stragglers had left, with many thanks and expressions of interest in the coming exhibition. Hosting an event like this was far from Margaret's favourite part of her job, but she couldn't afford to ignore any fundraising possibility for the Dior exhibition. So she reached down to excavate an extroverted side of herself that was usually unavailable, and she performed. Behind the performance was something that never went away—the joy she felt at Dior's swirl of a skirt, the set of a collar or the embroidered buds scattered over a ball gown.

Returning to her office, she was waylaid by the overworked secretary for Fashion and Textiles, Greek and Roman, Europe, South Asia (and just about every other department in the Art and Culture side of the museum). "Gareth would like to see you when you have a chance."

Gareth Wong was Vice President, Art and Culture, and constitutionally averse to texting or even emailing. No doubt he would prefer the extinct system of pneumatic mail where messages flew through pressurized air tubes around the tops of walls in department stores and offices. Slightly cross and very hungry, she left the crowded corridors of Fashion and made her way across cul-de-sacs, detours, passages and stairs in the backstage warren of offices and labs.

Margaret was a tall redhead who bumped into things—not because her limbs were too long to be controlled, but because she was often thinking about something other than the tables, chairs and people standing between her and her destination. She was absent-minded, except when she focused. Her husband did the cooking, since she tended to forget the key ingredient in a recipe. But she baked well, because she had a sweet tooth. Now, on the way to Gareth's office, fretting about the rising costs of the exhibit, she had a few gentle collisions with coat racks and recycling bins.

She stopped at Gareth's open door. "You wanted to see me?"

"Yes, Margaret. Come in. I have a surprise for you."

She felt an inquiring expression was called for, so she put one on while she took a seat. Gareth was genial, and a surprise sounded pleasant. Later, when she looked back on this moment, she reflected that their innocence was almost touching.

"Someone has sent us something, and I thought we should open it together."

"Sent *us* something?"

"Here it is."

The flat, square package he put on the desk was indeed addressed to Gareth Wong and Margaret Abrams, with no return address.

"Do you think it's a very thin bomb, or maybe anthrax?"

She was joking, but he said, "Security has had a look."

Trust Gareth.

Security had returned the contents to the brown paper wrapping and taped it back together loosely. Sandwiched between two squares of cardboard was a silky scarf with a sentimental pattern of hearts, flowers, hot-air balloons and pairs of dogs. A flower-framed oval in the centre pictured two hands clasping under the word *Love*. A note pinned to the scarf said, in neat printing, "Something you will want to consider."

Gareth made a move to touch the scarf, but Margaret said, "Don't." Automatically, she reached in her pocket for her gloves.

"Why?" Gareth asked. "It's just a cheap scarf."

"It's old," she said. "Maybe mid-twentieth century. Probably synthetic, maybe one of the new materials developed in the forties and fifties. I'll ask one of the conservators to check it out."

"But what does it mean? Why would we want to 'consider' it?"

"I have no idea," Margaret said, running her gloved fingers over the hot-air balloons and nosegays. "The Staffordshire dogs are less predictable than the other lovey-dovey pictures, but I suppose they read as 'cozy.'"

"What are Staffordshire dogs?"

Before his ascension to the vice-presidency, Gareth had been a curator in Archaeology of the Americas, so his ignorance of nineteenth-century English pottery was forgivable.

Pointing to the two King Charles spaniels, she said, "Cheap ceramic dogs, often mirror images like these two, decorated more humble Victorian mantelpieces than you could imagine. Named for the West Midlands area where they were made."

"So the scarf is English?"

"I don't know. The conservator might have an idea."

"But why the two of us?" Gareth asked.

"Well, it's a textile," Margaret said, "so that could be me. And you're my boss—is that enough?"

They agreed it was a weak link. And more important, they couldn't imagine what it was they should be considering.

She gathered the parcel up, wrapping paper and all. "Probably just some crackpot. I'll let you know what the conservator thinks."

Gareth looked uncertain. "Even for crackpots, this is a very weird one," he said.

Margaret bought a sandwich in the cafeteria, resisted a saucer-sized molasses cookie and dropped the scarf off at Conservation with a note of explanation. In her office, she read an email from a journalist at *The New York Times* whose name she did not recognize, asking if she could answer a few questions about the New Look exhibit. That was odd, as the May opening was four months away. Looking on the bright side, maybe this indicated an unusual level of interest for a fashion exhibition.

She called the journalist's number, and he went straight to the point.

"I'm wondering what your plans are for the collaborationist angle in your exhibition."

Luckily, she had the presence of mind to bite back "What collaborationist angle?" just before it left her mouth. There was a sizable overlap between the museum's members and *Times* subscribers, and she needed to be careful.

"Exactly what angle are you referring to?"

"Lucien Lelong, naturally. In addition to being a mentor when Dior worked in Lelong's salon during the German occupation, I don't have to tell you that he was the head of the couture association. In that role, he was responsible for all kinds of economic collaboration with the Nazis from 1940 to '44. I wondered how you are planning to handle that?"

Margaret took a deep breath. "Well, congratulations on your research so far in advance of the exhibit. As for Lelong, people in his position had no choice but to co-operate with the Germans. When it was enthusiastic or the French side profited too much, this was seen as collaboration, but the difference between coercion and choice wasn't always clear. You've probably read that many people considered Lelong a hero. He convinced the Nazis, who were determined to move the couture industry to Berlin, that it had to stay in Paris or die. Without all its attendant French trades, like embroiderers, button makers, lace makers and the like, it couldn't have survived. After the occupation, he supported a commission to investigate couture's links with the Germans—and no charges were laid."

The reporter, whoever he was, did not sound impressed. "And no doubt you know that all that is very debatable. The postwar commissions were notorious for bending the rules to accommodate important people. I'm just curious about how Lelong fits in to your exhibit."

The thin ice under Margaret was cracking. She had no plans whatsoever for Lelong. It occurred to her that besides being annoyingly knowledgeable, this reporter sounded a little inexperienced.

"Sorry, Alexander—it is Alexander, isn't it?—but I don't think we've talked before. Are you in Arts? Or News?"

There was a flicker of silence. "I'm an intern, working wherever they need me."

"I see. Why don't we talk again, closer to the opening? I'll be able to give you a much fuller picture then. Good luck with your internship and thanks so much for your interest."

Once she had hung up, Margaret sat for a few minutes with what felt like an incipient case of pit-rot. That call had come straight from left field. Never in her wildest ideas for the exhibit had she considered paying any attention to Dior's competent and less-famous mentor, but now she grasped that the relationship with Lelong was bound to arouse suspicion. Margaret had always seen him as doing a skilful, conscientious job at the tightrope act fate had forced upon him. Dior, on the other hand, who was still learning his trade in obscurity, would not have attracted any attention from the Germans. Part of her reassured the rest of herself that there was no reason to be overly concerned with the opaque workings of the occupation.

But she did not need reminding that the museum had designed exhibitions in the past several years on topics previously considered uncontroversial—eighteenth-century porcelain cups and saucers for drinking chocolate and, a few Christmases ago, the history of Santa Claus—that had led to accusations of blindness and insensitivity. In retrospect, the relationship between the Dutch Saint Nicholas and his helper, Zwarte Piet or Black Piet, was bound to arouse discomfort and questions. And behind those "charming" chocolate sets lay the colonial cruelties of cocoa production. The last thing the museum needed was more bad publicity. Much as she wanted to, Margaret could not afford to dismiss the intern out of hand.

SHE DECIDED TO WALK HOME. Once the snow and ice had melted, it was a half-hour transition between work and family, but now, in January, she added five minutes for more deliberate walking. She had a choice between South Goodman and Meigs Street and today she chose tranquil, working-class Meigs. Margaret lived on Rockingham Street, not far from the hip bars and small restaurants on South Clinton, but more residential and less cool.

Still, Rockingham was appealing, lined with mature trees that were in leaf seven or eight months of the year, depending on the winter. The houses on a rise to the south, as the street climbed toward Highland Park, were more expensive and the ones on the flat northern side were more affordable. Margaret and Will had stretched their budget to buy on the flat side when Will's first mystery, *Murder in the Vestry*, made the bestseller list. The rooms were generous, and the house had a few aspirational early twentieth-century touches, including leaded windows and gumwood interior trim, but eight years after they had moved in, the kitchen and bathrooms remained unrenovated.

The smell of baked ziti, one of Will's specialties, greeted Margaret before she succeeded in finding a hook for her coat. Everyone in the family except Margaret, who still carried a torch for what she called "good wool," had at least two puffy coats. They took up so much room in the narrow entrance that Margaret referred to it as the padded cell.

The cook was not in the kitchen, but Bee was, winding her brown hair around a finger while she read "The Case of the Missing Lady." Margaret kissed the top of her head and asked, "Where's Daddy? Where's your sister?"

Bee responded, "What's your favourite Agatha Christie?"

"*4.50 from Paddington*. Where's Daddy?"

This constant what's-your-favourite must be a twelve-year-old thing. "The Case of the Missing Lady" was part of Christie's Tommy and Tuppence series, not high on Margaret's list, but she would not mention that to Bee.

Now there was a clattering on the back stairs, followed by the arrival of Nancy and Will. Nancy was blond and wiry, compared with her twin's brunette sturdiness. Will took the bubbling ziti out of the oven, Margaret was entrusted with the salad—including separate bowls of green onions, which Nancy did not eat, and avocados, which Will did not eat—and the girls set the table.

When the girls were born, Margaret had been determined to give them classic names, as nickname-proof as possible. She hoped they would spend many more years as powerful middle-aged and old women than as winsome toddlers and had named them accordingly: Anne and Beatrice. But Will's formidable mother, who knew these things, announced that since the name Nancy had begun as a nickname for Anne, she would call her granddaughter that. It was her idea of a joke, although Margaret in her more irritable moments called it passive-aggressive, and the name caught on. And Beatrice inevitably became Bee.

Once they were all seated, Will said of the pasta, "It's a little overcooked."

"No, Daddy, it's perfect," Nancy said. "Thank you for making it."

Ninety seconds older than Bee, she had the first child's sense of affiliation with her parents.

Bee asked, "What's your favourite pasta?"

"Ziti," Margaret and Nancy answered in unison. Hoping to forestall more questions like that, Margaret asked Will how his day had gone.

"Not too bad," he said. "I'm afraid the verger, who's also the parish janitor, is going to die next."

When they married, Will had been a high school history teacher who loved mysteries. Now, to everyone's surprise including Will's, he was the author of a successful series centred on Crispin Applegate, a young Anglo-Catholic priest with a dwindling parish in the small town of Tisdale, Saskatchewan. Struggling to balance the needs of his aging parishioners with his devotion to the Anglo-Catholic ritual, Crispin had a knack for solving the frequent murders that blemished the snowy fields and forlorn streets of Tisdale.

"How will the verger die?" Nancy asked. "Maybe hit on the head by one of the church bells?"

"That's been done," Will said. "*Nine Tailors* by Dorothy Sayers. Besides, St. Hilda's is too poor to have real bells. They use a recording. If the murder happens in the verger's office, he may be crushed to death under the bookcase with all the hymnals. If it's in the janitor's workroom, probably just a plain old hammer to the head."

Will looked as if he favoured death by hymnals.

After dinner, looking for something in which to store the leftover avocados—no one would eat them, but Will did not countenance throwing out food until it was inedible—Margaret took down an oval bowl from far back on the top shelf. It was decorated with a faded blue-and-white Italian scene.

When he saw it, Will said sharply, "No!" and removed it from Margaret's dangerous hands. "That's part of the Spode set."

Margaret retreated from the bowl, now safely on the counter, as if it were radioactive. The Spode china had been parcelled out to members of Will's family, and her ordinarily sensible husband had inherited what she considered an excessive reverence for dishes that had seen better days.

"It can be chipped or cracked or stained, but if it's part of the ancestral Spode, it's holy," Margaret complained to her sisters.

She didn't really believe her mother-in-law cared that her WASP family was a step or two above the Abramses on the social ladder; Helena's complacent superiority rested more on her stores of arcane knowledge. But just in case she thought their difference in class was even slightly significant, Margaret made a contrarian point of underlining her own family's commitment to public schools, unfancy Y summer camps, thrift shops, garage sales and end-of-season reductions. She knew it was literally humble-bragging and she tried, usually unsuccessfully, to restrain it. She also suspected that she cared more about Helena's opinion than she wanted to admit.

Now, as she tried to cover the pan of leftover ziti with one of those beeswax sheets that never co-operated, she said to Will, "I had a kind of worrying call today."

Will took the beeswax sheet away from her and replaced it with the pan's own cover, lying in plain sight on the counter. Unabashed, she told him about the reporter and his suspicions about Lucien Lelong.

"The silliest thing," she concluded, "would be if Dior were considered guilty by association. But that happens a lot these days."

"What do you think about this reporter's attitude to Lelong?"

"It depends. Obviously, the occupation was a national trauma, with all kinds of betrayals, recriminations and cover-ups. Owners of the couture houses had to make nice with Nazis, and some of them did that with more energy than others."

Still brooding over the ziti, Will was rereading the recipe. "I think I'll bake it at 325 next time, not 350. But where does Lelong fit into that?"

"As the head of the couture industry, Lelong saved more than ninety percent of it, and postwar France was desperate for the foreign money it could generate. So the purification commission, as it was called, may have looked the other way occasionally when it reviewed his practices. But this exhibit is about Dior's beautiful clothes! It isn't about tawdry deals and Nazis."

The former history teacher in Will shook his head at her. "You know as well as I do that beautiful clothes can owe something to tawdry deals and horrible behaviour. But this reporter will probably get overwhelmed with other assignments and you won't hear from him again."

Reassured, Margaret remembered the other notable event of the day. "Something else happened today, but not worrying. Just weird," she said, and told him the story of the scarf. "What do you think?"

Like Gareth, Will looked briefly uneasy. "Probably just some crackpot. But he or she sounds a little dodgy. I hope this is a one-shot thing."

AT ELEVEN THAT NIGHT, Margaret knelt by the side of the bed in her nightgown. She was not praying but searching in the unsteady pile of books about Dior she kept there "for emergencies," as Will said. He meant that when an idea visited her in the middle of the night, she would turn on the light and rummage in the stack for more information. She found the book she wanted, toppling the pile, and got into bed with it.

"Why are you sighing?" Will asked without looking up from his Kindle.

"Because someone told me that a curator at the Fashion Museum acquired a dress that I would give anything . . . Her name's Sharon Singer. I don't know if she bought it or if it's a bequest . . . I was sure it was in this . . ."

The riffling of pages stopped and Will heard an "Aha," said with a mixture of exaltation and mourning. Exaltation because the dress never failed to move Margaret, mourning because she had lost it. It was a covered-up black day dress in fine wool from Dior's first 1947 collection, feminine and strict at the same time.

The slim pleats at the side were firmly stitched down over the hips and then allowed to flow with the wearer's walk. The tiny waist was emphasized by a self-belt with three small buttons. And most captivating of all were the strange, vaguely oblong pleated details at the breasts. It was a dress that said, *I may look like the most exquisitely behaved* jeune fille, *but there are surprises here.*

Will looked at the dress briefly, but spent more time on the ball gown on the opposite page, with a daringly low neckline and pushed-up breasts. "That's sexy."

"Yeah, it is. Well, he was all about breasts and waists, especially in the forties. This day dress came with its own built-in waist cincher, but I wonder if he helped along the hourglass shape with a little padding at the hips."

Will tried to close the book and take her in his arms, but she resisted.

"No, Will, I'm not done here. I just want to see if there's any mention of hip enhancement."

"How many times have you looked at and read about that dress?"

"Not enough. Damn Sharon Singer."

"And how is it that a dead, gay Frenchman who looks like the Pillsbury Doughboy has become my rival in the bedroom?"

She smiled. "Okay, you want to talk about sexy, just look at those loose pleats at the bust."

But Will had had enough Dior and returned to his Kindle. She looked over at him. His reading glasses suited him. Plus, the ziti had been very good. She balanced the book on the fallen pile, turned out her light and said, "Come here."

ZEMIRE

DIOR'S *CROQUIS*, OR SKETCH, FOR a short, full-skirted cocktail dress is dated June 21, 1955. A sample of the black silk he intended for it is pinned on the page, and he wrote two names. Hélène was entrusted with its sewing and Renée was the model on whom it would be fitted and who would wear it for all viewings, public and private. Their full names are not recorded. The dress was called *Zemire*, after the heroine of an eighteenth-century comic opera.

Insofar as the right dress can guarantee a good time,

Zemire promises a delightful cocktail party. Although Dior first thought of it in black, it is most itself in the full-blooded red version. Produced in France's finest silk faille, a fabric both crisp and sensuous, its top is simple, a deep and wide undecorated V-neck and three-quarter sleeves. All the interest is reserved for the waist and hips. A broad band of the silk appears on each side just above the waist and meets in the front at hip level, making an unexpected and graphic Y. To ensure that no one misses the bold shaping, the Y continues to the hem, with four large buttons covered in the red silk.

Zemire looks undemanding, even relaxed, but that's because Dior did all the work, on the inside. He ensured its flattery with a waist-cinching, breast-lifting built-in corset that includes eleven bones and fifteen hooks. There are five layers of crinoline for the voluminous but disciplined skirt—flat in front so as not to upstage the Y and pouffed out in the back with a bonus layer of crinoline. The wearer needs only to add earrings, heels and the party.

TWO

Red Silk for Cocktails

Margaret was edgy. Her day included a department meeting and dozens of decisions about the exhibit, and as usual, the contents of her closet disappointed her. Had there ever been a fashion historian or curator who dressed with style? Her colleagues in textile history, the ones who laboured over faded pieces of medieval Hungarian homespun, tended to dress like academic dowdies. They might have been studying coal production for all the interest in textiles they demonstrated in their own wardrobes. The fashion curators were better, but most of them dressed like gallerists in attention-shunning black whose details were so subtle as to be almost invisible. Like shoemakers' children, they seemed unable or unwilling to do more than that for their own wardrobes. No doubt money played a part there, and constant exposure to high fashion was probably intimidating as well as exhausting.

Including herself in that category, Margaret chose a thick grey knitted dress that zipped up the front from Cos, with black tights and the heavy oxfords the girls called nuns' shoes. She looked in the mirror as briefly as possible. Outfit: not inspired or original, but okay. Margaret: pale, unfreckled because it was winter, with an underlay of harassment. She thought she looked more carefree with a summer's dusting of freckles. Her only remarkable feature was her hair, described by admirers as copper and by her family as carrot-coloured. Nancy would always add, "But the carrots are organic."

Margaret called down the hall, "Twins! It's time to get up."

She was well aware that one was supposed to not use the words *twins* or *twin*, to allow people in what was called a multiple birth situation to become their full, individual selves. *Girls* or *sisters* were preferable. But every once in a while Margaret called her teenaged daughters twins just to be transgressive. She was not worried about the individuation of fizzy Bee and dreamy, conscientious Nancy.

In the kitchen, Will was stirring oatmeal. She kissed him with the warmth that lingered from last night. Nancy appeared, fully dressed, and looked her mother over.

"What about your Bakelite bar pin? The red one. It would look nice on that grey."

Eating her oatmeal standing up, Margaret said, "Sweetie, what a good idea. Would you be an angel and get it for me?"

Five minutes later, bar pin in place, Margaret was ready to leave, but the family, which now included Bee in pyjamas, was not done with her.

Nancy tilted her head to one side and asked, "What about her hair?"

"I like it up," Will said, and Nancy agreed.

"But maybe some French braids at her temples, so it's not so severe," Bee said.

"No, that's too fussy," Nancy said. "She could just roll it into a soft bun at the back of her neck."

Margaret never knew what to do with her best feature, and any suggestions made her feel even more hopeless about it than usual. She was tired of being talked about in the third person and was late for work.

"Soft buns, whatever they are, and French braids are above my pay grade. Why don't we reconvene this beauty parlour on the weekend when I have more time?"

She kissed them all quickly in semi-gratitude and, buttoning her coat and pulling her cloche down over her unsatisfactory hair, she said to Will, "Have fun killing off the verger."

AMBITIOUS CURATORS, INTENT on using Harkness as a stepping stone to better-known museums in New York City or London, sometimes described it as an outstanding museum tacked on to an unexciting city in upstate New York. Margaret's feelings about the degree of excitement Rochester afforded waxed and waned, but it was unfair to suggest that Harkness was the only game in town. George Eastman, the man who put his stamp and his name all over Rochester after he founded Kodak, had lavishly supported the Eastman School of Music, the George Eastman Museum of photography and the Memorial Art Gallery. The first two had international reputations and the art gallery was one of the state's best outside New York City. Harkness, also the beneficiary of Eastman's munificence, had plenty of company.

Beginning in the 1950s, a canny curator at Harkness had successfully wooed Rochester's wealthy women with the conviction that their Schiaparellis and Chanels were not frivolous extravagances but museum-quality artifacts. The donations that flowed from that continued, as women liked to say, "Oh, that little Lanvin suit? I'd worn it so much I finally gave it to Harkness."

In her office, Margaret dangled her coat on a hanger that already held a few discarded sweaters and squared her shoulders for the department meeting. They were unpredictable at the best of times because, like every department in the museum, they brought together experts with wildly differing agendas. There were the scholarly curators who saw the museum as a gigantic repository of objects that must be preserved and stored in perpetuity, preferably never seen by the public. Every decade or so they would squeeze out a monograph on the jawlines of a few dinosaurs or the underglaze on a Qing vase. There were the less scholarly types, such as Margaret, who wanted to curate the museum's treasures to inform and delight the public. And there were growing numbers of support staff—in Learning, Design, Diversity, Audience, Children and Family Programs, among others—who complicated, frustrated and sometimes helped the curators.

Margaret found a chair against the wall in the Fashion and Textiles conference room, but Claire Minichiello stopped her.

"No, Margaret, I know we'll have a lot of questions about *The New Look*, so we need you here at the table."

Claire was the Chief Curator, Fashion and Textiles, and she would chair the meeting. On paper, Margaret reported to Gareth Wong about her exhibition, but it was Claire who would supervise everything up to the final rubber stamp of approval. She was robust and motherly, with a mass of honey-coloured hair. Margaret marvelled at Claire's ponytails, twists and top-of-the-head poufs—a hairdressing talent as remote to her as riding a unicycle.

Claire began by taking questions that were not about *The New Look*.

Andrew Carr, the curator whose office was across the corridor from Margaret's, asked if there was any news on his proposal for a show called *The End of Mourning*, tracing the gradual demise of mourning clothes since World War One.

"Not yet, I'm afraid," Claire said. "I'll keep you posted."

There was a general feeling that Andrew's obsession with mourning clothes needed a rest, and people avoided looking at him.

Claire said, "Keitha, I see you're writing. Could I ask you to take notes?"

"I'm doing that, Claire." Even by intern standards, Keitha Richards was exceptionally keen.

A curator in Asian textiles, Derek Parfitt, complained about a small exhibit that connected nineteenth-century French floral embroideries and watercolours. "I know I'm so ancient I could qualify for a niche in Greek and Roman"—they had all heard his tired, cross joke more than a few times—"but I am probably the person here closest in age to our average visitor. So could I beg Design in the future to hold off on the pale-grey type on white backgrounds for the labels and text panels? It may be the latest thing in design circles, but it is profoundly hard to read."

Margaret guessed that several people around the table, including herself, agreed with Derek, but his complaints were so predictably sour that no one supported him. The woman from Design, who was rumoured to be having an affair with him, looked exasperated. She said, "Noted. Thank you, Derek."

Margaret marvelled, as always, at the ability of someone so negative to pursue an intimate connection, much less to have it reciprocated.

"So if there aren't any more questions," Claire said, "I'll ask Margaret to give us an update on *The New Look*." Turning to Margaret, she remembered something. "By the way, I sent on a reporter to you yesterday. What was that about?"

"Oh, he had a few questions about the historical background," Margaret said vaguely. "We're going to talk closer to the opening."

No sense in giving this crowd any ideas for objections. Margaret found that she was looking at the man from Diversity, who was sitting directly across the table from her, with a certain foreboding. Haute couture was far from inclusive. No one who worked in a museum in the twenty-first century could be oblivious to legitimate concerns about white privilege, colonialism and microaggressions, and Margaret agreed that most exhibits benefited from a context that was as broad as possible. At the same time, she nursed a stubborn conviction—one that, admittedly, she shrank from examining too closely—that Dior's clothes had no need for apologies or qualifications. Only when she was sleepless in the most despairing hours of the night did she worry that she was being an ostrich.

Pushing doubt from her mind, Margaret began talking about the exhibit. Choosing the clothes, all from the museum's collection, had been painful, she said, but her team had agreed on about 75 percent of them. At this point, Alan Shea interrupted.

"I heard Sharon Singer beat you to a particularly fine day dress from Dior's first collection."

She had never liked Alan. He was the other Senior Curator, and when Claire retired, which would happen almost immediately after *The New Look* opened, he and Margaret were the obvious contenders for her job. Alan made no secret of his interest in the position, and his credentials were impressive. Among his more obnoxious talents was a gift for managing up, cultivating his bosses while subtly undermining his peers or underlings.

Margaret gave him a wide smile. "Fortunately, we have an embarrassment of riches when it comes to day dresses from 1947. And we were never in the running for that dress. The owner has had a pretty exclusive relationship with the Fashion Museum for a long time."

She returned to the exhibit, talking about the fine points of the mounts for the clothes, but the grumpy Asian textiles curator had another complaint.

"Sorry, Margaret, but I have a request that won't surprise any of you. Could we please have the labels at a height we can read while standing? Call me old-fashioned, but I believe that is the usual position while going through an exhibition. Recently, at the African art exhibit, I had to crouch so much to read that I put out my back."

"Well," the woman from Design said snappishly, "Margaret wants a circle of pieces on mounts in the middle of the exhibition hall, so where would you suggest we put the labels, other than on the low rim around the circle?"

Margaret said mildly—at least she tried to make it sound mild—that she wanted to showcase some of the most exceptional designs, dramatically lit, without the clutter of labels on stands. She was hoping Design could come up with some bright idea to make that possible. There were dubious looks around the table about Design's ability to do that, most balefully from the Asian textile curator.

Before that could be addressed, the woman from Children and Family Programs said, "Margaret, Diana from Learning and I have been talking, and we're very excited about putting a few of the clothes into the Learning pod so that the kids could try them on. What do you think?"

My God, Margaret thought, how did this woman get hired? She murmured something about the extraordinary cost and fragility of the Diors, and the woman said defensively that the Wallace Collection in London allowed children to try on medieval armour and mail.

"From the Middle Ages!" she emphasized, as if Margaret wouldn't understand what *medieval* meant.

If she couldn't see the difference between metal and silk, Margaret didn't know where to start, but now the woman had another idea. What about getting some cheap knock-offs of the Diors and kids could play with them?

Straightforward but kind, Claire said that the museum wasn't really in the business of knock-offs, but they might consider putting some clothes in mid-century styles in the Learning pod. And so it went, for another half-hour of criss-crossing suggestions, objections and queries that often went nowhere.

Limp and hollowed out, Margaret left the room first, with the intern Keitha close on her heels.

"Margaret, I think your exhibit sounds fantastic. I did an MA thesis in history about postwar France, so this is right up my alley, if that isn't too presumptuous. Just the idea that while everything in France was still so shaky, Dior came along and resurrected a big part of its self-image . . . when even bread was severely rationed . . ." She shook her head. "Sorry, I'm rambling. I just wanted to say I would love to help you out wherever I can, either as part of my normal duties or in the evenings and weekends." Perhaps as a way of controlling her enthusiasm or her self-consciousness—or both—Keitha pressed her lips together into a thin line between sentences, like an additional piece of punctuation.

Margaret thanked her. She promised to be in touch. That was what she needed to concentrate on, the rebirth of French couture, with Dior the unlikely person who turned an industry around while rescuing femininity from the ruins of war. The ravishing suits and ball dresses. And people like Keitha, not the burned-out naysayers in her department.

And now surely she deserved a molasses cookie, if not a piece of the cafeteria's surprisingly good yellow layer cake. Walking to the basement, she received a text from David Hillman. She had been told more than once not to read while walking, but she could not resist.

The text said, "I have something to show you that I think you'll like. Can I come by this afternoon around four?"

She liked David as much as she disliked Alan Shea. He was an odd duck, a city librarian who had turned out to have an excellent eye for couture. She would shake her head in admiration at the finds he brought her from used clothing and consignment shops, garage and estate sales, saying, "How do you do it?" He had bought his first piece of couture years ago, when the library sent him to the Hadassah bazaar to look over the books. He had drifted into the vast clothing section and bought a Balmain cocktail suit from the 1950s for his wife to wear to costume parties.

While Margaret waited for 4 p.m., she met with Dom Bianchi, the assistant curator who was about to start drafting some of the text panels. Today he was concentrating on the first room, about Dior's boyhood in an affluent Norman family.

"I love the story of Dior's mother thinking it was vulgar to put your name on your business," Dom said. "That's rich, from a woman whose husband's fortune came from manure. When the winds blew from the wrong direction, people in their town would say, 'It smells of Dior today.' Luckily, Madame Dior had died by 1947, so her son could put up a tasteful plaque saying 'Christian Dior' over the door at 30 avenue Montaigne. And I want to write about how lilies of the valley, one of the Dior trademarks, came from his memories of his mother's garden. I'm thinking of—"

"Dom," she interrupted. "No. Calm down. You know these panels are cruelly short. Apparently the average visitor gives them two seconds. They're standing up and people don't like to read standing up. You have one hundred words to introduce a new section. So, enjoy your delicious details, but when it comes to writing, you're going to have to kill most of your darlings."

Dom knew all that, and Margaret knew that his finished panels would be crisp and to the point. He just liked talking about his discoveries. Surely that was one of the rewards of working in a museum.

Promptly at four, the guard at the rear entrance called to tell Margaret that David Hillman was waiting for her to pick him up. Mr. Hillman had a garment bag, the guard said furtively, as if it were a semi-secret, but he had unzipped it and it seemed okay.

She went down to meet him. David looked like a dentist or an accountant, reliable and bland. Or like a librarian in charge of Special Collections, which he was. He was trying but failing to carry his garment bag with nonchalance.

In the elevator, she said, "So, you've been shopping. Where?"

"Newish consignment shop, on Elmwood Avenue," David said. "Proceeds go to a cancer hospice. The woman pricing the clothes seems to know a thing or two, and the dress was expensive. But the label was cut out or it would have been more expensive."

Clearly, he had decided that the dress was too much of a find not to buy it immediately. In her office, Margaret put on her gloves and unzipped the garment bag. David's standards were not museological ones, and no matter how much she nagged him, she doubted he was conscientious about gloves. The state of his garment bag would have made Conservation shudder.

"I'm afraid it's been dry cleaned," he said, as a faint chemical smell wafted out from the bag, "and probably not following your guidelines."

But what emerged made Margaret forget about dry cleaners and worrying garment bags. She hung the dress on a pole in her office and walked around it for about thirty seconds. Then she hugged David. She had done this before, but not often. He seemed to accept it as his due, without embarrassment.

"David, David. What a prince you are. Do you know what this is?"

"I'm guessing Balenciaga or Dior. Late forties or early fifties."

She nodded. "It's called *Zemire* and it's from Dior's fall and winter collection, in the mid-fifties." She looked at the inside of the back of the V-neck, on the right, where the label would be. "I don't see any sign that the label was cut out."

"Nor did I," he said. "The cutter must have been superlatively careful and the needle marks where it was sewn must have faded with time."

"Strange," Margaret said. "Obviously, the consignment shop isn't going to tell you the identity of the owner. I'd love to know if there is more where this came from."

"Is it too late to figure in your exhibit? I thought it was devoted to the 1947 collections."

"The bulk of it is from those first two collections, but there are representative pieces from the 1950s that embody the New Look spirit. There's no way I wouldn't show this beauty."

They moved on to money. First Fashion and Textiles had to officially attest that it was an original Dior. David would set a price, which usually included a reasonable finder's fee. The Acquisitions Committee would okay the purchase and then, ideally, a sponsor would be sought for all or part of the cost. For the time being, the dress would stay at the museum.

"I can't thank you enough, David," Margaret said in farewell. "You've made my month. I'll keep you posted as we clear each hurdle."

Once Margaret was alone with the dress, she petted and prodded carefully. Straightening out the layers of organza under the skirt, her fingers came upon something stiff and papery. It was a stub from Savos Dry Cleaners, stapled into the depths of the underskirts.

Cramming David's unseemly garment bag into the bottom drawer of her desk, she called Conservation. Together they sheathed the dress in a paper covering and moved it to its own compartment in Storage.

In spite of the department meeting, it had been an excellent day and she found herself humming as she walked to the South Goodman bus. Her parents had loved mid-twentieth-century musicals, especially *South Pacific*. Borrowing from the heroine's song about a wonderful guy, Margaret hummed to herself, "I'm in love, I'm in love, I'm in love with a wonderful dress."

THREE

Wedding Party with Vogue Patterns

The mail at home that day included an envelope from her sisters. Their father had died three months ago and Constance, who had lived near him in Syracuse, and Lydia, who lived in Boston, were clearing out his condo. Inside a folded piece of paper on which Lydia had written "Doesn't this say everything?" was a photograph of a wedding party.

Nancy and Bee seated themselves on either side of Margaret on the couch. They stuck themselves close to their mother, as if to soften her sadness about her father's death.

Bee said, "Tell us about these people."

They knew the picture and the cast of characters, more or less, but they liked to start at the beginning.

"The bride is my great-aunt Helen, and the woman next to her, who was called the matron of honour, is her sister, my grandmother."

"And now tell us the story of the flower girl."

They were done with the grown-ups, and this was their favourite part.

"That's my mother. She was only two and far too young to be a flower girl, but she was unusually well-behaved. The story is that my grandmother, who had made the bridal dress and all the bridesmaid dresses from Vogue patterns, woke in the night two days before the wedding and decided that her little girl had to be a flower girl. She didn't have a pattern, so she adapted the bridesmaid dress in organza for a two-year-old, filled in the neckline, and added these rows of crunchy-looking ruffles around the sleeves and on the skirt. Whenever she saw this picture, my mother would remember how scratchy the organza was."

"But she looks very cute," Nancy said.

The girls remembered their grandmother, who had died five years before.

"That's called reverse engineering, what she did for Grandma's dress," Nancy said.

Bee tried to argue that it wasn't exactly reverse engineering as there was a pattern, although for a grown-up, but Nancy cut her off, asking Margaret, "Was her husband nice?"

"Who? Oh, the bridegroom, my great-uncle. Yes, I think he was a good guy."

As usual in wedding pictures, the groom, best man and ushers were also-rans. They balanced the picture, but could not compete with bouquets, long white gloves and silk whose swish was almost audible.

Coincidentally, the wedding took place in 1947, but Margaret doubted that word of Dior's New Look had penetrated to this family in Syracuse. The bride's parents had emigrated from Germany in the 1920s, and her father worked in a tool and die shop. The bride herself, beautiful in a slim, long-sleeved dress, was eighteen and a long-distance telephone operator. Her two bridesmaids were also recent high school graduates doing low-paying jobs. Their dresses were even prettier than the bride's, with sweetheart necklines bordered by deep bands of Alençon lace and fullish skirts. It was not a fancy family, but something about the refinement of the dresses—"Well, they were Vogue patterns!" someone in the family would always interject at this point—gave the group a style that had endured.

Margaret's grandmother had more natural elegance than anyone else in the picture. Eight years older than her sister the bride, she had been born in Germany and christened Maria Margareta. In America, that became Mary Margaret, but she was always called Marg. She could do anything with cloth or yarn or thread—sew, knit, crochet, embroider (including broderie anglaise) and needlepoint (including petit point). Margaret had been named for her, although the only people who called her Mary Margaret were Will and her sisters, when they wanted to take her bossiness or sanctimoniousness down a peg.

Nancy and Bee were still welded to Margaret's sides, although she could feel from the way they were shifting their positions that her time was almost up.

"Why does Aunt Lydia say the picture 'says everything'?" Nancy asked.

"I guess because we all love cloth and clothes and well-made things. My sisters, especially your aunt Constance, can sew, although not a fraction as well as our mother and grandmother. I only learned to knit, which is a shame. But any time either of you wants to try knitting again, I would be happy to teach you."

Bee rolled her eyes to indicate this would never happen, and Nancy put her hand on her mother's, which was her way of saying the same thing.

Nancy asked if Aunt Constance could do reverse engineering, but before they could start to argue again about its precise meaning, Will appeared to announce dinner.

At the table, he asked, "So how's the iconic photograph? Is Grandma still clutching her little nosegay as if her life depended on it? Is Marg still wearing—shocking!—gloves that end below the elbow, while the bridesmaids' are above the elbow?"

He was a veteran of many perusings and parsings of the photograph, usually around the kitchen table in his parents-in-laws' condo.

Margaret's father had not figured in the talk about the photograph, but he was in the air.

Now Nancy said matter-of-factly, as if continuing a conversation, "Matilda said that Grandpa was Jewish." Matilda was her cousin on Will's side of the family.

"Well, my father never told me that he was," Margaret said, trying not to sound as if she had covered this ground before. Even when she thought she had answered the question of her father's Jewishness definitively, it had a way of reappearing. "And he converted to Catholicism before he married my mother."

Will looked wary, as if he was trying not to blurt something that he would regret. But he stayed silent, so she carried on.

"And besides, there's the—"

"Here we go, girls! The iconic christening dress is coming up!"

Margaret turned on him. "Would you stop calling things my family holds dear 'iconic'! We can do without your sarcasm."

The girls chewed their chicken with blank faces, not looking at their horrible parents.

Will retreated. "Okay, I'm sorry. You'd better finish the story," he said, looking briefly at Margaret.

"Well, everyone has heard it before, but I was just going to repeat that we have a christening dress that came from my father's family, a long white dress with tucks in the front and about a hundred mother-of-pearl buttons up the back. My sisters and I were baptized in it. A Jewish family wouldn't have a christening dress. Just saying."

And because everyone had heard that story before, there was no need to comment. Or even to look at each other.

WILL APOLOGIZED AGAIN, in bed, and she kissed him good night. The question of her father's possible Jewishness—or was it her reaction to her father's possible Jewishness?—roused something in him that puzzled her, and her feelings were bruised. But now she needed to sleep. In spite of Will's peevishness, the wedding photograph had stirred good memories of standing on a stool in a new dress while the hem was measured or the waistband taken in, of cloth billowing out over her mother's sewing table, of her grandmother narrowing her eyes as she appraised a lining.

When she was a little girl, her mother would take Margaret to the patterns section of Syracuse's department stores and hoist her up on the long-legged chairs in front of the pattern catalogues. Lydia was already at school and Constance was at home with a babysitter. While her mother made careful notes comparing styles and yardages, Margaret treated the big catalogues like stories, making up lives for the women and children pictured there. She knew from a tender age that Butterick and Simplicity were the plain Janes of patterns—the straightforward illustrations reminded her of the drawings in Lydia's early readers. McCall's held the middle range, and Vogue was the sophisticated apex. All that was part of Mary Margaret Abrams, Senior Curator, Fashion and Textiles.

As for her father, everyone outside her family assumed that Michael Abrams, the son of Hester and a tailor named Sol, was Jewish. So why did she resist? In her heart of hearts, she accepted that almost certainly he must have come from a Jewish family. But did that make him Jewish? He had usually sidestepped the question, and when Lydia occasionally pressed him, he flatly denied it. Margaret wondered why it mattered—to him, or to her. Or if it did matter.

When she thought about it, she came back to the fact that her aversion stemmed from her father's: If he didn't want to talk about it, who was she to barge in? When she tried to think about it, she felt as if she was rummaging through a box of papers he wanted to keep private. She didn't understand his reluctance to talk about his childhood, but she respected it. And there was another, deeper reason for her unwillingness to look at the subject more closely, something that was hard to consider, something she glimpsed quickly and then shut out. It was a disappointment in her father.

She knew she should also try to understand Will's antagonism when the subject was raised, but she avoided that too. Her sisters had no trouble arguing and saying uncomfortable things, but not Margaret. She had inherited her parents' dislike of confrontation.

Meanwhile, she had something more pressing to do. In the next weeks she had to get *The New Look* on its feet, funded properly and ideologically unassailable. And, most of all, wonderful.

Hours later, dreaming happily of the red cocktail dress, she saw again the little stub stapled to the underskirt that said "Savos Dry Cleaners." When she'd found it, it hadn't looked like a useful piece of information, but in her dream she changed her mind. She woke up, turned on the light and opened her tablet. Savos Dry Cleaners was on Monroe Avenue, near Twelve Corners in Brighton, and it opened at 8 a.m. She had an appointment with her committee about the mounts for the clothes at ten, so that would work.

When Will walked into the kitchen at seven thirty, Margaret was dressed and drinking coffee.

"You're up early."

They kissed, a little formally.

"I need to be in Twelve Corners by eight. I'll explain later. Do you need the car?"

At eight o'clock, a rumpled man unlocked the door at what looked like a run-of-the-mill neighbourhood dry cleaner, and she went in. It seemed simplest to tell the truth, so she explained about the museum and the dress in the consignment shop and her wish to talk with the owner, on behalf of the museum, of course.

"The reason I've come here is that I discovered one of your stubs in the dress's underskirt." She showed him the picture of the dress on her phone.

And then she had a piece of luck. While the man, perhaps Mr. Savos, was beginning to explain in a soft-spoken but definite voice that they never identified any of their clients, a voice about thirty feet away, midway down the ranks of plastic-wrapped clothes, body visible only from the trousers down, was heard to say, "Sounds like Mrs. Slaney."

Or perhaps he had said "Mrs. Skaney," but instantly the man at the desk whipped around and told the headless voice to shut up. Margaret pretended she hadn't heard, assured the man at the desk that of course she understood about client confidentiality, she just hadn't thought of that, and wished him a good day. She sent a silent blessing toward the man lost in plastic.

In the car on the way to the museum, she thought, *Slaney*. That was how she imagined it was spelled, but it could be Slany or Slanie or Skaney, Skany or even Skani. But she thought it was Slaney—rather unfortunately, because that sounded Irish, and while the Italians in Rochester outnumbered the Irish, there could be hordes of Slaneys in the phone book. Margaret assumed that the dress's owner was older, if not old, and still had a land line.

She arrived in her office shortly after nine, with plenty of time before her meeting, so she asked the secretary if she could bring her that quaint artifact, a telephone book. Opening its floppy heft, she imagined an exhibit in the near future on old-time communications, where the telephone book would be featured along with electric typewriters, cassette players and telephone booths. With a map of the neighbourhood around Savos Dry Cleaners on her laptop, she found no Skanys or Skanis and only a few Skaneys in the phone book. They lived far from the dry cleaners. There were no Slanies, two Slanys and perhaps thirty Slaneys, not as many as she had feared. Eliminating the Slanys, who lived in the wrong neighbourhoods, she began going methodically through the Slaneys. She noted a few possibilities, until she came to L. Slaney. L. Slaney lived on Penarrow Road. In a nice piece of triangulation, Penarrow Road was about six blocks from the dry cleaners and four blocks from the consignment shop.

Margaret grinned at the map and at L. Slaney's address and phone number. She knew exactly how Crispin Applegate, Will's priest-detective, must feel when a significant clue landed in his lap. Now, what was she going to do with this precious information? Crispin Applegate would have called the woman immediately. (She presumed L. Slaney was a woman.) But Margaret thought David Hillman would do a better job. He was so sure-footed, so patient with wary owners. She could turn on the charm for a while, but was shyer and scratchier, not always sure where to go next when faced with reluctance. David could find out if L. Slaney had more couture clothes, and if she was interested in donating or selling them. Margaret would call David after her meeting.

PONDICHÉRY

IN 1948, PONDICHÉRY WAS a French colony in southeastern India, a tranquil blend of Gallic and Indian cultures. Although he never set foot in India, Dior translated something of the enclave's hot-weather glamour into an evening jacket he designed for his spring/summer collection of that year.

It is a short, swing-style jacket in white linen lined in emerald silk, embroidered in silver- and gold-coloured threads. With his usual sleight of hand, Dior managed to avoid almost all seams by cutting the front, back and sleeves in one piece. For its April 1948 issue, *Harper's Bazaar* posed its model in *Pondichéry* seen from the back and the side, all the better to appreciate the deep, dramatic back pleat that is also fully embroidered. The model clasps her arms at shoulder height for a view of the exaggerated generosity of the cuffed, elbow-length sleeves.

Nodding to the opulent Indian exports of the seventeenth and eighteenth centuries, the embroidery studio Maison Rébé sent Dior a sample of multicoloured flora and fauna on black velvet. But Dior wanted something more freewheeling and tropical for his loose jacket, with no fastenings and the tiniest of mandarin collars. He exchanged Rébé's design for a coarse white linen with stylized birds, flowers and butterflies embroidered in silver and gold. The sequins, mother-of-pearl beads and tiny glass tubes lined with silver used in the embroidery might have been overwhelming, but Dior left liberal stretches of untouched linen.

When Bee asked her, "What's your favourite Dior this week?" Margaret always answered, "The *Pondichéry* jacket." Most of Dior's seventy-year-old pieces looked like gorgeous retro styles, but *Pondichéry* was totally contemporary. If Margaret won the lottery and the jacket ever came on the market, she would just slip it on over a black cashmere pullover, slim black pants and ballet flats and go out for the evening.

FOUR

The Pondichéry Jacket

It had taken a week for Mrs. Slaney—yes, it was a woman—to agree to meet David for coffee in her neighbourhood. She admitted, reluctantly, to having "some" couture pieces, and no, she was not interested in donating or selling them. The cocktail dress had been an exception. There was a boy in her apartment building with a talent for the cello, and she wanted him to have a better, more expensive teacher; the proceeds from the sale went there.

But she sounded interested—"cagily interested," said David over the phone—in the museum's fashion holdings. After thinking about it for a few minutes, she agreed to come with him to meet Margaret and see some of the collection.

"What's she like?" Margaret asked.

"Reserved. Resistant to what you call my charm. At first, she was worried about how we had found her, but she seemed relieved when I told her the story of the dry cleaners. Fairly tall, and probably was taller. There's a tiny remnant of an accent, but I don't know from where."

"What was she wearing?"

David sighed. "You know I'm better at clothes on hangers than on people. Let me think. She wore either a long camel jacket or a short camel coat. Looked to be good quality, but not couture. Black slacks. And a Hermès scarf, but not one of the horsey ones with bridles and stirrups."

"You're improving," Margaret said. "Will you ask her what kind of pieces she'd like to see? And let's say next Thursday, at two?"

"Oh, and one more thing. She's got all her marbles, but she's old."

"I assumed that."

"I'm not talking eighties. She's into her nineties."

MARGARET HAD SETTLED ON CLASSIC, headless mounts for *The New Look*, and she and Keitha went to the mount makers' studio to inspect them. "The mount is supposed to be as invisible as possible," she told Keitha, "but making one is a complicated business of padding a standard dress form with polyester wadding at points and paring away at others."

Nodding at a form that had undergone considerable surgery, Margaret said to the mount maker, "Nice. You really nailed Dior's hourglass shape here."

She explained to Keitha, "Now it will be covered with stretch jersey. Sometimes, even after a dress or jacket is buttoned onto the mount, it happens that the mount maker has to shove in an extra slab of wadding or winkle some out."

As they left the studio, Keitha said, "You mentioned Dior's hourglass shape, and that's something I want to ask you about, Margaret. How many women really have that ultra-slim, high-breasted, round-hipped silhouette? Especially the ultra-slim part. And yet Dior designed all his clothes on that fantasy. What about all the women whose bodies didn't fit his ideal?"

"That's why he designed the built-in corsets in his clothes," Margaret began, but Keitha interrupted.

"Exactly. And that's why I wonder if his corsets and his attitude to the female body don't deserve a little section to themselves in the exhibit. Not in the centre, but off a bit to the side. A place to get people thinking about how he shaped women—not just physically, but psychologically."

Margaret nodded, taking that into consideration. She agreed with Keitha that museums had a social mission. But they were more than teaching tools about feminism and body image; they were also shrines to craftsmanship, artistry and unapologetic beauty. Margaret wasn't interested in an alcove that scolded or condescended to Dior. Still, Keitha was doing an excellent job. She didn't want to shelve her idea outright.

"That's an appealing proposal, and I'm going to think about it," she said carefully. "But I think it's a mistake to apply our standards to a man who was born at the start of the twentieth century."

Keitha had begun to talk in some detail about how Dior's ideal body was still all too current when Margaret's phone pinged. It was a text from a man from Learning who wanted to schedule a meeting to discuss the school tours for *The New Look*. What did she have in mind for online Further Reading? Did she have any plans for smoothing any ruffled feathers? Learning now assumed that viewers of some stripe would be riled at most exhibits.

Margaret glanced at Keitha for any sign of disturbed feathers. The intern looked composed but eager to return to the argument. Usually, Margaret enjoyed talking with Learning, but now, not so much. Keitha was interested in history; maybe she could send her to the meeting in her stead. No, she needed to go herself, but she would take Keitha with her.

As she started to answer Learning, her phone rang. It was Gareth's secretary, who passed on the news that they had received another package, this one containing a brooch. Two weeks after the arrival of the scarf, Gareth was already tired of the drama of unwrapping it together.

"I'm bringing him some gloves," she told the secretary, "and I'll be right over." What was the point of Gareth wearing gloves? she asked herself on the way to his office. Was she thinking of having the pin dusted for fingerprints? She was taking her new Nancy Drew personality too seriously. One lucky break did not make her a detective.

The brooch was a bird in a gilded cage, his body and head probably made of artificial stones, the cage gold-painted metal. A note printed in the same hand as the one that had accompanied the scarf said, "This is right up your alley, isn't it?"

"Right up our alley," Margaret murmured as she turned over the brooch. There was no identification on the back.

Gareth was alternating between parking his hands in his pockets and crossing his arms above his belt. The first position suggested nonchalance, the second looked self-protective.

"I wonder if we shouldn't be taking this more seriously," he said. "I'll have a word with the head of Security."

"It's some nutcase," Margaret said. "I have to assume he—or she—is harmless."

She had no basis for her assumption, but she was more baffled than worried. Aside from their probable age, there was no connection she could think of between the scarf and the pin. Conservation had confirmed that the scarf was made of twill woven cellulose fibre, likely from the 1940s and more probably European than North American, but nothing more.

"The pin looks mid-twentieth century, like the scarf. It reminds me of something I've seen, but I don't know what. I'll ask our jewellery guy if he recognizes it."

The department's jewellery expert, Jerry Sorensen, was always terse. His outstanding feature was a luxuriant moustache, which seemed almost too large for his small frame. Margaret imagined him combing it in the morning with the same no-nonsense briskness he brought to jewellery. Now he trained his loupe on the brooch.

"Cheap," he pronounced. "Very cheap. Could be a knock-off of a good piece, and I think it is, because it looks familiar . . ." He moved toward his laptop.

"Is it American?" Margaret asked.

"My hunch is it's French," he said, typing a few words and scrolling through screens full of giraffes, zebras and horses in enamel or gold, their realism compromised by the occasional pearl or diamond in an ear or collar. Domestic animals followed— coquettish cats, ingratiating puppies and finally birds.

"Bingo. Here's the original, with the addition of this silly bow of turquoises fixed to the side of the cage. The bird is made of two pieces of tourmaline, green for the body and blue for the head."

"Cartier, 1942," Margaret read. "*Captive Bird*."

Jerry handed the pin back to her. "So, what?" he asked.

Margaret said, "My sentiments exactly."

MRS. SLANEY HAD TOLD DAVID she would be interested in seeing some Dior pieces from the 1940s and '50s, and Margaret had put some choice examples on mounts in the storage room. She had moved a chair in there, too, in case her guest wanted to sit, and had reserved the Director's sitting room for tea afterwards.

But the woman who came out of the elevator with David seemed to have no trouble walking and standing. Her skin was papery, as you might expect from her age, and pleated when she smiled. But she did not smile often, and her wrinkles were less noticeable than her strong cheekbones and blue eyes. She wore a navy reefer that was old but well-made, and her white hair was skilfully cut. She was a bit fragile around the edges—it took a while for David to divest her of her coat—but she shook Margaret's hand firmly and repeated her name back to her.

"Margaret Abrams. *Mary* Margaret Abrams. There's a story there."

Taken aback, Margaret laughed. "Maybe someday when we don't have dresses to look at, I'll tell it to you."

Which was an odd response, because Margaret didn't know what story she was proposing to tell Mrs. Slaney. The fact that she'd used Margaret's almost unknown first name must mean that the woman had googled her.

Judging by the red cocktail dress, she was a kindred spirit, so Margaret had chosen eight of her favourite Diors. The guaranteed crowd-pleaser was *Venus*, a diaphanous, pale-pink cloud of a strapless ball dress, although it looked as if Mrs. Slaney, like Margaret, was more drawn to the suits and day dresses. Even so, Margaret could not resist the dress's shimmering tiers of scallops, embroidered in an abstract pattern that used ten different kinds of crystals, paillettes and sequins.

Mrs. Slaney greeted several pieces like old friends, others with more reservations but familiarly. Of a double-breasted suit whose buttons slanted down from the bust to the impossibly tiny waist, she said, "The New York collection." It was not said with unalloyed admiration. She was right: the suit came from Dior's first New York line, in 1949, designed for American tastes. It had been one of David's first purchases, at a downtown antiques market, and he looked ever so slightly put out at her hint of dismissal.

How did Mrs. Slaney come to be on such close terms with all these pieces? Margaret was getting the feeling that it was better not to ask. She and David would find out, or not, according to their guest's agenda.

Of a wool coat dress, called *Cocotte*, Mrs. Slaney murmured, "Mine was better."

"You owned this model?"

"Yes, but I got rid of it years ago. Yours must have been modified for the North American market—the belt has been removed and the quite saucy bustle effect is toned down here."

From the front, the slim dress was perfectly behaved, with a velvet collar and set-in pockets. At the back, flamboyantly in the original and more decorously here, the wool draped into an upstanding bustle. It was as if a modest bird had suddenly revealed a raucous, attention-seeking tail. Dior's 1948 preoccupation with women's backsides was so obvious that the press called the collection "the Paris *derrière*."

"Actually, the owner of the dress bought Dior's original design," Margaret told Mrs. Slaney, "but she had the bustle adjusted."

Her visitor softened. "She was probably right. It was hard to wear a coat with it, and impossible to sit. I didn't wear it often, and when I did, it was with the feeling that I was wearing a *tour de force*. Not the most comfortable thing."

From the minute Mrs. Slaney entered the hall, she had been eyeing but not approaching something at the far end. She was saving it for last. Now she circled the *Pondichéry* jacket slowly.

"I worked on this design," she said matter-of-factly. "I was rather known for my back pleats. This one, as you see, opens up the whole jacket and gives it its swing."

David's and Margaret's mouths dropped in unison.

"You worked on this? You worked at Dior?"

"Yes, I was in the *atelier flou*. But could I be rather rude and remind you that you promised me a cup of tea? I would love to have that now, but only if you will permit me to come back here very briefly just to see *Pondichéry* once more."

The Director's sitting room was small, warmly lit and furnished with lovely things that were not needed at the moment for display. On a table by the window, an eighteenth-century leather picnic case lay open to show cups, saucers and plates in yellow-and-white Derby porcelain. Their own tea things waited on top of a Japanese *tansu* chest, which David eyed anxiously.

"Come sit here by me, Mrs. Slaney. You don't want to be too close to Margaret. She's a spiller."

As if to oblige, Margaret made a bit of a mess pouring her tea.

Once Mrs. Slaney was settled with her cup of jasmine tea, well away from Margaret's wayward elbows, the questions began.

"What years did you work at Dior?"

"Well, I began as a *petite main,* you would say a seamstress, a few months before the opening of the house, on that mercilessly cold day of February 12, 1947"—she looked as if she invoked that historic date at least partly ironically—"and I stayed until the mid-fifties."

"And you worked in the *atelier flou* the whole time?"

Remembering that David did not know the inner workings of a couture house, Margaret explained that soft things like dresses and gowns were made in the *atelier flou* and tailored suits and coats were made in the *atelier tailleur*.

"Yes, I worked in the *flou*. I wanted to learn to tailor and eventually work in the *atelier tailleur,* but it was never the right time. *Pondichéry* was an exception in that I was seconded to the *tailleur* for that piece. Perhaps it was my so-called expertise in the inverted back pleat"—she smiled without looking too modest—"and sewing a fabric with that heavy embroidery wasn't easy. It wasn't that the *atelier tailleur* was more prestigious than the *flou,* but I craved the rigour of the tailoring, its strictness." She sipped her tea. "I think I have a rather strict personality."

Their guest was relaxing.

Margaret asked, "When you were working there, did you have a sense that Dior was turning the couture world upside down, that he was making a revolution?"

Even before Mrs. Slaney said, "Nonsense!" Margaret could see that she had been naive.

"There were other designers before the war and during it who were making dresses with big skirts, who rounded the shoulders and plunged the necklines. Even Chanel, who became famous for her straight-up-and-down silhouettes, designed such a dress in '39. Balmain made one in '45, and also Balenciaga. But Dior got all the credit. Revolution, my eye!"

In that surprising outburst, something about the pronunciation of her old-fashioned "my eye!" reminded Margaret that English was not their guest's first language.

David must have reacted to something similar because he asked, changing the sensitive subject, "So, you are French?"

Mrs. Slaney paused, becoming impassive again. "I was born in Hungary. But I came with my parents to Paris as a ten-year-old."

David was having better luck with questions than Margaret. Returning to the earlier topic, he asked, "So, why did Dior get all the credit for the newness of the New Look?"

"Because he had everything. He had the elegance of his premises at 30 avenue Montaigne. He had all the money he needed from his patron. He had an uncanny gift for public relations that was new to the French. It was his novel idea to make the shows as dramatic as possible—fashion shows before Dior had been as dull and formal as you could imagine—and to provide the press with all kinds of helpful information they had never had. Although he was a shrewd businessman, he came across as humble and friendly.

"And it goes without saying," she added almost reluctantly, "his clothes were breathtaking."

Margaret dared to ask, "What was he like?"

Now Mrs. Slaney's pause seemed shot almost with pain. She said slowly, "I think he was very kind."

A thought derailed Margaret's train of thought and she blurted, "Now I see why the cocktail dress has no label!"

David looked puzzled, but Mrs. Slaney laughed. "Yes, we *petites mains* and the other staff could buy pieces that had been worn in the fashion shows or the private viewings quite cheaply. Each piece was made to a particular model's body and was worn only by her. I didn't have Dior's perfect mannequin body, but I managed to acquire some pieces. And you are right, we only put labels in pieces that were sold in the regular way."

The conversation ricocheted between Margaret and David's curiosity and Mrs. Slaney's willingness to respond, but on her terms. She filled in a few biographical facts. While still working for Dior in the early 1950s, she met an American who worked in the embassy, for the US Agency for International Development. When he was recalled to the States, they married and ultimately settled in Rochester, where he taught development issues at the university. She taught French at the Alliance Française. It sounded to Margaret as if there had been no children, but she was not going to ask that. Presumably, Mrs. Slaney was a widow, and Margaret was not going to ask that either.

The woman drinking jasmine tea on the loveseat had lived in America for more than sixty years. Most of the time, except for that slim slice of foreignness in her accent, she seemed comfortably American. But when she talked about her life as a *petite main*, the Frenchwoman emerged.

Mrs. Slaney had warmed to them, but now she began to look tired. Margaret took her back to the storage hall to say adieu to *Pondichéry* and pressed an invitation into her hand.

"It's for a talk we're putting on next week about the context of Dior's 1947 collection, by a visiting English fashion historian. The talk is open to the public, and this card will let you into a reception afterwards. And Mrs. Slaney, what a treat to meet you. I hope you will visit again."

"Now you must call me Léa." She addressed both Margaret and David.

"Then, Léa, I hope to see you next week."

NOTHING CONCRETE HAD COME OUT of the visit from Léa, but building a relationship with a possible donor was a long game. Plus, the thought of being so close to Dior himself exhilarated Margaret.

Meanwhile, Alexander Beyle, the intern at the *Times*, had left her another message. She had assured him they could talk again closer to the opening, but some instinct made her return his call now.

He got right to the point. "I'm interested in what part Marcel Boussac is going to play in your exhibition."

Conversation with Alexander was like a history quiz. Margaret knew the history, but she stalled for time.

"Boussac, yes. The so-called Cotton King. When he offered, out of the blue, to set Dior up in a couture business of his own, Dior hesitated. It was his clairvoyant, Madame Delahaye, who finally convinced him to accept."

Alexander was not distracted by talk of Dior's clairvoyant. Margaret assumed he knew that the designer never made an important decision without consulting Madame Delahaye, and Alexander was nothing if not focused.

"Boussac's economic collaboration with the Germans was widespread and very well-known," he said sternly. "His connections with German officers and the Vichy Ministry of Industrial Production meant that his textile company stayed in business throughout the occupation. He supported *Le Nouveau Temps*, a pro-Nazi paper, as well as encouraging ultra-collaboration among many sectors of the French economy. Unlike most Frenchmen, the Cotton King did very well in the occupation." Now he sounded as if he were reading notes.

"Yes," Margaret said. "But if all that was so well-known, why was Boussac not even investigated by the purification committees?"

"During the war," Alexander recited, "he had continued to pay the salaries of his employees who were deported to Germany, only then to their families, and people think that may have been a self-protective tactic. The families' gratitude, which he made sure to publicize, covered a multitude of sins. Probably even more important, as one of France's biggest textile manufacturers, he would play a crucial role in the postwar return of couture's international business. With Lucien Lelong as his mentor and Boussac as his patron, it's obvious that Dior and his house were deeply compromised."

Will's prediction that the reporter would move on or be moved on to a new preoccupation hadn't happened, and Margaret felt a dull ache of worry. Flirtation was not one of her strengths, but she tried a confiding kind of flattery.

"Alexander, your research is awesome. I'm so impressed. Did you study history?"

"No."

She soldiered on. "It's just that it's hard for me to believe that your services aren't needed elsewhere in the paper. Where do you find the time to study this in so much detail?"

This line of inquiry seemed to work better, because he said, "Please don't repeat this, but someone is sending anonymous letters to the news editor about your exhibit. And so the editor wants me to check out the facts. To tell the truth, I think he's planning on this being a big feature."

Margaret had told Nancy and Bee more than once not to say "to tell the truth," because it implied that everything up until then had been a lie. Will said she was being pedantic.

"You know, Alexander, I think it's you who should be writing the big feature on this. You've done all the legwork. And once you know the whole story, which I'll be able to tell you in the final lead-up to the opening, it will be that much richer."

She implied, but did not say, that he would be one of the few reporters, if not the only one, to receive the full story.

Then, remembering Sun Tzu's advice about keeping your enemies close, she promised to send him an invitation to next week's lecture and reception. It was a stretch to think of the ingenuous Alexander as an enemy, but his source's persistence was making her nervous.

FIVE

Doc Martens Mary Janes

Margaret had never expected to live permanently in Rochester. She assumed that after she had finished her graduate work at the university, she would move away from upstate New York—perhaps to New England or to bigger places like Chicago or Seattle. She met Will Jackson, who was also doing an MA in history, at the university. He had grown up in Rochester but did not seem particularly attached to it. When they became a couple, "Where should we live after Rochester?" was one of their favourite conversations.

But life intervened. After Will finished his MA, he got a job teaching high school while he waited for Margaret to finish her PhD. Whatever period of history Margaret studied, it was the clothes that snared her. Jerkins, codpieces, slashed sleeves, bloomers, semi-transparent dresses with empire waists, hoop skirts, chemise dresses, whatever weird and ingenious and lovely things people had done with cloth before they put it on their bodies fascinated her. She loved knowing that the word *candidate* came from the shining white (*candidus*) togas men running for office in ancient Rome wore for maximum visibility. When she discovered the English writer Aileen Ribeiro and her series of costume histories, she found an intellectual home and a midden of irresistible details. How could you not marvel at the fact that French aristocrats who wanted to express their solidarity with those who had been guillotined in the Reign of Terror wore a red ribbon or thread at the point on their neck where the blade would have fallen?

Margaret became a fashion historian and was planning a thesis about the vogue for cotton clothes in late eighteenth-century England. Unlike brocades, velvets and silks, the simpler cotton styles could be washed. Clean clothes made unwashed bodies more noticeable, and standards of hygiene rose. Cotton was relatively cheap, so it became a force for democracy—all but the poorest classes could look presentable. But when Margaret was in the early stages of writing, one of her professors told her about a temporary job at Harkness, filling in for someone on maternity leave.

She never went back to her PhD. The backstage world of Fashion and Textiles at the museum was a revelation—she never could have imagined that a small army of people restoring, conserving, researching, discussing and presenting the museum's holdings would share her passionate interest in the invention of the zipper or seventeenth-century nightshirts. Individually, her colleagues could annoy her mightily, and their ideas could be at best kooky and at worst almost fanatical. Right now, Margaret was watching Claire trying to persuade Molly Raines, the timid, secretive curator in the next office, that the world was not ready for an exhibition about contemporary fashion inspired by the medieval nun-composer Saint Hildegard of Bingen. Margaret doubted that, if she got Claire's job, she would be as patient and sympathetic. But even the fixated Molly—perhaps especially the fixated Molly, she thought in her darker moments—was in some ways a soulmate.

The only thing that wasn't completely happy about the story of how things had turned out was that now Margaret Abrams,

MA, was competing with Alan Shea, PhD, for the job of Chief Curator, Fashion and Textiles.

A POSTER OUTSIDE THE MUSEUM announced that Dr. Deirdre Ferrar of the Victoria and Albert Museum would give an illustrated lecture, "The Frivolous French: Anglo-American Reactions to Paris Couture in the 1940s," on January 25 at 8 p.m. Margaret had suggested using a picture of one of Dior's designs on the poster, but Deirdre had insisted on a photograph of some anti–New Look protesters in Chicago. It showed a woman carrying a sign that said *Mr. Dior/ We Abhor/ Dresses to the Floor*. Afterwards, Margaret thought this should have been her first clue that things were not going to go as she wished.

At seven thirty on the night of the lecture, Margaret was waiting for the staff elevator when she heard someone behind her. It was Gareth, and an expression she could not define crossed his face when he saw her. It was perhaps guarded, perhaps tired.

"There's another one," he announced curtly, which was unlike him. "Come up with me and I'll show it to you."

"I'm a little tight for time, Gareth. I have to get my notes to introduce the speaker, in my office . . ." She looked more closely at his face. "Okay, but just for a minute."

Gareth unlocked his office and took the latest arrival from a desk drawer. It was a plaid woman's handkerchief, about six inches square, with intersecting stripes of white, green, blue and yellow against the scarlet background.

"It's the Stewart tartan," Gareth said, and to Margaret's look of surprise he added, "My wife is a Campbell. I sent her a picture."

More disconcerting than the well-worn cotton handkerchief was the accompanying note. It asked, "What side are you on?"

That seemed to signal a rise in aggression, and Margaret and Gareth sighed together. A scarf with syrupy images, a piece of costume jewellery and a tartan handkerchief. What sides was the sender thinking of?

"I have to run, Gareth. We'll talk about this tomorrow."

"Break a leg."

The museum followed the wrong-headed policy of having someone introduce the person who was going to introduce the speaker, which made the evening longer and more tedious. The General Director of the museum was introducing Margaret, which should have made her pay attention, but as usual when someone listed her achievements, she zoned out. Her accomplishments interested her less than her shortcomings and failings. From her seat on the stage next to Deirdre Ferrar, she surveyed the sizable audience. She had asked Keitha to keep an eye out for Léa Slaney, and now she saw them sitting together. Good girl. There was Will in the third row. He believed in sitting as close to the front as possible. David Hillman and his wife Jill were roughly in the middle. Wondering briefly why Jill Hillman always seemed so discontented, Margaret spotted someone she knew vaguely from National Public Radio, along with a few donors and most of her department.

Deirdre Ferrar was an exception to Margaret's belief that fashion historians and curators didn't dress with style. In her mid-thirties and an impressive scholar, she dyed her hair fire-engine red and wore it in an ear-length bob with bangs. Besides her signature round, black-rimmed glasses à la Philip Johnson and Doc Martens Mary Janes, tonight she wore a black, unconstructed jacket (later identified by a colleague who specialized in contemporary fashion as "techno stretch, Prada or a knock-off") and a floaty, tie-dyed chiffon skirt.

After an introduction that Margaret tried to keep brief and not cloying, Deirdre took the stage. Once her Mary Janes and lace-trimmed socks were hidden by the podium, she looked more like a grown-up. And, as always in America, a British accent had more cachet than several PhDs.

She began by contrasting the experience of war on the home front in Britain and North America with that of the German occupation of Paris. Limited to rationed food and clothing, and isolated from news of France during the four years of the occupation, the Allies assumed that life under the Germans in France was at least similarly bleak. Here Deirdre showed PowerPoint pictures of British and North American women in mannish suits, with short, straight skirts that used a minimum of rationed yard goods. Wearing their boxy clothes with hand-knitted sweaters, they were seen cheerfully serving in the civilian guard, learning how to cook with food shortages, knitting for soldiers and entertaining them in canteens.

After these edifying images, Deirdre said, "The German occupation had its very real sorrows and dangers, of course, but French *joie de vivre* found a few escape hatches, especially when it came to fashion. And the Allied journalists and military who arrived immediately after Paris was liberated in August 1944 were completely unprepared for what they saw there."

Now she showed rapidly changing pictures of French women wearing peculiar, towering turbans, exaggeratedly big sleeves and full, swirling skirts. Fascinated by their curvaceous shapes, platform sandals and the clouds of perfume in which they moved, the American photojournalist Lee Miller watched the GIs watching Parisian women. They gasped at a town full of pin-ups, she wrote, and thought that "tales of wild women in Paris had come true."

Margaret was starting to feel as if she had a barely discernible pain somewhere she couldn't quite locate, but she had to admit that Deirdre's presentation was unusually adept. Weaving back and forth between her script and her images, her timing was note-perfect.

"Here's a rather startling picture taken by the American war photographer Bob Landry, a few weeks after liberation," she said.

On a shabby Paris street, a model wearing a smart coat dress, high heels and a hat that looked like a throw pillow rested her gloved hand on a damaged American tank. Behind the model, a man hunched on the ground with his few possessions in bags.

Deirdre purred that the photograph "brought the two extremes of war and fashion very close together..."

Silently, Margaret finished her sentence, "in a way that is borderline distasteful." Wearing a cap, the man sitting on the street stared straight ahead, ignoring the woman. What was in Landry's mind, Margaret wondered, to juxtapose the smiling, elegantly dressed model with the battered tank and the distressed man? She had never met a woman who would fondle a filthy tank in kid gloves. Even if the intent was to document a "Look! We have come through" kind of moment, it struck her as monumentally insensitive.

Deirdre quoted *The New York Times*, which asked sarcastically on September 1, five days after liberation, "What is this happy, prosperous place whose beautifully shod women our own style-conscious women can only envy?... It now seems that Fashion never actually departed from the banks of the Seine. Apparently, it needs a much larger German occupation than four years to undermine the prestige of centuries."

Deirdre continued, "All of that would have been at most an amusing look at the Gallic talent for glamour and"—lowering her voice confidentially—"shall we say, superficiality"—laughter, slightly tentative, from the audience—"except for one thing: the Allies and the French still had to fight—together—to win the war. And this disparity between sacrifices at home and what they saw in Paris grated on the Allies. Plus, it looked as if Paris was partying while American boys were still dying on French soil."

Looking out from the stage, Margaret could see that this was a new idea for many in the audience. Deirdre explained that irritation at French frivolity had to be squelched as soon as possible. British and American journalists were assigned to quiet their compatriots' suspicions. Dutifully, they claimed that the over-decorated styles Paris had produced during the occupation were a make-work project to keep couture and its accompanying trades employed. That the flamboyant designs and their reckless use of cloth were a way to mock the Germans, or to flaunt the regulations, or to appeal to the vulgar tastes of the Nazi wives and mistresses. None of these excuses were convincing, and the last was particularly untrue, as the vast majority of couture sales during the occupation were to French women.

Now Deirdre fast-forwarded to February 1947. The war had been won, but France was far from recovered. Almost half a million buildings were still in ruins, and sabotaged dams had flooded vast tracts of land. The French were obsessed with the food they could not buy, and on the morning of February 12, the daily bread ration was lowered from 350 grams to 200. Deirdre illustrated this with images of derelict fields and hungry-looking people on war-torn streets. After about a dozen of these, she began intercutting them with pictures of a classically detailed stone building with an elegant sign above the door announcing, *Christian Dior*.

On that same morning when the bread ration was lowered, Deirdre intoned (as if to suggest some sinister connection between the ration and the new business, Margaret thought huffily), a group of about one hundred people waited in below-zero temperatures outside 30 avenue Montaigne. The doors opened at 10 a.m., and half an hour later, when the first floor was so packed that guests had to sit on the stairs, Dior launched his house and its first collection. Deirdre began flipping rapidly through images of the collection, the white shantung peplum jacket with the black pleated skirt that became the symbol of the New Look, the dresses whose padded hips and breasts emphasized waists so tiny they looked as if they would snap, the décolleté necklines and abundant skirts.

"Many of you recognize these designs because they are part of fashion history," Deirdre said. "The uproar was fantastic, pro and con. The fashion press adored them. The woman in the street, not so much. The in-your-face extravagance of the clothes when many were still suffering roused actual violence in a Montmartre street market." She showed a famous photograph of an aborted fashion shoot where the model's dress was literally ripped off her back by three furious market women.

Reactions in North America were non-violent but strongly negative in some quarters. There were newspaper photos of a poker-faced Dior being met at the Chicago train station by protesters whose signs read *Christian Dior Go Home*, *Down with the New Look* and *Burn Christian Dior*. Chicagoans, who saw the new long skirts as reactionary and wasteful, founded the Little Below the Knee Club, which mushroomed in several cities. Men in Georgia started the League of Broke Husbands and hoped that their 30,000 members would "hold that hemline." More than 1,500 Canadian women supported the Society for the Prevention of Longer Skirts for Women.

"Obviously, there were several ways in which the world wasn't ready for Dior's New Look," Deirdre told her audience. "It relied on a radical reshaping of the female body. The longer, fuller skirts demanded almost unobtainable amounts of material. Men missed seeing women's legs. And yet, in spite of that, the New Look was a huge success. On the level of haute couture, women actually bought these styles. On the level of international publicity, the press worshipped the fledgling house and gave it unheard-of publicity. As for the ordinary woman whose budget would never stretch to couture, the designs worked their way down to affordable, wearable department store versions.

"And now"—she smiled with British faux humility—"I've talked far too long. Thank you for your patience, and I look forward to your questions."

After healthy applause, a few hands lifted and an intern, seconded from European History and Culture, carried a microphone to the people with questions. Some were designed to display the questioner's knowledge, others asked things that Deirdre had already answered in her lecture. Deirdre prefaced her responses by complimenting each speaker on a "brilliant" or at least a "very good" question.

When the questions slowed, Alan Shea stood up. The staff let the public lead the questions but chimed in when necessary to keep the Q & A going.

"Deirdre, that was absolutely marvellous," he began, to show that they were friends. No "Dr. Ferrar" for him. He asked, "Do you think that Dior was oblivious to what was going on in the wider world?"

Deirdre said, "Obliviousness wasn't a possibility for him. His younger sister Catherine, with whom he was very close, worked in intelligence in the Resistance. She was imprisoned and tortured, but she refused to inform on her colleagues. Finally, she was sent to the concentration camp at Ravensbrück and other work camps. When she returned to Paris in 1945, having been very probably raped by the Russian soldiers who enabled her escape, her brother barely recognized her. So, there was no way for Dior to avoid the horrors of the occupation.

"And yet, in spite of that, not as a brother but as a couturier, he *did* live in a particular kind of bubble—one he chose consciously and that was very much a reaction to the real world he knew. A couturier is selling a fantasy, an impossible and often beautiful dream. In his case, Dior sensed that women longed for relief from the dowdy making-do of the war years and a return to extravagance. And he was right."

Keitha raised her hand and stood up as the microphone neared her. She had continued lobbying for an alcove in *The New Look* devoted to Dior's corsets, and Margaret wondered if she would raise the underwear question now.

"Thank you, Dr. Ferrar, that was just wonderful," she said. "I'm wondering how British and North American women, some of whom had had seven or eight years of doing men's jobs by 1947, wearing clothes they could move and work in, wearing pants even—and I've read that Dior never, ever designed a pair of pants! But I'm rambling, sorry. I just wanted to ask, how did it make sense for those women to start wearing corsets so punishing that even taking a deep breath was difficult? And to wear clothes that were so complicated and heavy that they often needed help just getting into them?"

Flushed, Keitha sat down abruptly. Deirdre assured her that was a key question, absolutely key.

"One thing about fashion that I'm sure you've noticed is that 'sense' is not one of its most pressing goals." Approving chuckles from the audience. "But I think, at a deeper level, the New Look made psychological sense because women wanted to throw away their overalls and climb into party clothes, even if it was just in their imaginations."

Keitha did not look convinced, and she stood again and opened her mouth, perhaps to add something about Dior's punishing lingerie. But Margaret decided that the allotted twenty minutes for questions had run out, and she rose to thank Dr. Ferrar for a stimulating and provocative talk. Deirdre took a chair on the stage, to autograph copies of her newest book, *Always in Style: French Women and Their Clothes*. Those invited to the reception went to the small rotunda outside the European Furniture Gallery and started celebrating without her. Gareth would bring Deirdre once she had finished signing.

Jill Hillman, David's wife, came up to Margaret in the rotunda, as usual with the air that she was fulfilling an obligation. She spent many volunteer hours coordinating other museum volunteers, and her attitude to the museum was invariably proprietary and disapproving. After looking over the catering and the service, she said she thought it was a shame that no one had asked the speaker if she really did think the French were frivolous, since she had put that word in her title. She didn't approve of branding an entire country with one adjective. Margaret thought, *Then why didn't you ask that question?* Feeling more than a touch negative herself, she had no patience with negative people. Why were really nice people, like David, so often drawn to spend their lives with difficult people?

Handing her a flute of something bubbly that was bound to be a disappointment, Will whispered in her ear, "I thought it was very good, and much livelier than the usual. But I can tell you don't think so."

Horrified, Margaret asked through her teeth, "How do you know?"

"Because I know the difference between your approving-face mask and the real thing. But relax, no one else does. Plus, the real giveaway is that you're not eating the petits fours."

As if to hide her unhappiness, the next time the waiter swirled her way, she accepted one with a lemon flourish on top. Then she made her way to Léa Slaney, who was standing with Keitha.

Léa said it had been an excellent talk, with much to think about. Keitha agreed, although she had to be reassured that her question had not been totally stupid.

Margaret asked Léa, "You didn't think the speaker painted too negative a picture?"

Léa looked surprised. "Why would I think that? That's how things were. A mess in many ways, both before and after Dior's debut. But he was like cream, he always rose to the top. The American buyers who had come to Paris to see the spring collections hadn't even bothered to stay for the first collection of an unknown designer, and they flew back to the States. When they landed, they read Carmel Snow's glowing review in *Harper's Bazaar* and got back on a plane to return to Paris and place lots of orders. That's the kind of thing that happened to Dior."

Keitha lived not too far from Léa and had offered to drive her home. Margaret decided to be grateful for that kindness, and also not to resent Keitha's question, even if she had already heard enough from Keitha about Dior's responsibility for making women feel bad about their bodies.

She walked the two women over to the coat rack, but Léa gently batted away Margaret's offer to help with her coat. Keitha's coat was a large wool patchwork, like a cape with sleeves.

When Margaret admired it, Keitha said, "My patchwork tent, you mean. I got it at Century 21."

Why was even the modest Keitha more willing than Margaret to go out on a limb with her clothes?

Meanwhile, Deirdre had finished her signing duties and was holding court in the rotunda. She never seemed to tire of saying, "Actually, it's pronounced Deir-DREE, not Deir-DRUH." When Alan Shea made his way to her, they fell ostentatiously into each other's arms and cried, "Darling!"

The General Director and Gareth both seemed cheered that there were political and sociological elements involved in the New Look: the exhibition wouldn't have to be all hemlines. They looked forward to it more than ever, they told a poker-faced Margaret. She did manage to ask Gareth in an aside if he could send her the picture of the plaid handkerchief that he'd sent his wife.

Margaret had picked out a tall, skinny young man wearing glasses for Alexander Beyle, but the man who introduced himself to her as the *Times* intern was sturdier, blond, and looked at least a few years out of college.

"Alexander, I expected you to have a question or two for the speaker," she teased him.

He said, seriously, "I have an hour-long interview with Dr. Ferrar booked for tomorrow."

Of course he did.

Patricia Bertelli, an NPR producer Margaret knew slightly, approached. "I had no idea there was so much strife in the backstory of the New Look," she said happily. She was thinking of a documentary about those dark corners and she hoped she could count on Margaret's full co-operation. Patricia was a nice woman, and her children had been in daycare with Nancy and Bee. Margaret smiled wanly. Her head was starting to hurt.

She had already thanked Deir-DREE again, and she looked around for Will, to suggest that they could leave. He and David Hillman were deep in conversation, their flutes of Prosecco rising and falling with their opinions. On her way to Will, and trying mindfully not to collide with anyone, she was stopped by Rivkah Waldman. Rivkah was a lawyer who had made some important donations of her mother's couture wardrobe, and Margaret liked her. She was small and talked in excited bursts.

"Margaret, that was fascinating, just fascinating. It made me think about my mother and her Diors. And her life, which was cosseted and at the same time very stifled. And I wonder what you think of the idea of having a part of your exhibit devoted to the lives Dior's customers led? Not a big part of the show, don't worry! There must be some archival material, and we could talk about audiotapes and other things. Just in an alcove, maybe. I'm thinking out loud right now, but if you have time for coffee tomorrow, we could talk about it. I'm between trials, so my time is a bit freer. And I'm sure you have deadlines, so the sooner the better. If we could come to an agreement, I could see my way to doing something to support the exhibit."

How many people wanted to guest-curate a special-interest alcove, Margaret wondered. There was Keitha with corsetry, Rivkah with women's lives, and probably the General Director and Gareth would like one on couture's contribution to France's balance of payments. If her plans included any alcoves, which so far they did not, they would be devoted to something delicious—for example, the Roger Vivier shoes Dior had favoured for his clothes. But she could not ignore Rivkah's carrot. She invited her for coffee at 10 a.m.

MARGARET WAS DRIVING, because she had felt too dispirited to drink the museum's mediocre offerings. Will shifted in the passenger seat, unused to the space left for her long legs.

He asked, "So what didn't you like?"

"You're going to think this is silly, but the brilliant lecture left a bad taste in my mouth. I feel as if I had a gleaming, big red balloon and Deirdre stuck a few pins in it. You can't even see them, they're tiny and in an out-of-the-way place, but my balloon is slowly losing some of its shiny roundness."

Will turned to address her profile. "If one pin is the information that an important sector of the French economy tried to save itself during the occupation, while French women tried to look good, even if it meant some black market and other shady transactions, then yes, you are being silly. And if the other pin is that Dior started a couture house when a lot of people's lives were still very deprived, then you are being even sillier."

"I know, you're right. I know. But I don't get the point of tarnishing Dior's name with crimes and misdemeanours committed by other people in the occupation, when he was nothing but a minor cog in Lelong's house, or in the aftermath of the war. And I'm not saying Deirdre set out to do that, it just leaves a connection in people's minds."

"Margaret, you work in a museum. I don't believe you haven't noticed that one of the big projects of our time is to put absolutely everyone who exercised influence and power under the microscope. It doesn't matter that Dior was a nobody until 1947. Some investigator just might find something shameful about his doings in the occupation or after the war."

Margaret turned onto Rockingham Street. "But why? There are plenty of uncontroversially bad people to expose, rather than a shy man who just wanted to make women look beautiful."

"Why? Well, for starters, money and success. Dior had both. The potentially good side of all the revisionist hunting is that it could illuminate the complexity of the past. The problem is that the ransackers are only looking for the bad side. You're the opposite. You fiercely resent any suggestion that Dior was not a saint. Both you and the possible detractors need balance."

Margaret looked out the window. So Will was against her too. She knew she was over-invested in the idea of Dior being above reproach, but knowing that didn't affect her feelings.

When she was silent, he went on. "Sweetheart, this isn't a canonization you're working on. It's a museum show. What's wrong with this story: in a very imperfect world, a man incidentally benefited from the questionable doings of others and made beautiful clothes, which didn't appeal to everyone. What would you give up if you accepted that version? It sounds as if you're losing perspective. And I know it's going to be a great show."

"Will, I love you—"

He interrupted. "'—but I don't want to talk about it anymore tonight.'"

She shot him a questioning look.

"Because," he answered the look, "that's usually what you say when you start out with 'I love you.'"

Now did she have to add "bad wife" to her overflowing cup of troubles?

Will said, "That was a poignant story about Dior's sister."

"Yes. He named his first perfume Miss Dior in her honour."

There were very few pictures of Catherine Dior, and Margaret had a cloudy memory of having seen them in a biography of her brother. She remembered a square face and a distinct resemblance to Christian. But the face she could not get out of her mind was that of the man in Robert Landry's photograph, sitting impassive on the Paris sidewalk, staring at nothing, his belongings reduced to two bags. Even his posture, arms carelessly resting on his knees, spoke of the toll taken by war. Perhaps she had been too hard on Landry. Perhaps he had planned his photograph to suggest that while normal life, in the person of the chic model, might be returning, the horror of war remained just down the street.

At home, once Margaret had taken off her insuperably boring black pantsuit, she checked her email. Gareth had already sent the picture of the handkerchief. She forwarded that, along with pictures of the scarf and the brooch, to Deirdre Ferrar, explaining how they had come to her.

"This is confidential, of course," she wrote. "But you know this period so well, I just wonder if these things have anything in common except their age."

Deirdre was nothing if not efficient. Before Margaret had turned out her light, exhausted beyond anything, Deirdre texted back, "At first glance, I have absolutely no idea. But I'll keep thinking about it. Going out for supper with Alan now!"

Margaret tried to remember whose idea it had been to invite Deirdre Ferrar to speak. She was pretty sure it had been Alan's. Well, whoever's idea it had been, she was going to have to assume that it had nothing to do with undermining *The New Look*.

SIX

Bat Mitzvah by Dior

At breakfast the next morning, Margaret described Deirdre Ferrar's outfit to Nancy and Bee.

"Very cutting edge," Nancy concluded. Margaret nodded, glumly, and Nancy said consolingly, "Mom, your style is classic."

The girls were trying to call her Mom and not Mommy, which they'd decided was babyish, but it still sounded to Margaret like an effort. In spite of her low wardrobe self-esteem, Margaret felt better this morning. The lecture had aroused lots of interest, and she was going to concentrate on that, without worrying about possible consequences. Her anxiety that others' bad behaviour in the war might dim Dior's lustre was probably neurotic. Maybe she should give meditation another try. Or Cognitive Behavioural Therapy, which her therapist sister Lydia was always talking up.

She looked at Will, who was spreading marmalade lavishly on his toast, the way a mason might slather mortar on a brick. When she first knew him, he thought couture was innately silly, and at a deep level he probably still did. But eighteen years with Margaret had schooled him to see it like a series of Fabergé eggs, exquisitely designed and made but not useful.

"But it is useful," she would say. "Dior's clothes provide warmth and privacy."

"For the ultra-rich."

It was one of the founding arguments of their marriage, and they knew their parts well.

At this point, Margaret would remind him of Olympia Dukakis's line in *Steel Magnolias* that what distinguishes us from animals is our ability to accessorize. "Something else that sets us apart from animals," she would add, "is our ability to take a practical necessity like clothes and make them beautiful."

But she didn't need to go through their routine this morning. She felt grateful for Will's sturdy common sense. And sometime, as soon as *The New Look* was on budget and on schedule, she would think about his hint that she was reluctant to talk about sensitive things.

She asked, "What's Crispin up to today?"

"One of his elderly parishioners is convinced that someone—probably the murderer—has stolen the church's chalice and paten. Actually, the parishioner has put them away in the wrong cupboard, but the parish is in an uproar."

Bee wanted to know what a paten was—she could guess about the chalice. While Will explained, Margaret thought, *These heathen girls are learning odd bits and pieces about religion from murder mysteries.*

MARGARET TEXTED CONSERVATION. "I have a meeting at 10 a.m. with the younger sister of the Bat Mitzvah group. Could you put out all three dresses on mounts in the storage hall by then? Thank you."

She'd already had a text from Deirdre, who apparently did not need much sleep. "I have an idea about your gifts. I'm meeting a reporter at the museum at ten, so could we have coffee around eleven?"

Between Rivkah and Deirdre, it was shaping up to be a very caffeinated morning.

Margaret walked to work, taking Goodman Street and going past the staff entrance on Park. The museum's main entrance was on East Avenue, and before she went in, she wanted to rest her eyes for a minute on East Avenue's anthology of opulent mansions. It was the architectural equivalent of taking deep breaths.

Of the trio of Rust Belt cities in upstate New York—Rochester, Buffalo and Syracuse—Rochester was considered the snootiest and most full of itself. Its detractors liked to point to the title of a notorious book about the city, *Smugtown, USA*. When her friends from college and Syracuse asked what it was like to live in Rochester, Margaret always said it depended on your address. From Rockingham Street, the city's hospitals, colleges and museums, the Rochester Philharmonic and the network of parks designed by Frederick Law Olmsted could make you think you lived in a place of great privilege. (The exception was the city's underfunded school system. The twins' school was barely okay, and only Margaret and Will's belief in public schools kept them there.) On the other hand, if your address was north of the Inner Loop, on Joseph Avenue or the streets that crossed it, you lived in a racially segregated city with a poverty rate more than three times the national average, and a corresponding rate of crime.

Cynics said that Rochester was less than the sum of its parts. Margaret did not go that far, but she was uneasily aware that she mostly lived insulated from the city's serious problems. Now, as she walked, she tried to focus on East Avenue's stately houses and high-maintenance landscaping.

Half an hour later, she greeted Rivkah at the museum elevator with a pair of gloves.

"I thought you might want to say hello to some old friends before we sit down."

In 1957, Rivkah's older sister, Dina, made her bat mitzvah. The idea of including twelve-year-old girls in the Jewish ceremonial entrance into adulthood was novel in those days, and the girls' father had been doubtful. His wife persuaded him. She also arranged for Dior to dress her two daughters as well as herself for the dinner after the service.

Now the three dresses stood in a little family grouping in the middle of the storage hall. Rivkah laughed at the sight and touched Margaret's elbow.

"When I see what kids wear now for bar and bat mitzvahs, these are indescribably modest and old school."

The girls' dresses were so classic they looked almost undesigned, like something Margaret's grandmother would have drawn quickly on brown paper—plain tops, Rivkah's with a Peter Pan collar and puff sleeves, Dina's with a high, heart-shaped neckline and short sleeves, and full, ballerina-length skirts. The dresses relied entirely on France's best fabric, something not available to Margaret's grandmother—custom-made, hand-embroidered cotton organdy. Dina's was covered with white narcissi, lit up by bright-yellow centres. Her skirt was stiffened by eight layers of organza, net and horsehair, and for extra shape Dior added an interior ruffle that stretched from the thirteen-year-old's waist to her hip.

The organdy for Rivkah, who was then Rebecca—she adopted the Hebrew form of her name later, while living on a kibbutz—was all stylized white-on-white flowers, sometimes at wide intervals, sometimes thickly strewn, with eyelets and a scalloped hem.

"The part I loved most," Rivkah said, "although I couldn't see it when I was wearing it, were these twenty-eight covered buttons up the back, each one embroidered with a flower. For an eight-year-old princess, even if your sister was getting all the attention, what was there not to like?"

Her mother's dress had begun life in Dior's 1957 New York collection as a wedding dress, but by shortening the train it became a covered-up evening dress, with three-quarter sleeves, a shawl collar and sprays of blossoms woven into its shimmering *velours de coup* satin.

Walking around her mother's dress, Rivkah said, "Both Dina and I considered wearing it for our first weddings. But in the seventies it just looked dated, not 'vintage.' I got married in an Oscar de la Renta sheath with a scoop neckline and transparent chiffon sleeves instead. For my second wedding, I wore a pantsuit."

Close to seventy, still practising law and well put together, Rivkah said, "I'm not planning a third wedding, but you never know. This time, I think I'd go with something ultra-pure and uncompromising, like Jil Sander."

In Margaret's chaotic office, Rivkah moved a stack of books and papers from a chair onto an even more piled-upon chair and sat down on the empty one.

Sliding the cup of coffee Margaret gave her to a less dangerous place on the desk between them, she said, "That talk last night made me so excited about your exhibition, Margaret. It also made me think about my mother and her life. As the speaker said, Dior knew the customer he wanted—sophisticated, elegant, with deep pockets. Example A: Ruth Miriam Waldman. She loved dressing up, and her clothes often gave her deep joy. Not the bat mitzvah dress, I think. She was still young and fit, and it was matronly, although that was the style in 1957. Today the bat mitzvah mothers wear sexy, short, strapless dresses.

"Some of my mother's favourite Diors were that parade of impeccable tailored suits—a new one bought every two or so years—in which she chaired hundreds of Hadassah committee meetings. Those came to you, and you also have what I think was her most beloved piece of all, that wonderful black faille swing coat that she wore over dance dresses and out to dinner for years. When she put it on, she would swirl for us, and that silk faille caught the light. You had a poetic name for all those little tears in the faille."

Margaret laughed. "Depends on your idea of poetry. We call it 'inherent vice' when some instability in the fabric continues to cause splits no matter what we do. In the case of that silk faille, the silk makers immersed the threads in metallic salts to give the fabric more weight, and that was its doom. But the coat is such a marvel of construction, including its completely hidden lining, that we're coddling it with everything we have, from acid-free tissue to the right humidity and a totally dark environment."

"Well, my father coddled my mother too, on one level. There were the clothes, jewellery, trips to Florida in the winter and Europe in the spring and the cottage in the summer. From a less sentimental angle, her looks and clothes were important signs to other men that his law practice was doing well. And my mother, who was better suited to law than I am, had to satisfy her talent for strategy and organization with volunteer fundraising.

"Someone mentioned Dior's body shapers last night. My mother and her friends boasted that when you wore couture, you only needed to buy panties—everything else was built into the dress. But her life was like her corsetry. There wasn't much scope for individuality: the dress wore the woman. She loved her Diors, and her Balmains and Lanvins, but there was a bargain struck there."

Margaret thought of her own mother, a generation younger than Rivkah's and not rich. She too had loved clothes, the ones she bought on sale and the ones she made. The closest she ever came to couture was sewing a Vogue pattern based on a design by Dior or another designer, but Margaret imagined that her mother and Mrs. Waldman had felt a similar joy in the look and feel of a fabric, the sureness of a line, the inevitability of the perfect colour, the unapologetic *flattery* of the right dress. Rivkah saw her mother's clothes as a reward. Margaret saw her mother's as a refuge from the mostly happy stress of family life and her long-time job as a school principal.

Rivkah had paused, and Margaret returned to the present.

"Rivkah, I couldn't agree more. Your mother's generation paid a price when they accepted the traditional role for a woman— one a lot of them didn't realize until their daughters set out on another path. So, it's an important story. But is this the right place for it? It would be so drastically compressed in a corner of all this Dior glamour, it wouldn't get its due."

"I'm not looking for an in-depth investigation, Margaret. But since you're going to acknowledge the women whose clothes are the stars of the exhibition, wouldn't it interest people to get a glimpse into their lives? It could be quite simple—a few audiotapes with interviews of the women themselves or memories from their children. And pictures, any relevant videos. I could get you lots of archival stuff from the Jewish community. I'll leave the Gentiles to you."

At the mention of the Gentiles, Rivkah gave her an amused look that stopped just short of being conspiratorial. She had sent the look Margaret's way before, but had never followed it with a question. As Margaret usually did when she thought people were wondering if she was Jewish, she ignored it.

She stifled a sigh. It seemed as if everybody else knew how to curate an exhibit at least as well as Margaret. She considered: *The New Look* would occupy four generous rooms and the display staff could easily create one or more alcoves along the edges of the space. Rivkah was convincing, although Margaret would have preferred an alcove dedicated to the intricacies of silk production for Dior's fabrics. But why was she trying to shoot herself in the foot? There was the promise of badly needed money and, more important, Rivkah's idea wasn't a bad one. It was actually a good idea, even if it felt like sociology, not fashion history. Meanwhile, it was the end of January and the time for conceiving and planning an alcove was rapidly running out. She promised Rivkah that she would give her scheme serious thought.

They stopped in again at the bat mitzvah dresses before Rivkah left.

"Just look at the way the scalloped hem is lit up by those eyelets," Rivkah said of her dress. "What an innocent world."

Was it? Looked at in a certain way, Rochester in 1957 did seem innocent. But however safe and prosperous the Waldmans were in Rochester, Dina's bat mitzvah was a mere twelve years removed from the Second World War. Margaret had no idea how many of Rivkah's family had stayed in Europe, and how few of them had survived. For the Rochester Waldmans, the innocence and simplicity of Dior's dresses was a luxury. For the family members who had not left Europe in time, innocence was not an option.

Where were these dark thoughts coming from? Maybe the slide Deirdre Ferrar had shown of the man sitting on the Parisian sidewalk with his bags was still floating around in Margaret's unconscious. To distract herself, she said, "You know, I've never asked you what you wore for *your* bat mitzvah."

"Well, there was a sea change between Dina's bat mitzvah in 1957 and mine in 1962. I wore an early Courrèges, from his second season. They called it a minishift, although *mini* in those days meant a mere four inches above the knee. My mother went from horror when I first broached it to seeing the fun in it."

Green with longing, Margaret said, "I wonder what happened to that dress."

"My mother probably donated it to the Hadassah bazaar. She never saw Courrèges in the same class with Dior."

THIS MORNING, DEIRDRE WAS wearing crew socks with her Mary Janes and a linen apron over a long-sleeved, striped T-shirt.

The apron's broad straps crossed in the back and its generous sides usually but not always covered what Margaret's mother would have called her backside.

Taking the chair recently vacated by Rivkah, Deirdre dosed her coffee with milk and three spoonfuls of sugar. Margaret avoided looking at her own cup.

"That fellow from the newspaper is like a dog with a bone. The occupation has been over for seventy-five years, but to him it's brand new and filled with villains. Could I see your mystery gifts?"

Margaret laid the three items, in their packaging, on her desk.

Deirdre looked them over and said, "No surprises here. But I wanted to make sure. The obvious answer came to me this morning when I wasn't quite awake. I'm pretty confident they're all coded signals of the Resistance. Or at least of affiliation with Britain."

"Coded signals of the Resistance." Margaret hoped that by repeating that bizarre idea it might sink in faster.

"Yes. Women in Vichy France showed their allegiance to General Pétain and his conservative values by wearing rural, nostalgic prints and scarves decorated with images of Joan of Arc, Louis XIV and Pétain himself. At the other end of the political spectrum, women in the occupied zone found ways to cock a snook at the Germans without incriminating themselves, also through their clothes. If you look at the scarf, the giveaways are the English word *love* above two clasped hands in a garland and the Staffordshire dogs—lamentably twee but uniquely English. Wearing this scarf signalled your support for the only country still fighting the Germans by the summer of 1940.

"Similarly, the handkerchief. Tartan had been a French favourite for a long time, but during the war wearing it meant one thing—friendship with Britain. The only people in Paris who didn't know that were the Germans, so you could arrange this little dear in your breast pocket and wear it without any fear of reprisal."

"And the pin? I know it's a knock-off of a Cartier design."

"Cartier was a strong supporter of General de Gaulle, and the original bird in his gilded cage was a clear nod to the occupation. This pin is making the same point in plastics and painted metal."

"Deirdre, you are brilliant. I can't thank you enough. And just look at the messages that came with them. With the scarf, 'Something you will want to consider.' With the pin, 'This is right up your alley, isn't it?' And the handkerchief's message asks, 'What side are you on?'

"So," Margaret continued, going slowly as she tried to figure it out, "is the sender warning me not to forget the occupation? But what is it I should remember about the occupation? And why would I, or the exhibit, be on the Nazi side? None of this really touches on Dior."

Deirdre said, "Is the sender trying to remind you that Dior didn't just spring up out of nothing but, like all the French of his generation, had lived through a devastating decade?"

"No one is denying that," Margaret said, "but I wonder what I'm supposed to do with this information."

Deirdre looked more grave than Margaret had expected. "I don't know," she said. "But there's something creepy about it."

She had a plane to catch, so, after more expressions of gratitude from Margaret, she left, saying, "I don't think you've heard the last of this. Let me know about any further packages."

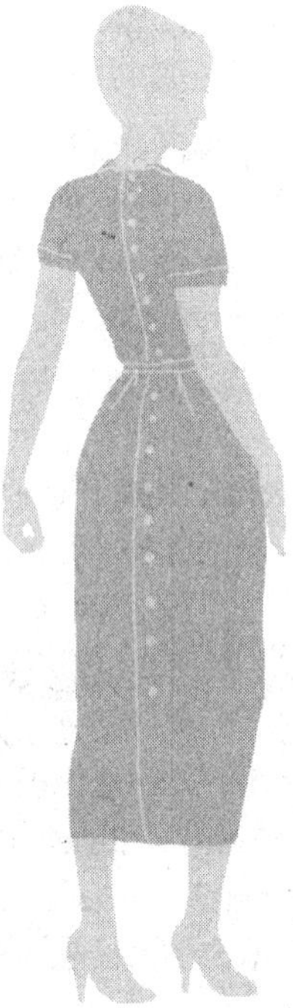

LONDRES

DIOR FOUNDED HIS HOUSE on the wish, as he put it, to design for a small group of supremely elegant women. In his mind, especially at the start of his career, his ideal client had a maid to help with getting in and out of her Diors. A dress that buttoned at the back, as did several of his 1947 designs, was no impediment for such a woman. *Londres*, with seventeen large, covered buttons that travel down the back from the neck to near the hem, is a case in point.

One of the more youthful and timeless designs of the fall 1947 collection, *Londres* is an effortless-looking sheath with short, cuffed sleeves and a rolled neck. Serge Balkin photographed it from the eye-catching back as the model ascends the curvaceous, wrought iron staircase in the Maison Dior—all the better to contrast with the dress's modernity. Only her accessories, seamed stockings and slingback wedge shoes give away the 1940s date.

Dior's original sketch had shown a black leather sash that ended in a plump bow at the back. Wisely, Margaret thought, he had changed his mind in favour of a more contemporary snakeskin belt.

SEVEN

A Snakeskin Belt

Things had been calm in the two weeks since Deirdre Ferrar's talk. There were no new packages, and no more calls from Alexander Beyle at the *Times*. Keitha remained the ideal intern, although her preoccupation with Dior's corsetry was inching up.

Alan Shea had just returned from Japan, where he had been nailing down experts and pieces for his forthcoming blockbuster show *Japonisme and Contemporary Fashion*. It would trace the Western infatuation with Japanese style, usually considered a nineteenth-century phenomenon, up to the present day. The exhibit was Alan's calling card for the job of Chief Curator, as *The New Look* was Margaret's. She was sorry to see him back. With Alan away, there had been no undermining comments at the department meetings about *The New Look*.

There was just one strange thing. Patricia Bertelli, the NPR producer, had telephoned her about an anonymous note she had received in the mail. It said, "There was only one Dior, but there were many Fanny Bergers. Look her up. You're going to hear more from her."

"Of course, I thought of you and your exhibit," Patricia said. "You probably know who she is, but I didn't."

"Never heard of her, but that doesn't mean anything. Who is she?"

"She designed hats and had her own atelier in Paris, beginning in the 1930s. Apparently that was rare for a woman. She was Jewish and that sealed her fate. She died in Auschwitz, in her early forties."

Margaret pushed her chair back from the desk and closed a few of its gaping drawers. "That's horrible," she said slowly. "But I still don't quite understand . . . why are you calling me?"

"Because I have no idea why this person sent me this note or what he or she means by saying that I'm going to hear more from Fanny Berger. How can you hear more from someone who is dead? The mention of 'only one Dior' made me think there's some connection to your exhibit. But it sounds like it's not ringing any bells."

"No, it isn't, but I'll let you know if anything occurs to me. In the meantime, could you send me a picture of the note?"

Margaret had the dismal feeling that it was going to look familiar. She was right: the note was written in the same careful printing that had accompanied the mystery packages.

THE CLOTHES FOR THE EXHIBITION had been finalized, the mounts were well under way, and Margaret needed to keep a close eye on the text panels and to meet with the lighting people. She had asked the design team to carve out two niches and two long, slim window boxes around the perimeter of the main hall. Her ideas for those spaces churned frequently. Other than Keitha's and Rivkah's suggestions, why not, for example, the work of the *petites mains,* the seamstresses who turned Dior's sketches into beautifully finished clothes in the ridiculously short space of three months? Or what about Dior's own inspirations, the flounces and ruchings of the Second Empire or the S-silhouettes of the belle époque styles worn by his adored mother in his early childhood? Rather than feeling exhilarated by her choices, Margaret felt bewildered. Usually she made decisions easily—perhaps too easily. Now she could not stop second-guessing herself.

She hadn't seen Léa Slaney since the night of Deirdre's talk, and then only briefly. But the older woman was on Margaret's mind, partly because David Hillman was sure she had a few pieces that would suit the exhibit, and she might be more persuadable now that she had seen some of the collection. Margaret invited her for lunch, at any place that would be convenient for Léa, and to her delight, Léa accepted.

MEANWHILE, HER SISTER Constance called, sounding resentful.

"We're still clearing things out, but Lydia has to pore over everything, so it takes forever. It seems Dad brought several boxes from Grandma Abrams' house when she died and just put them in the storage unit in the condo. I would throw it all out, but Lydia thinks there's buried treasure there. When are you coming to help us?"

"I feel awful that you two are doing all the work," Margaret said, and meant it. "But I don't know when I—"

"Yeah, your exhibit, I know."

Constance did not sound overwhelmed by the importance of *The New Look*.

"Right now, the timing is really tight and some odd things are happening. I'm hoping that I could come for a weekend in the next few weeks, maybe."

Silence from Constance.

Margaret asked, "Have you found anything at all interesting?"

"I don't think so, but Lydia does. We found Grandpa's employee card from Gordon-Pinkney Men's Clothing."

"What's interesting about that? We know that's where Grandpa worked."

"As I said, it's Lydia who finds this significant. Turns out he was a cutter. Another thing she's found is a bunch of cards and letters from people we never heard of, named Abramson."

Margaret thought about that. "Well, that's a common enough name."

"Lydia's taking another crack at her favourite daydream, 'Our Jewish Dad.' She's building a case that Grandma and Grandpa, or maybe their parents, changed their name from Abramson to Abrams so it would sound less Jewish. But it's Lydia who should be explaining this. By the way, Grandma had kept all of Dad's high school yearbooks, which won't surprise you. I'll email you copies of some of his class pictures. And try and come by the end of the month. Lydia's going home next week, but she'll be back then."

After they hung up, Margaret thought, with surprise and gratification: *So, Grandpa was a cutter.* She had only known that he worked for Gordon-Pinkney, a quality men's tailoring company. If he had lived in Paris rather than Syracuse and been a very good cutter, he might have worked in Dior's *atelier tailleur*. That made her feel closer to him.

She had barely known her father's father, who had died when she was about five. There was one photograph of him in the family album, a staged-looking picture taken at a picnic table outside her grandparents' chicken barn. They were both in their sixties, and her grandmother rather formally presented a platter of corn on the cob to her husband. He was a bald, smiling man, and Margaret's grandmother looked uncharacteristically eager to please. She was a tiny, compelling character who wore her dark hair wound around her head in braids.

Grandma Abrams's religion, as far as Margaret understood from family stories, had seemed to be the teachings of Bernarr Macfadden and other early twentieth-century health faddists. She'd followed their doctrines closely—strict vegetarianism, no alcohol, no caffeine, no medicine, no doctors. When Margaret was prescribed glasses for nearsightedness as a child, her grandmother fed her curds and whey, like Little Miss Muffet. If she ate them regularly, her grandmother said, her nearsightedness would disappear and she could throw her glasses away. Grandma Abrams was so eccentric that nothing she said surprised Margaret, much less persuaded her to follow her advice.

She'd approved of Margaret and Lydia, both serious, bookish girls, and had less time for Constance.

"She wrote me off as shallow," Constance once said placidly. She did not care.

Their father had experienced his mother's convictions more intensely. Meat or fish had never touched his lips until, rebelliously, he'd eaten a hot dog at a Cub Scout picnic. He remembered it as one of the most wonderful sensations he'd ever had. To the end of her long life, Grandma Abrams never knew that her son drank an occasional beer.

Where her grandparents had lived before they landed in New York City in the 1920s was unclear to Margaret. Sometimes Vienna or Cracow was mentioned, but when Margaret had asked her father, he said he didn't know. Nor did he show any interest in finding out. Even their first language was a mystery.

The morning after Constance's call, Margaret woke early and could not go back to sleep. She felt as if something doomy, like a rectangular, dark-grey cloud, was hanging over her head. In the kitchen before 7 a.m., she drank tea and downloaded the yearbook pictures Constance had sent. Here was her father in all four years of high school, beginning in 1949 when he was fourteen. Crinkly dark hair that stood up from a high forehead, and a big grin. Something about the disposition of his features reminded her of Bee.

There were two surprises here. The first was that her father's freshman and sophomore pictures were labelled "Moe Abrams." By his junior year he had become "Mike Abrams," the only name Margaret had known for him. Where had this Moe come from? As far as she could remember, his mother always called him Michael.

The second surprise was that Margaret was weeping. There was enough of the man she knew in those happy teenage pictures to send tears streaming down her face. When people learned that her father had died three months before, they said how sorry they were. Margaret would thank them and explain that his death was a blessing, he had been suffering from cancer for more than a year, they had had ample time to say their goodbyes, et cetera. All clichés, but they were true, too. And *The New Look* was so engrossing that she could go hours without remembering that her father was dead. But then she would remember.

She thought of the Japanese poem,

> *This world of dew*
> *is a world of dew,*
> *and yet, and yet.*

And yet, her gentle father was dead. She had always felt she was his favourite, but probably Constance was sure she was his favourite, and Lydia had the same conviction. He thought all three of his daughters were beyond wonderful, and that made her cry more.

She heard Will's heavy tread on the stairs and dried her face on her nightgown.

"You're up early." He opened his sleepy eyes a little further. "Are you okay?"

"Yes, fine. I think this must be my allergies."

Why did she shy away from talking with Will about missing her father? Sometimes she felt that, if she confided in him, it would make the sorrow more real. It was simpler to keep a lid on things.

"There's Claritin in the medicine cabinet if you want some."
She shook her head.

Will was easier to fool than the girls. When they appeared half an hour later, although Margaret's spell of sadness was over, they saw something in her face and they moved their chairs as close to hers as they could. Nancy was getting so tall she could put an arm around Margaret's shoulder. Bee picked up her mother's phone.

"What are you looking at?"

Margaret showed them, and they smiled at their grandfather's ready-for-anything freshman face.

"But why is he called Moe?"

"I don't know. I'd never heard about that. Sometimes kids just choose a nickname for a few years and it fades away. Could be that."

On her way to work, Margaret read a text from Molly Raines, the woman in the next office whose kindred spirit was Saint Hildegard of Bingen. She had been seconded to help with *The New Look*. The text said, "You don't have the snakeskin belt that goes on *Londres*, do you?"

It was faster for Margaret to call her. "Definitely not. Once Conservation has okayed them, we're putting all the pieces that are confirmed for the show in the smaller storage hall. Are you sure it isn't there? Maybe someone put it in one of the thin drawers instead of on the dress?"

"We've looked everywhere in both storage halls."

"I'm coming to your office."

Molly's office was hung with several portraits of Saint Hildegard, the most worrying of which showed her head in flames as she wrote. Margaret raised her eyebrows at that one, and Molly explained, "The flames symbolize inspiration."

Later, when she thought back to that scene, Margaret would

find it odd that she had been unworried enough to notice the painting at all.

She turned away from the painting and focused on the matter at hand. "When was the last time someone saw the belt?"

To answer that, Molly looked up the register of pieces, which noted when and with whom they had left the storage room, on her computer. For a medievalist, she was impressively tech-savvy. Margaret still regularly walked to the storage room to look at the physical register.

"Let's see," Molly said. "The dress and belt were moved to the small storage room about a week ago. Two days ago, a docent named Trudy Schneiderman was giving a tour of the permanent fashion collection. She took a small cart of accessories with her to illustrate some of her points—a few hats, shoes, costume jewellery and the snakeskin belt. There's no mention that the belt was returned to the dress."

A furious Margaret called the director of tours and demanded to know why a docent had been allowed to take the belt out of the storage room.

Sounding understandably flustered, the director said, "Trudy Schneiderman is one of our most trusted and experienced docents. She made a good case for the belt demonstrating the care Dior took with the smallest details. Another of our most reliable docents, Jill Hillman, was assisting her."

Margaret felt a momentary, dark near-pleasure that the crabby Jill Hillman was involved in this misadventure, but there was no time to dwell on it. Calls went out immediately to Trudy Schneiderman and Jill. Jill enjoyed bragging that she almost never carried her phone. The implication was that, unlike most people, she did not live in craven servitude to it. As expected, there was no answer from her landline or cell. Trudy was horrified that the belt had been mislaid and could not understand how it had happened. She had been in a rush to get home after the tour, and she and Jill had split up the contents of her cart. Someone she didn't know from Conservation had come in to help and she couldn't recall who had returned the belt to the dress. She thought it must be one of the other two women, because she would have remembered doing it.

Jill, when she returned Margaret's call a few hours later, said more or less the same thing. Between the lines, there was a predictable whiff of satisfaction, as if her feeling that the museum was badly run on every level was vindicated once again. She didn't know the woman from Conservation who had pitched in and she had been so busy she hadn't noticed what she looked like. She thought the woman wore glasses. The head of Conservation texted her department, looking for the helpful conservator who'd assisted with the Dior tour, but without saying the belt was missing. No one came forward.

At first Margaret was calm. The belt had been misplaced and it would turn up. Who would want to steal a consummately simple black snakeskin belt, so unassuming that even the buckle was snakeskin? She asked the four people who knew the situation to keep it confidential for now, and no, she did not plan on telling Claire Minichiello, who had enough to deal with.

Margaret decided that she would look in on *Londres*. Maybe someone had made a mistake and the belt was hanging inside the dress instead of outside. Maybe it had fallen to the floor of its locker and been overlooked. Of course, nothing of the sort had happened. When Margaret brought the dress out briefly into the light, she realized that in some crazy way she wanted to apologize to it. She wanted to sympathize with its loss and beg its pardon. The original meaning of *curator* was "a keeper or custodian," and she had failed the dress.

She could hear Will saying, "It doesn't even need a belt. No one would miss it if they didn't know it had been there."

He was wrong: much depended on that slim black line of punctuation, that division between the ribs and hips. The dress was bereft.

Several hours later, as she was leaving for the day, Alan Shea stepped into the elevator with her. Whatever jet lag remained three or so days after his return from Japan was dimmed by the glow of his *schadenfreude*.

"Margaret, what terrible news about the robbery of the belt. Just terrible. What in the world will you do to replace it?"

So much for confidentiality.

"Calling it a robbery is a stretch. It's just misplaced, and it's going to turn up."

Looking dubious and even sadder, if possible, Alan hoped that she was right. "Because that dress would be such a terrible loss to the show."

Margaret smiled at him and tried to think of some catastrophe that would sink his wretched *Japonisme* exhibit. Nothing came to mind immediately, but she would work on it.

MISS DIOR

THE PHOTOGRAPH OF Catherine Dior dates from 1947, around two years after she escaped a forced march from a German camp in April 1945. It shows her in profile, with short, curly dark hair brushed off her forehead, a strong, straight nose and a chin lifted high. Resembling her older brother Christian, she looks uncompromising, even slightly tragic. A serious beauty. It's easy to imagine her looking like that as she sat in the audience for the debut of her brother's couture house on February 12, 1947.

The public rooms at 30 avenue Montaigne that day were sprayed with a new perfume commissioned by Dior. It was still anonymous and would not be for sale until December 1 of that year. In 1946, a boyhood friend named Serge Heftler-Louiche had suggested to Dior that they start a fragrance company together. Heftler-Louiche was a director for the Coty perfume company, but, other than his love of scent and flowers, Dior was not an obvious choice as a partner. Still, he agreed. Marcel Boussac, who bankrolled the couture house, provided the money, rounding out the trio of partners in the Christian Dior perfume company.

Dior asked a respected "nose," Paul Vacher, to create "a perfume that smells of love." Vacher paired with another celebrated nose, Jean Carles, and the result is known to perfumers as a green chypre, a kind of olfactory sandwich with citrus notes and bergamot on top, a middle that concentrates on jasmine, roses and other floral tones, and a woody base starring sandalwood, patchouli and oakmoss.

But what to call this perfume, which Dior said was born on a summer night in Provence, a place beloved by his sister and himself? The story has it that one day while he was casting about for a name, Catherine Dior entered the room and Dior's assistant, Mizza Bricard, announced, *"Tiens! Voilà Miss Dior!"* ("Look! Here comes Miss Dior!") A tribute to his heroic sister—that was the name, including the English *Miss* rather than *Mademoiselle*, that had eluded Dior.

Originally, Miss Dior came in a bottle shaped like a curvy, narrow-necked Greek amphora. But in 1950 Dior changed its look, using a severely rectangular bottle, "cut like a suit," with brawny shoulders and a bow tie of a ribbon. Its Baccarat glass was etched in a houndstooth design, a nod to British tailoring and a perennial Dior favourite. The perfume's name, the houndstooth motif and even the Edwardian font of its lettering stemmed from Dior's anglophilia. Considering Catherine Dior's part in the war, it could also be read as a homage to the English who fought the Nazis alone until 1942.

Fashion did not play a large part in Catherine Dior's life. Her only piece of jewellery was a bracelet engraved with the dates of her imprisonment and liberation, but she wore Miss Dior daily for the rest of her life. Outliving her brother by more than fifty years, she died at ninety-one in 2008.

EIGHT

Miss Dior

Léa had chosen a small Middle Eastern restaurant near her apartment for lunch, and Margaret showed up at three minutes past the appointed time, trying not to seem too eager but still punctual. She was still worrying about the missing snakeskin belt, which she would not mention to her guest. A distraction would be welcome. Léa appeared a few minutes later, and after she settled, she suggested they could share a platter of baba ghanoush, grilled halloumi and tabbouleh to start, and order kebabs after that if they were still hungry. She refused wine, so they both drank mint tea.

"Forgive me if I ask too many questions," Margaret said, taking the bull by the less dangerous horn, "but I'm so curious about your work in Dior's atelier. Was it your first job?"

"My first job after leaving school was in a millinery atelier. My mother had been a hat maker in Budapest, so I knew the vocabulary and it seemed familiar. There was some sewing, of course, but a great deal of pressing felt and straw into the required shapes. I can still remember the smell of heated and ironed felt."

"What was the atelier called?"

"Oh, it's long gone, I don't remember. And within a few years I knew I wanted to work with cloth, not scratchy straw or steaming felt. I got a job as a *petite main* at Lucien Lelong's house, which is where I met Dior. 'Met' is an exaggeration, because he and Balmain, the two designers, didn't have much to do with us seamstresses, but he recognized me when I applied for a job at his new house. Lelong's designs were quite conservative, and I hoped that Dior would be fresher and newer."

"When you went to work for Lelong," Margaret asked, backing up a step, "was it during the occupation?"

"Yes, it was in '43. And I stayed until '46, when Dior began to assemble his house." Léa fiddled with her pita and was quiet for a minute. "Of course, we *petites mains* were far from any discussions Lelong might have been having with the Germans about textiles, taxes or other problems, but we felt the stress in the air.

"After the war, people sometimes talked about the improvisations we lived with in the occupation, as if they were fun. I remember getting ready to go to a nightclub we liked, near the atelier, and having my hair set at a salon. The electricity failed that day, as it did frequently, and as usual, two men were sent to the basement, where they pedalled furiously on bicycles to power the hair dryers. That kind of novelty might have been amusing the first time it happened, but not when it went on for four years.

"We worked our way around all kinds of shortages. Elizabeth Arden sold a special iodine leg stain that was intended to fool people into thinking you were wearing impossible-to-get stockings. The stain came in three shades—'flesh,' 'gilded flesh' and 'tanned flesh.' I wore 'flesh' in the daytime and 'gilded' in the evening. The hard part was getting a friend who could draw a perfectly straight line up the back of your leg to look like a seam."

Margaret tried to imagine that. "Did they use rulers?"

"Measuring tape. I do remember shrieking with laughter at the wandering lines on the backs of our legs. But there was so much that was not fun, so many rumours, so much anxiety, resentment and outright danger. We lived with the constant threat of being denounced and the fear that someone you loved would be charged for some trivial offence. Sometimes the simplest, most human thing required bravery. I remember seeing the couturier Marcel Rochas coming across one of his clients on the Champs-Élysées. The client was wearing a yellow Star of David, as ordered by the Germans. Rochas went out of his way not to greet her."

Léa pushed her plate to the side and sat up a little straighter. "I hate to think what happened to that woman. So you see, the house of Dior was not only this elegant mansion smelling of lilies of the valley. It was planted very shallowly on soil that still felt unsteady for many people."

Echoing Will's comment after the lecture, Margaret said, "I found Deirdre Ferrar's mention of Catherine Dior in her talk very poignant."

Léa nodded. "I never met her, but I would see her at the openings. I was rather surprised when she was pointed out to me at the first one. Her torture and her time in the camps doing forced labour had left her looking older than her years. She would usually wear the most subtle and covered-up suit in the new collection, but her look was entirely different from the chic, chattering people who crowded the openings. She kept to herself and focused on the collection."

"So, she was interested in fashion?"

"Perhaps she had some interest before the occupation, I don't know. She fascinated us *petites mains,* but most of our knowledge about her was third-hand. She would never talk about her time in the Resistance except during her testimony at the war crimes tribunals."

They were silent for a minute, staring at the table covered with dishes, until Léa picked up the thread.

"You ask about Catherine Dior's interest in fashion . . ." She touched her brow briefly. Something about the gesture suggested to Margaret the superficiality of her question, and she was abashed. But Léa seemed to be thinking about it. "Perhaps her appearance at the openings was a sign of loyalty to her brother, nothing more. Certainly she was not a typical guest: three countries—France, Great Britain and Poland—had awarded her some of their most important medals for her bravery. In a way, her presence in the midst of so much frivolity was like a ghost at the banquet."

"What did she do after the war?"

"She and her partner supplied florists with fresh flowers, which involved her getting up every morning at four a.m. to go to the flower market at Les Halles. She was not able to have children, and people wondered if that was a result of her torture. Whatever the truth of that, her time working in the camps and the forced march afterwards left her with physical and psychological problems for the rest of her life. She would never return to Germany or use any German products, and she hated to hear German spoken."

Léa smoothed her linen napkin and paused. "Christian was twelve years older than Catherine and died young, in his fifties. He had planted his garden in Provence with acres of jasmine, lavender and roses, and Catherine tended them, as well as his reputation, until she died."

Margaret thought about the differences between Catherine's and Christian's wars. While he learned his trade in Lelong's studio, she risked her life. While she shunned anything German after the war, her brother began taking shows and collections to Germany beginning as early as the late 1940s. No doubt, differences like these existed in many French families. And the brother and sister had remained devoted to each other.

It seemed gauche to change the subject, but continuing to question Léa about Catherine Dior felt like pressing on a bruise.

"When you said you were hoping for fresher looks at Dior, is that what you found?"

"Yes and no. From some points of view, he returned to the look women had in his boyhood at the turn of the twentieth century, but in a way that seemed new."

"Do you mean the ultra-femininity?"

"I suppose so. You have to remember how humiliating the occupation had been. For men, it was emasculating. Dior thought it was the reverse for women. In their straight-shouldered, rectangular suits, he said they were 'women-soldiers built like boxers.' He wanted women-flowers, and his description of them—their blooming busts, their slim waists like vines and big skirts like petals—sounds very strange now."

Margaret tried and failed to imagine her waist as a vine.

"He loved women," Léa continued. "But they had to meet his standards, and that meant reshaping their bodies. In the twenties, women were supposed to look like straight-up-and-down boys, then in the thirties like mature women with no foundation garments under their slinky bias-cut gowns. Their low-slung breasts always looked to me as if they had dropped two *ficelles*, those short baguettes, underneath their dresses. The *ficelles* just lay there, on top of their ribs. And then came the occupation, when there was no time or taste for fripperies like good bras or girdles. So Dior had to revive corset-making to create the bodies that his clothes demanded."

"I love the idea of women dropping *ficelles* down their blouses," Margaret said. "I'll think of that from now on when I watch movies from the thirties."

Both wearing well-fitting bras, they smiled at each other. Things were going well, Margaret thought, and proposed splitting a lamb kebab and a chicken one.

Feeling she had nothing to lose, Margaret said, "David got the idea that you might have other pieces from the 1940s."

Léa said firmly, "I am not selling any of the others."

That was a blow, but not unexpected.

Even without plans to sell, and looking slightly reluctant, Léa could not resist itemizing her collection. "I own a navy afternoon dress from 1947, the one with three-quarter sleeves with deep cuffs and the skirt made from gores that form very large pleats. I wore that for decades, I think. I have two suits, one double-breasted with deep lapels and the other a tweed 'morning suit,' which meant you were to do your errands in it. Monsieur Dior called it *Zigomar*."

Margaret nodded weakly. She worshipped *Zigomar*.

"The trick to it, as you probably know," Léa said, "is those wide pockets with flaps just under the shoulder. Quite unusable, but their width and the roomy skirt makes the wearer's waist look small by comparison.

"Let me think, what else do I have from the forties? A summer dress from the second collection, the most unassuming thing imaginable, all done in medium-size pleats with short, cuffed sleeves and a little bow at the neck. But when you walked in it on a day with a slight breeze, the pleats lifted and separated in the air and it was delightfully cool."

Margaret could see that dress spotlit in the central circle of the exhibit. Could the technical people rig up a discreet fan to show the pleats opening and closing in the breeze? No, she was overreaching, and anyway it was a fantasy. She wanted all Léa's Diors, and *Zigomar* illustrated so much about his brilliant ways with construction, but she felt especially sorrowful at the thought of the summer dress.

The waiter brought coffee cups and asked if they were interested in dessert. They did not want dessert, but ordered coffee.

Then Léa said, as if it were nothing, "And of course, I have an early version of *Bar*."

Margaret sent her coffee cup, fortunately still empty, skating across the table until it collided with Léa's. She thought, *God help me. You have a version of* Bar, *the suit that means "New*

Look" to people who know the barest minimum about Dior, the suit that Deirdre Ferrar showed first when she came to the inaugural collection, the suit that every creative director at Dior had revisited and tried to make their own. The suit—now that she knew Léa had one—without which she could not possibly mount her exhibition.

Finally, she managed to say, "Why do you say 'an early version'?"

"Because the jacket was originally made up in a very pale cream-coloured shantung. Monsieur Dior thought the curvy little jacket above the voluptuous black skirt was almost, but not quite, perfect. He fussed and fussed, as he did, and finally saw the light. He changed the cream to ivory shantung. He was right: the ivory works better with the black skirt."

The coffee had arrived, and Léa added a very small teaspoon of sugar to hers.

Margaret's head was bursting. A close-to-final version of *Bar* was in Léa's apartment at this very minute. Lying flat and shrouded in tissue paper, she hoped. And tragically unavailable.

"I would love to see it," she said faintly. Forlorn hope.

Léa was not to be swayed. She lifted her coffee cup. "But you already know what it looks like."

Margaret's head throbbed now for two reasons: the story of Catherine Dior, whose life was a new and disquieting vantage point from which to see her brother, and the unattainable suit.

ON WEDNESDAY, FIVE DAYS after the belt had gone missing, Gareth called her.

"They found it. Or rather, a guard did. Meet me at the entrance to the Greek and Roman galleries."

Margaret visited the Greek vases on an irregular basis and always meant to go more often. She preferred the ones painted with small domestic scenes—the young girl carefully holding her folded dress while she poured water into her washstand, the boy tempting a bird with seeds—to those that celebrated the bravado of gods and heroes. But she rarely ventured into the Etruscan Gallery, which angled off in a kind of preamble to the Romans. It was easy to forge straight ahead to the Romans, and most visitors did.

Gareth led her to the last of the Etruscan rooms, dominated by a double row of statues and sarcophagi. At the corner in the row closest to the wall, a statue of a middle-aged woman rested on her sarcophagus. With the curator side of her brain, Margaret noticed that the details of her terracotta dress included a delicate border at the neck, made in what looked like netting. The woman had the typical Etruscan almond-shaped eyes and emphatic eyebrows, and she held a mirror. Around her neck, as tight as her plentiful braids allowed, was a slim snakeskin belt. The buckle was at her back, and the set-up suggested an incompetent attempt at a garroting.

"I wanted you to see it in situ," Gareth explained. "And I've had pictures taken."

Was Gareth falling for the glamour of a mystery? He seemed energized by the discovery, even slightly triumphant. Margaret felt relieved, but dumbfounded and alarmed. The figure had been strangled.

"Doesn't anything show on the security camera?"

"The perp chose that corner sarcophagus carefully," Gareth answered. "It's out of the camera range."

Margaret wondered if Gareth's use of the word *perp* was correct. He had probably learned it from watching cop shows. They stared accusingly at the camera, mounted too close to the sarcophagus in question to capture it.

Margaret said, "All we know is that three people—the docent Trudy Schneiderman, Jill Hillman and the unknown person from Conservation—had access to the belt on the day it was used for the tour. Two days after the tour, all the other accessories borrowed on that day were found in their proper places. But that check was only done once the belt was discovered to be missing."

"So," Gareth said, "anyone who had access to the combination in the storage rooms could have taken the belt in the two days between the tour and the discovery that it was missing."

Margaret nodded. It was clear they needed to talk with Claire about changing the combination and strictly limiting the number of staff who knew it. Who could have done this, and even more mysterious, why?

NANCY AND BEE WERE excited about "The Mystery at the Museum," as Nancy had titled a new notebook.

Bee asked, "What's your favourite mystery set in a museum?"

Margaret had to think about that. "Most of the ones I've read take place in art museums, not a general one like ours. I would say *The Golden Child* by Penelope Fitzgerald. She does a good job with the pecking order and rivalries among the curators at the British Museum."

Nancy wanted to get back to the real business, and she turned to a blank page in her notebook. "So, who are your possible thieves?"

Margaret went through the three she had mentioned to Gareth, and Nancy made a list, with comments.

"Unless I find out something about her, I can't suspect Trudy Schneiderman," Margaret said. "The person from Conservation who helped the volunteers is still an unknown. And Jill Hillman is a pretty grumpy character, but why would she want to sabotage the exhibit?"

"I think it's Trudy," Nancy said. "You're going to find out that she has a grudge against Fashion and Textiles—maybe something to do with a donation her family made a long time ago."

"No," Bee said. "It's the mystery person from Conservation."

Later, when the girls were in bed, Margaret mentioned another possibility to Will. It was not someone she could bring up with Gareth.

"I wonder about Alan Shea. He has access and motivation, in that if *The New Look* fails, he's in a better position to become Chief Curator."

Will nodded. "Yes, I thought about him. In a way, he's obvious, so suspicion would fall on him and he would be a natural contender for the villain if this were a book. Close to the end, a stronger possibility would emerge and just as readers had forgotten about Alan, he would be revealed as the villain after all."

"Will, do I need to remind you this is not a book? This is life. And it could be very bad for my career. As well as a botched opportunity for a wonderful exhibit."

"Yes, sorry. I have a case of what the French call *la déformation professionnelle*. My job is warping your reality."

She took his hand. "Do I have that too, a *déformation professionnelle*?"

"Do you mean, are you fixated on Dior? Of course."

NINE

A Corsage with Stars of David

Feeling as if she needed to prepare for something menacing, Margaret had obeyed Patricia Bertelli's anonymous correspondent—"Look her up"—and read everything about Fanny Berger that was available online. Berger's atelier had been just off the Champs-Élysées and her talent promised continuing success, until the German occupation changed everything. Beyond that, there was only the bare outline Patricia had communicated, and no mention at all of Dior. The only slim lead Margaret found was the title of a book about Paris fashion under the Nazis. The following Friday, with a little time to spare before catching a train to Syracuse for the weekend, she went to look for it in the department library.

At the far table, Keitha was poring over one of the library's treasures, a boxed set of eighteenth-century Neapolitan fashion journals.

"*Giornale della Nuove Mode di Francia e d'Inghilterra,*" Margaret read. "Do I take it you're interested in Marie Antoinette–era French and English fashions as seen by the Italians?"

"A bit," Keitha said, turning pages carefully so that Margaret could see pictures of women wearing bustles, stomachers and hats like small boats. "What I'm really interested in is the book they made of the journals. Look at these beautifully tipped-in illustrations. And the binding they designed, covered with what look like dots until you realize they are small buttons."

Margaret looked instead at the models' drastically flattened chests, exaggerated derrières and skirts so wide they must have turned parties into obstacle courses. "So, Dior was not the first to distort women's bodies," she murmured, and instantly regretted it. No need to underscore Keitha's preoccupation. Looking for something else to say, she added, "I didn't know you were a connoisseur of books."

"Not really," Keitha said. "My mother was a bookbinder, that's all."

"Is she still working?"

"Not full-time anymore. She's had some health problems."

"I'm sorry." Without prying, there was nothing more to say. Keitha asked, "Was there something you want me to do?"

"No, thanks, I'm just looking for a particular volume here."

The book, *Paris Fashion Under the Nazis*, was shelved with others that documented happier eras of French style. Margaret sat down to read.

Odette Fanny Bernstein, she learned, was born to Jewish parents in the comfortable neighbourhood of Neuilly, just west of Paris, on July 2, 1901. Her father was a businessman and her mother kept house. As a girl, she was called Fanny, but other than that there was almost no information about her childhood and youth. Reading between the lines, Margaret had the sense that her mother was not happy with her daughter's unconventional plans for a career, but that was only a guess. Fanny opened a *salon du modiste* at the age of thirty-one, designing and making hats for a fashionable clientele. The salon was at 4 rue Balzac, and both the business and the designer were called Fanny Berger.

There were two photographs of Fanny. In the first one, probably taken when the woman and the century were in their twenties, she wears a rather daring one-shouldered dress. Her hair is short, with a spit curl on her forehead, and her lipstick is bright. She is slim, but her exposed shoulder, arm and hand have a roundness that is both girlish and seductive.

The second photograph, taken perhaps in the late 1930s, shows an attractive woman wearing a sleeveless white blouse with two soft folds of the material falling from the neck. Her shapely arms slant away from her body, resting on a couch. The most striking thing about the photograph is her expression as she faces the photographer—candid, full of affection and trust.

Margaret stared at the photographs for a long time. She thought she preferred the confidence of the woman in her thirties, but the flapper's insouciant charm was undeniable. No matter how many times she read or heard or watched stories about the Holocaust, something in Margaret found it impossible to make sense of the undeniable facts. That this smiling woman had been brutally snuffed out seemed incomprehensible.

Margaret left the library, her head still cloudy with the idea of killing a hat maker, and retrieved her suitcase from her office. She had just enough time for a quick lunch in the cafeteria before her train.

Jill Hillman was eating alone, and Margaret asked her, "May I join you?"

"I'm almost done, but sure, sit down."

Jill Hillman didn't look as if lunch with Margaret was her idea of a good time, but Margaret was determined to be friendly for David's sake. She wheeled her suitcase to Jill's table in the cafeteria's basement gloom and for a minute the two women sat silently.

Finally Jill said, looking at Margaret's suitcase, "You're going somewhere. No doubt somewhere glamorous."

Her tone suggested that while Margaret flew off to do something frivolous, she stayed behind working without pay to undo the staff's mistakes.

"'Glamour' doesn't quite describe it," Margaret said. "I'm going to Syracuse for the weekend to help my sisters clear out our father's condo. He died a few months ago."

Jill nodded curtly, which Margaret took to be her way to express condolences. There was silence again, until Margaret attempted a bridge to her truculent neighbour.

She said, "You know, choosing the clothes for this New Look exhibit, I've been struck all over again by how much David has done for Fashion and Textiles. Many of the best Dior pieces came thanks to him and his infallible eye. I remember his first big find—that Balmain cocktail suit. He bought it for you, didn't he? He thought you might wear it for Halloween."

Jill sniffed. "Do I strike you as the kind of person who likes to dress up in costumes? That's the thing about David. He gets so involved in his own hobbies it doesn't occur to him that other people have no interest in extreme, wildly expensive clothes. Now, of course, *you* get first dibs on all the pieces he finds."

In just a few sentences, Jill managed to pour scorn on David's finds while implying that Margaret had usurped her rightful place as the beneficiary of her husband's foraging. Margaret couldn't imagine how to respond to this tangle of resentment. Fortunately, she didn't need to.

Jill asked, "Have you figured out who took the snakeskin belt yet? I always thought it's a mistake to let docents take away parts of the collection, but Claire Minichiello pays no attention to that sensible rule. Frankly, I think the person who said they were from Conservation is an imposter, and that's where you should be looking. Because, believe me, that isn't going to be the last try at sabotaging your exhibit."

And with that prophecy, delivered with relish, Jill said she had to get back to work. Learning's new approach to school tours was proving to be the disaster she had foreseen, and she was late for a meeting with them. The two women parted eagerly.

On her way to the station and the 3:35 train, Margaret wondered again if Jill's gloomy suspicions of everyone pointed to something darker.

The Amtrak station, just off the Inner Loop, was fairly new and soulless. The chief decoration in the waiting room was a bank of vending machines and the American motto in big, silvery letters over the exit to the track. *E Pluribus Unum.* Out of Many, One. The sign looked both grandiose and enigmatic. Was it supposed to suggest that Americans from all races and walks of life took the train and became one? Far fewer people did take the train now, of course, and the six platforms of the original station had been reduced to one.

Just as she was about to board the train, Margaret glanced at her phone. There was a text from Gareth's executive assistant. He knew she was going away for the weekend, so he had leaned on his assistant to send a note to Margaret that another package had arrived. The assistant had included a picture of a corsage of black, flat-petalled flowers like anemones, with a yellow Star of David in the centre of each flower. It was made of felt, and the note with it said, "Meanwhile, in the real world . . ."

This fourth anonymous package struck Margaret more heavily than the first three. The disappearance of the snakeskin belt had significantly raised the stakes. Whoever the saboteur was, he or she meant business. She thought for a moment, then sent the picture on to Deirdre, writing, "Obviously, this is Jewish, but you may know more?"

Brooding on the Star of David corsage as well as Fanny Berger's cruelly shortened career and life, Margaret found her seat next to a grimy window. Luckily, no one appeared to claim the aisle seat, so she would not be subjected to small talk, phone conversations or uninhibited chewing and paper crumpling. She gave in to her sense of disappointment and menace and, taking out her tablet, began searching for details of Catherine Dior's capture and interrogation.

Léa had mentioned a notorious apartment on the rue de la Pompe that the Nazis had set up for grilling their captives. Now, Margaret began to read the details. The Nazis had brought in two experienced torturers from Tbilisi. A resident doctor revived unconscious prisoners with camphor injections so the interrogations could resume. The apartment's barman had to order enough ice every day for cocktails as well as to fill the bathtubs for those being tortured. Nazi officers cuddled pets on a bed in a room where someone was being tortured, while others played Bach on the piano in the drawing room—but not loudly enough to drown out the screams.

In this circle of hell, the Germans tried to make Catherine Dior reveal her colleagues' names and activities. They punched, slapped and kicked her, but their chief technique was submerging her in a bathtub filled with icy water for long periods, with her hands tied behind her back. Every so often they would push her head under water until she almost drowned, and then resume the interrogation. She never cracked.

The apartment in the rue de la Pompe was the nadir of her imprisonment, but in August 1944 she was sent to Germany, first to Ravensbrück concentration camp and from there to three sub-camps to do forced labour with munitions and military engines. As the Allies approached and the war wound down, the poor conditions in the camps deteriorated further—punishingly long working hours, no latrines, very little food and a cold cement floor for sleeping.

Finally, on April 13, 1945, the SS officers evacuated Catherine Dior's sub-camp and sent the prisoners on a forced march through German-controlled land. For about a third of the prisoners, malnourished and ill, these evacuations were literally death marches. Catherine was one of the lucky ones. She escaped into Dresden on April 21. When she arrived in Paris a month later, almost unrecognizable, her brother met her at the train station and took her to his apartment in the rue Royale, in the heart of the couture district. She was unable to eat the festive dinner he had prepared for her.

Margaret closed her tablet. One of the things she found hardest to understand about the cruelties of the war was how the world had managed to put itself more or less back together afterwards. She spent the rest of the trip staring out the window at the small towns of upstate New York.

HER SISTERS PICKED HER UP at the station. Two years older than Margaret, Lydia had the first child's authority alongside a broad streak of empathy, which Margaret assumed a therapist must need. Constance was one year younger than Margaret, and although she seemed more happy-go-lucky than her sisters, she ran a successful event-planning company. The weekend would be given over to sorting, donating and disposing, alongside the inevitable spats, memories and fits of laughter that erupted whenever the sisters got together. All of this was overlaid now with their father's death and the fact that they were orphans.

Adjusting the front passenger seat of Constance's car as far back as it could go, Margaret asked, "So, what is our mission this weekend?"

"More of the same," Lydia said. "Most of the big furniture has been spoken for, but there are hundreds of small things. And tons of paper. What is it about teachers and paper?"

Their parents had both been principals, their mother at a high school and their father at an elementary school.

"But we're not working tonight," Lydia said, not so much taking charge as simply continuing in what she saw as her natural role. "We're having pizza and red wine, and we'll start the sorting early tomorrow morning."

Constance groaned. She would have happily worked far into the night and skipped the morning. Margaret had heard this argument between her sisters a few hundred times, so she concentrated on the landmarks on 81 South. After a brief glimpse of Onondaga Lake, they drove by the Syracuse Mets' baseball stadium, then the huge mall grandiosely named Destiny USA. Just before they left the highway, they passed St. Joseph's Hospital, where their father had died.

Constance lived in a condo in Franklin Square, converted from what had been a typewriter factory when Syracuse was the typewriter centre of the country. She was "between men," as she put it, which was fortuitous because her condo was not large and her sisters were sleeping there. Margaret had liked the last incumbent, a sweet, rather vague piano teacher, but according to Constance, her energy had overwhelmed him.

Over the pizza and wine, they navigated their usual voyage back into intimacy. First they reported on everyone in the family, from Lydia's son's girlfriend to Margaret's mother-in-law, then moved on to any notable behaviour or misbehaviour at their father's funeral, before settling on their evolving feelings about his death. Lydia and Margaret teared up and Constance, always the last to cry, did not. Reversing Nancy's and Bee's movement from Mommy to Mom, they started the evening calling their father Dad and soon relapsed into Daddy. Lydia made no mention of what Constance called her "Jewish Dad daydream," but Margaret knew it would return.

She greeted Saturday morning under-slept and with a few new bruises on her shins. The pullout bed in Constance's office was not quite long enough for her and, as usual in a place that was not perfectly familiar, she had bumped into her sister's desk several times while undressing and dressing.

Their father's condo was in Fayetteville, which the family thought of as a suburb of Syracuse but was officially a village. Named for the Marquis de Lafayette, it made itself known from the highway by a mall. Behind that was an enclave of carefully tended Colonial Revival houses and gardens. The sisters had grown up in one of them, on Academy Street, and when their parents retired, they had moved a few blocks from the family house to the condo.

At nine o'clock, Constance unlocked their father's door. Inside, Margaret, who had not been to the condo since her father's death and funeral, saw a picture of achingly slow withdrawal from the life that had been lived there. Some things, like their parents' bed, were gone already, to a charity that helped immigrants furnish their places. Others were earmarked for donation once the sisters had finished clearing out. Lydia was taking a small Parsons table and Constance a chair she had always liked, but, like Margaret, they already had full houses. The dining room table, a remnant from the family house that was too big for the condo, was a sea of papers.

Lydia pointed to the coffee table, covered with knick-knacks and small things. "Lots of those were presents from us, so you may want to reclaim one or two."

Margaret wished her girls could be here. They would have loved going through the ornamental boxes and pieces of pottery. Constance lifted a chunky crucifix in shiny blond wood and said, "For sure you'll want this, Margaret. I remember when you gave it to Mom and Dad."

"Very funny," Margaret said. The central part of the crucifix, where the body of Jesus hung, slid up to reveal a cavity with two candles, a handkerchief, a spoon and a bottle of oil—the objects necessary to perform the Anointing of the Sick. At the height of her girlish religiosity, perhaps eleven or twelve, and feeling that no Catholic home should be without one, she had bought it at Syracuse's religious gift shop and presented it to her nonplussed parents.

"Can you believe they kept this all those years? And imagine what they thought of it. They kept straight faces, of course, and thanked you."

"But they never hung it up," Margaret said, shaking her head in mock disappointment, and her sisters grinned. Although their parents had sent their children to the parish school and went with them to Sunday Mass, they would not have given houseroom to the kitschier branches of Catholicism.

"I do have colleagues who would take this very seriously as a piece of material culture," Margaret said, putting the crucifix firmly on the Not Wanted side of the coffee table.

They sat down at the dining table, and Lydia handed Margaret a plastic bag filled with letters, cards, photographs, insurance certificates and report cards. These had originally come from their grandmother Abrams, and Lydia insisted that each piece of paper should be looked at.

At first Margaret enjoyed looking at a dozen snaps of her late aunt Dorothy's young husband fondling the family cats, who for some reason were all named Bunny. Or a paper certifying that the same aunt, her father's shy older sister, had insured a leopard coat for six hundred dollars in 1958.

"Aunt Dorothy in leopard! Who knew?"

Constance was charged with separating the family pictures. The ones they wanted would be digitized, but all three sisters had a fetishistic interest in the originals. Lydia was rapidly making her way through their father's voluminous correspondence with salespeople, mechanics, real estate agents and former teachers from his school.

Lydia was angular except for her face, which was an appealing series of roundnesses—cheeks, lips, chin. Margaret, glancing at her, thought her looks echoed the disparity between her motherliness and her sharpness.

"When it came to obsessiveness, Daddy was no slouch," Lydia said.

"It's Saturday," Constance said. "Why don't you take a day off from playing therapist?"

That was the way they talked to each other. It could sound rough, but at heart it was affectionate.

Looking over Margaret's pile of yellowing cards and letters, Lydia said, "I see you've reached the Abramsons."

The Abramsons, whom none of the sisters had ever met or heard mentioned before, were apparently scattered in a few east coast states. For years they had sent matter-of-fact accounts of family doings to Margaret's grandparents, whom they called Hester and Sol, or Aunt Hester and Uncle Sol, with inquiries about the Syracuse family, their garden and the weather. Since the Abramsons clearly assumed that Hester and Sol knew the ins and outs of their relatives near and far, it was odd, Margaret thought, that they were news to her and Lydia and Constance.

"So, are we related to them?" Constance asked.

"I'm not sure," Margaret said. "'Aunt' and 'Uncle' could be just courtesy titles for an older couple, or they could be in-laws of some kind, or maybe distant family."

"Are there any envelopes from their letters?"

"Mostly no," Margaret said, dealing out the letters and cards on the table like a pack of cards, "but here are a few."

"Aha! Do you see this?" Lydia said triumphantly, jabbing the address on one with her finger. "It's addressed to Hester and Sol Abramson! And so is this one. And this one. They could date from before the name change, or maybe the rest of the family never got behind the change and kept writing to Abramsons. I rest my case."

"I don't know what you're so excited about," Margaret said. "So our grandparents shortened their name, that's no big deal."

"Margaret, let's think about that for a minute. A family in the 1930s tries to make their name sound less Jewish—doesn't that suggest anything to you?"

Margaret made one last stand. "We simply don't have any hard evidence that the family was Jewish."

Lydia must have been good at sensing when her clients were bluffing. "Margaret, I really don't believe you doubt Grandma and Grandpa's Jewishness anymore. What is that pile of cards you're covering with your hand?"

There was no point in hiding them, so Margaret pushed the little pile of paper to the centre of the table. All except one of the cards were from Ruth Abramson. She stood out from the other Abramsons for her devotion to their grandmother, especially after Hester was widowed, sending lively descriptions of teaching high school English, volunteering and enjoying regular package tours to cultural landmarks.

The cards included Hanukkah and Passover greetings, the former with menorahs and Stars of David, the latter with dogwood blossoms and other signs of spring, one with a bespectacled rabbi in tallit and yarmulke reading from a bible. There must have been a year when Ruth couldn't find a Passover card, so she repurposed an Easter card with a duckling ("Just ducking in to say Happy Easter") by adding "And also a Joyous Passover." One of the Rosh Hashanah cards was a handsome modern one, with Hebrew letters and stylized lilies, but most were in the Hallmark vein, with bearded rabbis blowing shofars or romantic scenes of Jerusalem. The exception in this festive bunch, the only card not from Ruth Abramson, was a Christmas card with a picture of a fifteenth-century Madonna and child by Hans Memling. Margaret, then in her early twenties, had written Christmas greetings to her grandmother and aunt Dorothy on the inside.

"Mary Margaret strikes again," Constance said with a laugh. "The Catholic schoolgirl in you never gave up, did you?"

"First of all, what is so strange about sending Grandma and Aunt Dorothy, who liked art, a picture of a masterpiece? And they kept it, didn't they?" Margaret pretended to look closely at the Madonna's costume. "And just look at that brocade border at the hem of her dress. Isn't that beautiful?"

"Margaret, it's Saturday," Lydia said with a superior smile, "so you can drop the Fashion curator card for today."

Constance had been cooing over a First Communion picture of herself, but now she looked up to ask, "What else do we know about Ruth Abramson?"

Margaret said, "She mentions in a letter that her father had been a master tailor who learned his trade making uniforms for Austrian army officers before he came to America."

Lydia leaned across the table toward Margaret. "What part of this obvious story don't you get? Our grandfather was a tailor named Sol Abramson or Abrams. It hardly matters. Ruth Abramson's father, who was probably Grandpa's brother, was also a tailor. She sent our grandparents Hanukkah, Passover and Rosh Hashanah cards."

"And this Ruth Abramson was a committed Jew," Margaret said. "That doesn't mean our grandparents were, once they were adults."

"I don't see that it matters what people were or weren't in the past," Constance said, then added, helpfully, "Grandma never had a Christmas tree."

"But she gave us a Christmas present every year," Margaret countered.

"And that could be just because she loved us," Constance said. "Why do you care what they were? But since you care, why don't you two just go on Ancestry.com or 23andMe and settle the whole thing instead of this endless bickering?"

Margaret said, "Because that would only tell us about the family DNA, not what Dad felt about who he was."

Lydia sighed. "Margaret, this is a no-brainer. Why are you balking?"

"Because when you asked him, Daddy said he wasn't Jewish. Isn't that enough?"

"How naive are you? Do you take everyone's word for everything they say?"

"No, but I do when it's our father."

"I don't understand what you're trying to protect here. I don't think your childhood Catholicism means any more to you now than it does to Constance and me, so it's not that."

Margaret said, "What is Jewish, anyway? If you don't want to be Jewish, are you still Jewish? You can reject Jewish theology and still consider yourself a Jew. But if you don't feel part of the culture, are you still a Jew?"

"Well, why couldn't Daddy just say, 'My parents were born into Jewish families but they didn't seem attached to Judaism. And I didn't want to be Jewish'?" Lydia countered. "Why did he always act as if he had no knowledge of his parents' origins and had never thought about being Jewish? Isn't that the question we can't answer? What would you give up if you had to admit he was disingenuous about this?"

Lydia's question reminded Margaret of Will. His tone had been much the same when he had asked her what she would lose if she let some of the mess of the occupation and the war into the atelier in which Dior made his immaculate clothes. But now, even more than with Will's question, she did not want to probe too closely for an answer.

Lydia had more to say. "You're always trying to tidy awkward things up, Margaret, or put something unseemly back in the box where it hides. You romanticize our grandmother Meier and obsess over her sewing, but the Meiers were hardly an ideal family. And you work hard at ignoring the obvious about Daddy's family."

"Look, we didn't come here to psychoanalyze Margaret," Constance said. "Not that she couldn't use it, but first let's get this table cleared off."

AT THE END OF THE DAY, after an hour at Constance's where they happily retreated to their rooms and did not speak, the sisters went out together to dinner. They talked sentimentally about the Dinosaur Bar-B-Que on Willow Street, a rowdy favourite of their youth, but knew it would be too noisy. They went instead to Francesca's Cucina, in Little Italy on North Salina Street. It was dim, with hanging clusters of plastic grapes, and looked as if the management had only recently dispensed with candles in Chianti bottles wrapped in straw. They felt very fond of each other and had reached an unspoken agreement that there would be no talk of the elephant in the room during dinner.

Although their mother had been dead for five years, also from cancer, and they had become used to visiting their father in the apartment without her, Margaret had felt her presence all day. Margaret could never decide whether her mother had been shy or simply never wanted to be the centre of attention. It was probably the latter, but her husband's devotion and the understated perfectionism with which she ran the household ensured that the family revolved around her. Inside the condo, the mugs, the serving platters, the candlesticks, the lap rugs she had knitted all bore her imprint. So did documents, recipes and anniversary cards to her husband—all inscribed with her rounded, perfectly balanced Palmer penmanship. Like her sewing and knitting, its flawless regularity was almost uncanny.

"Grandma's sewing looks like it was done by a machine," a preschool Bee had said about one of her quilts, and she meant it as a compliment.

Sitting between her sisters in the restaurant, Constance was wearing a long black jacket, unstructured and buttonless, over jeans. Margaret and Lydia recognized it as part of a suit their mother had worn and they began rubbing the wool between their fingers.

"What are you two doing, and stop it!" Constance said, shaking her wild brown mane. Unlike many people with naturally curly hair, she loved hers and used it for emphasis.

"What do you think we're doing?" Margaret said. "We're trying to figure out if it's Forstmann wool."

They laughed, even Constance. They had grown up in a house where Forstmann wool and Moygashel linen were things to be longed for, although they could be afforded only when on sale. As a small child, Margaret had thought they were single words—*Forstmannwool* and *Moygashellinen*.

When she shopped, their mother took each dress, each sweater, each hank of wool or piece of yard goods between her fingers and assessed it. Its touch was the first test it had to pass, and Lydia and Margaret were applying that test now to Constance's jacket.

"The light is too low in here," Margaret said. "I can see it's twill, but I don't know if it's Forstmann."

"Trust Margaret to know the word *twill*," Lydia said.

"Well, just think of all the words Mom threw around—*faille*, *piqué*, *pongee*, *matelassé*, *dotted swiss*, *jacquard*. That was her element."

Their mother had kept a cupboard in the closet they called the sewing room crammed with wools, linens and cottons she intended to sew someday, and she had strong opinions about their relative merits.

"Do you remember how she despised rayon?" Constance asked. "I still feel slightly guilty when I buy anything made of rayon."

This topic was a well that never ran dry, and they moved happily on to memories of homemade prom dresses, new Easter coats covered with snow in Syracuse's predictably horrible climate and the struggles their mother had had with the crepe of Lydia's wedding dress.

Now that the wine, the memories and the muted light had softened their sharp edges, Constance asked Lydia, "Why did you say earlier that Margaret romanticizes the Meier family?"

"Their sewing, especially our grandmother's and Mom's, was impeccable. Their family life wasn't. But Margaret keeps her eyes firmly fixed on the needles and thread. Sewing is all about control, but it's not so easy to control people."

"What was so wrong with their family life?" Margaret was trying not to sound defensive.

"How about our grandmother's brother who spent the last twenty or so years of his life in the upstairs bedroom of his parents' house? Probably an alcoholic and definitely a hermit, but no one talked about it. And I don't think our grandparents' marriage was any bed of roses either. Marg and Grandpa seemed to travel on two separate tracks, with the occasional collision."

"You're talking as an adult and a therapist," Margaret said. "I was a child, and I loved my grandmother. It was normal that I didn't know about things that happened between grown-ups and behind closed doors."

"I think you were probably aware of some of it, on some level," Lydia said. "I just read an essay where the writer says that family is the handful of stories we never tell. That's extreme, but I do think the unspoken stories in a family are like the load-bearing parts of a house. And that children sense their presence, even if they don't understand the content."

Neither was about to prove the other wrong, Margaret realized. She began talking about clothes they should never have given away and still regretted.

That night, Margaret dreamed of her grandparents' brass bed. Marg's parents had bought it soon after they arrived in Syracuse in the 1920s, and unlike the familiar Victorian curvaceous design, it was an austere combination of vertical and horizontal poles. It was already old-fashioned when Marg and Grandpa married, and why the unsentimental Marg adopted it was a mystery. When she and Grandpa moved to single beds late in their lives, they offered the bed to Margaret. She declined, she hoped tactfully.

In the dream, the bed acquired a demonic life of its own. Furious at her rejection, it followed her from Syracuse to Rochester. Too large for her bedroom, it bruised her with its corners and ran over her feet with its mean little casters. No matter how often she broke it into its constituent parts of headboard and footboard and hauled it out onto the street for pickup or delivered it to the nearest Goodwill, when she returned from work, there it would be, taking up all the oxygen in her bedroom.

Margaret lay awake in the dark and thought about her grandfather. Tall and handsome, he did not talk much. He liked playing his accordion, usually in his workroom in the basement because Marg did not appreciate his music. One day when she was about nine or ten, Margaret was giving her friend Sallie a tour of her grandparents' house. Above her grandfather's workbench in the basement were three pictures of big-breasted, smiling women without any clothes on. Margaret had not known much if anything about sex back then, but she felt the pictures were somehow unfair to her grandmother. And that they could give Sallie the wrong idea of her family. She ripped them down and threw them in the wastebasket, telling Sallie they must have been left by people who had rented the house. Now, lying in Constance's inadequate bed, Margaret was impressed at the speed of her childish lie. Her grandparents never mentioned the pictures to her. She supposed Lydia would say the incident was one in the "handful of stories we never tell" that make up a family.

THERE WAS AN EMAIL from Deirdre waiting for Margaret early on Sunday morning.

> Hi Margaret. Never a dull minute at your shop. Actually, you're only half right about the felt corsage. Obviously, the Stars of David on the flowers reference things happening to Jews, but it was made for and worn by Gentiles. Before you start gasping at my cleverness, let me say this is not my area of expertise. I sent the picture on to a historian friend at Cambridge. Here's his response:
>
> "Theoretically this could come from any of the occupied countries in WW2, but my guess is France, as they objected particularly strenuously to the decree of June, 1942, that ordered Jews to wear yellow stars. To show their solidarity with Jews, Gentiles—many but not all of them Gaullists and Communists—devised their own wearable protests. A dog had a Jewish star attached to his collar. Some embroidered crosses or their Christian names on Stars of David and wore them. One woman attached eight yellow stars to her belt, each with a letter in the centre that spelled out *Victoire*. Offences like these were punished by three weeks in the internment camp at Drancy. Hope this helps."

Blessed academics, Margaret thought. *Nothing, not weekends or families, keeps them from their email.* She wondered how the corsage had survived. Presumably the Germans had confiscated the pieces that got their owners sent to Drancy, but the corsage's owner must have escaped arrest and hidden it.

So many separate but overlapping sorrows, she thought. Fanny Berger. Catherine Dior. The Jews whom the wearer of the corsage wanted to support. By the time Constance knocked on her door with coffee, Margaret had spent half an hour googling the plight of French Jews in the occupation. The nastiest, most petty thing about the order to wear a yellow star was that the Jews had to buy them using their minimal clothing rations. The Nazis were saying, Not only are we forcing you to wear a humiliating symbol that will make it easy to identify you for your ghastly fate, you have to sacrifice your precious clothing allowance to procure it.

She showed Constance the picture of the corsage.

Her sister said, "Pretty."

"Yes. And brave too."

Margaret explained the probable origin and meaning of the felt flowers.

Constance was confused. "So you think the Abramsons were *French* Jews?"

She made the French part sound more exotic than the Jewish part. At first Margaret smiled at her sister's mistake and then she realized with a kind of dull thud that in a deeper sense Constance was correct. Not that the Abramsons were French, but that the family members who had not emigrated to America probably lived in a country where they too had been forced to wear yellow stars. And most of them very likely were exterminated during the Nazi regime. Thinking about Abramsons who'd stayed in Europe was a disturbing idea, and pursuing it felt daunting. Aunt Dorothy, who might have known something about the European branch of the family, was dead. As was her father—although he would have been an unlikely source of information.

Perhaps because she had been dreaming about her mother's family, her mind leaped to the Meiers who had stayed in Europe. Had one side of her family, the German Christians, loathed the other side—or worse? Would she now have to think about the Meiers' role in the war?

To stop those thoughts, Margaret told Constance about the mysterious packages sent to the museum.

"But what do they have to do with your exhibit?"

"I wish I knew. It seems that someone wants us to think about the years before Dior founded his house, in the chaos of the occupation and the war, but I don't understand why."

THE SISTERS HAD MADE progress in the condo. It had lost more personality and looked increasingly bereft, but at the same time it seemed as if it might have a future as someone else's home. The space was cluttered with huge black bags of non-recyclables, boxes of books for the hospital second-hand shop, tables and chairs marked "Furniture Depot." Margaret had been charged with all the rusty can openers and odd mugs still in the kitchen. Lydia and Constance were sorting through the last of the miscellaneous papers.

"Seriously, do neither of you want this sweet little creamer in the shape of a cow?" Margaret asked. "I brought them this from France."

"Absolutely not," Lydia said. "I notice you haven't taken any of your lapses in taste, so why should we?"

"Hey, here's something," Constance said.

It was the registration for kindergarten in Summerhill Public School for Michael ("Moe") Abrams, dated 1940.

"So," Lydia calculated, "they had changed their name by 1940. I wonder exactly when it happened."

Part of the answer came sooner than expected. A small envelope labelled "Birth Certificates" in their grandmother's faded handwriting had strayed into a manila envelope of yet more insurance papers, and Constance fished it out. Inside were birth certificates for Dorothy Rachel, born in 1928, and their father, born in 1935. That is, for Dorothy Rachel Abramson and Moses Michael Abramson.

"There you have it," Lydia said, sounding surprisingly dispassionate. "At some time between 1935 and 1940, they shortened their name."

"But wait a minute," Constance said. "*Moses* Michael Abramson?"

Lydia shrugged. "Obviously, that's the source of 'Moe,' which Daddy dropped halfway through high school. Jewish people, like many others, have a custom of naming children after dead family members, and I bet if we had a family tree, we would find a grandfather or great-grandfather, maybe, named Moses."

They left it at that. Margaret longed to be by herself and let things settle. Constance locked the condo. She could do the rest herself, and her sisters would not be here again. Margaret put her hand on the door, in one more farewell to her mother and father. When she was in Syracuse, she sometimes drove by their old house on Academy Street, but nothing about this building would call her back. The sisters had never really liked the condo, but their parents had lived an old age there that was contented enough until cancer invaded it.

Constance and Lydia drove Margaret to the train station in the early evening and hugged and kissed her goodbye. They would see her next at the opening of *The New Look*.

TEN

Eleven Bones, Fourteen Hooks and Eyes, Horsehair and Net

The girls were asleep when Margaret arrived home, and she gave Will an unexpurgated account of the weekend. On Monday morning at breakfast, Nancy and Bee got a shorter version, but she felt honour bound to mention the Jewish cards and the birth certificate.

Bee asked, "So, when we make our bat mitzvahs, can we have Dior dresses like your friend Rivkah?"

The girls had gone through a preschool period when they drew Rivkah and Dina Waldman's bat mitzvah dresses over and over.

"Absolutely, as long as I inherit a fortune or *The Mystery of the Chalice and Paten* is on *The New York Times* bestseller list for a year."

"That means no," Nancy told her twin.

Looking slightly alarmed, Will pulled her into their old-fashioned pantry and shut the door.

"You're kidding, right? About the bat mitzvahs?"

"Yes, I'm kidding. But I'm not sure Bee is."

She rubbed her nose against his cheek. She found his face when he was bewildered especially appealing.

She made a mental note to tell Rivkah about Bee's question. She would be amused.

IN THE AFTERNOON SHE WAS giving a talk about Dior's corsets to a graduate seminar in fashion history at the university. She had invited the department volunteers, rather grandly called the Friends of Costume History and Design. And she had written to Léa, "You should be giving this seminar, not me. But if you think it would be at all diverting, please join us. And feel free to correct the speaker!"

Margaret felt distracted, touchy, unfocused, weak and aggressive. She did not know what to make of the petty and not so petty ways the exhibition was being undermined. When it came to the belt, undermined was too weak a word—that was sabotage. She did not know how to rescue *her* Dior, devoted to women and their beauty, from the rumours and mysteries that were swirling around him. And in her own life, what was she supposed to make of the Abramsons and all those holiday cards?

She unlocked the door to the storage hall—doors were being locked more conscientiously now—and went inside. The staff had put the pieces she was planning to talk about that afternoon on mannequins, and they would be moved to the department boardroom closer to the time of the seminar. The mannequins stood in an odd cluster, since women in dressmaker suits, day dresses, sexy cocktail dresses and gowns fit for an embassy dance would not normally huddle together.

Margaret walked around them a few times. She admired again the smoothness of Dior's shoulders and the way the sleeves emerged seamlessly, literally, from the body of the dress or suit. His idea of cutting the bodice and sleeves as often as possible from a single piece of fabric gave the finished piece a soft, organic look. It was not like a completed puzzle, cut, sewn together and helped along with the occasional dart, but rather as if the wearer had extruded a second skin of flannel or silk.

Then, feeling ridiculous but compelled, Margaret moved a metal chair into the very middle of the group and sat there almost hidden by sequined embroidery, skirts stiffened by horsehair, and wool dresses so precisely tailored they looked carved. She did not, of course, but she *could* have touched side-seam pockets, self-buttons and flawless jacket linings that were content almost never to be seen. Anyone coming in would have thought she was mad. But she felt at home, for the first time in weeks. This was her Dior, master of cut and colour, he who exalted the smallest details to unimagined perfection. That was enough. This was why the exhibition was important.

Sitting there surrounded by his clothes, like a child playing hide-and-seek, made her miss her mother. The highlights of her trips to Rochester had always been their visits to the collection, where they pored over the precision and ingenuity of the sewing. Margaret imagined showing her the interfacings on the lining of the grey wool dress that stood at her shoulder. In her laconic way, her mother would have shaken her head and said, "Look at that. I wouldn't want to have to sew those." No greater compliment.

At two o'clock, eight graduate students, their professor and a healthy sprinkling of volunteers sat around the board table. Just as Margaret was about to begin, a door opened at the back of the room and an elderly woman came in. One of the grad students seated close to the door pulled out a chair for her and Léa Slaney lowered herself carefully into it.

The mannequins were grouped behind Margaret, like a phantom choir. With help from Keitha, who was acting as her assistant, she moved one wearing a strapless white dress to the front. Called *Avril* and embroidered with violets, the dress was from the spring 1955 collection and intended for a garden party or a dance.

Margaret said, "What you see here on the outside of the dress is freedom, youth, gaiety. Inside is a prison, with the human body the prisoner. I'm going to show you some of these prisons today. But while you watch Keitha detach the top from the skirt and open it up—please notice that this will involve no fewer than eighteen hooks and eyes and a zipper—I'll just say a few words about body shaping before Dior."

If Margaret had expected the graduate students to look even mildly interested at that prospect, she would have been disappointed. They slouched, looking at their phones, and she carried on.

"In the aftermath of the First World War, people threw out many things, including corsets. Women said goodbye to tight lacing and whalebone stays and went from being full-breasted pouter pigeons to looking as boyish and natural as possible in the 1920s. If you had a big bust, looking 'natural' could involve binding it. But corsets were Victorian and beyond the pale—no one imagined a comeback for them. When Dior opened his house in 1947, you could not buy a corset in England without a prescription from a doctor. They were meant for medical problems, not to enhance your figure."

One student, the lone male in the class, did have the grace to make a note about that.

"Among the unexpected things Dior did was to reimagine women's bodies. He saw the woman wearing his clothes as shaped like an hourglass, with natural shoulders and rounded hips and stomach. His staff had to learn the lost art of corset-making, including cinchers that could take two inches off a waist. And Dior went one better—or worse, depending on your budget—than the nineteenth-century corsets. Instead of a woman owning a separate corset that she wore under all her good dresses, Dior's were custom-made for each dress and sewn into it."

By now Keitha had detached the bodice, undone its fastenings and laid it inside out on the board table, like a spatchcocked chicken. People at the end of the table stood up for a better view, but Léa remained sitting.

"What you see," Margaret said, running her gloved fingers over it, "is that this simple strapless bodice is really nothing but a corset covered with a top skin of silk organza. You can count eleven stays, or bones, set in these long channels—seven for the front, two at the back and one on each side."

The students sat back in their chairs with their arms folded or bent over their tablets and phones. One or two seemed to be taking notes. Margaret did not get the feeling they were impressed with Dior's ingenuity.

One raised her hand. "What do you think about Chanel's reaction to the New Look—'Elegance means being free to move without restrictions'?"

Keitha, Margaret couldn't help noticing, looked gratified by that question. Léa looked bored.

"Thank you for bringing up Chanel's quote, which sums up a lot of the opposition to Dior's New Look," Margaret said. "Chanel's attitude to clothes is the modern one, that we should be free and unselfconscious in them. Dior belongs to an earlier sensibility. He would have agreed with the expression 'Beauty Knows No Pains'—in other words, you have to be prepared to suffer to be beautiful."

She suggested that they ask any technical questions about construction that arose while looking at the individual pieces and save the big-picture comments for the end. With Keitha's help, she moved *Zemire*, the showstopper in the group of mannequins, front and centre. *Zemire* was the red cocktail dress David had discovered in the consignment shop, now the museum's property thanks to a generous donation. Margaret flashed a comradely glance at Léa, but she knew better than to mention its former owner.

Now Margaret watched as a few of the students finally sat up a little straighter in their chairs. Was it the dress's brave colour or the crisp delicacy of the silk faille? Both, she imagined. Any simplicity or naturalness was illusory, she told her listeners. The dress relied on the usual discipline of an eleven-boned corset and numerous hooks and eyes, and the skirt was buoyed with five layers of crinoline.

Talking of the crinoline led her to the sheer size of a Dior dress and its weight. A dress, even an apparently simple one, weighed twenty-two pounds on average. A dress with a full skirt could use forty-five yards of silk. Lifted by crinolines and net, it rustled. When he compared the short, straight wartime skirts to his generous ones, Dior called their whoosh "the sound of peace."

A student asked Margaret about the hip enhancers Dior favoured.

"That might be the one part of Dior's ideal figure that has been modified a bit," Margaret said. "In general, his ideal is pretty close to ours, but we favour a slimmer hip and usually not a pronounced derrière. Unless, of course, you're a Kardashian."

She showed them small pads of horsehair or pleated pieces of linen, like flat pincushions, that were attached to skirts at hip level to produce a more curvaceous shape. Dior's reshaped hips were subtle. The same could not be said for his late-1940s focus on the buttocks. The most extreme result of his fascination with women's bottoms was *Cocotte*, and Keitha turned the mannequin so that the gravity-defying folds of its naughty bustle faced the board table.

"And who in the world would wear such a ridiculous thing?" one of the volunteers asked abruptly.

So far, the volunteers had seemed too intimidated by the students to ask their own questions. The students greeted this unexpected query with what looked like a mixture of approval and uncertainty. They seemed to have a sixth sense that this brusque woman was not one of their people. She did not deify Dior, which was good, but something told them not to expect solidarity, either. They had nothing against the wearing of ridiculous things as long as they were not sexist, racist or classist.

Before answering the volunteer, who now looked mortified, Margaret sent a complicit smile, just for a second, to Léa, who had also owned *Cocotte*.

"That's an interesting question, because the dress does look quite extreme. Dior had a habit of designing one or two really *outré* pieces for each collection, which he called Trafalgars. He said they were to wake up the audience, which could wilt in ninety minutes of rapid-fire entrances and exits. The Trafalgars were almost never put into production, because Dior didn't expect them to sell. I don't think *Cocotte* was designed as a Trafalgar, and as a matter of fact it sold quite well."

When it came time for general questions, the student who had quoted Chanel said, "You're probably familiar with Simone de Beauvoir's comment in *The Second Sex* that the New Look was 'elegance as bondage.' How do you react to that?"

Clearly, this pupil had done her homework.

Before Margaret could decide how to respond, another student added, "Since you bring up bondage, Pauline Réage must have been thinking of the New Look when she wrote *Story of O*. All those confining, fantasy-inducing garments the heroine wears, as ordered by her lover—with the pushed-up young breasts, the confined waist—I think they sound very Dior."

Margaret nodded. "I've been thinking about *Story of O* and Dior's New Look for some time now. The novel was written in

1954, when the New Look was still very hot. The heroine is a fashion photographer and the book is shot through with references to high fashion. I think Réage tapped into the erotic appeal of the New Look not just for the observer but also *for the wearer*. I think it's undeniable that the constraints, the 'bondage' as Simone de Beauvoir calls it, were erotic for many women. It's a long continuum, from Dior's corsets that might prevent you taking a deep breath to the abuse and bondage practised by the heroine's lover, but Réage believed that there was a connection between masochism and female arousal. What do you think about that?"

No one answered. Perhaps the students needed time to absorb this uncomfortable idea, or perhaps they had decided there was no point in discussion. Finally, one of them broke the silence with a question of her own.

"I notice that you talk about dresses as prisons, about impossibly heavy clothes you can't get into or out of by yourself, about a designer who doesn't adjust his designs to women's bodies but rather adjusts women's bodies to his clothes. Does that bother you?"

There it was, the heart of the matter. And Margaret might as well be hanged for a sheep as for a lamb.

"No. I believe Dior loved women, but probably not in the way you or I would like to be loved. His vision of women was literally and symbolically constrained. And constraining. And no, the fit he wanted wasn't comfortable. But it wasn't the worst thing either. And it wasn't irrevocable. Many of the clothes in our collection have been altered to make them more comfortable by the real women who wore them—darts were relaxed, stays taken out, waist-cinchers made more forgiving."

Since she had started, she decided to finish. "There are different ways to look at these clothes—as historical artifacts, as instruments of domination if not mild torture, as toys and status symbols for the rich, as homages to women and their beauty, as expressions of disdain for women, as examples of the highest achievements in design and craft and sometimes even artistry. Speaking personally, I try to hold as many of those possibilities in my head as possible. The clothes are complicated, and my response is complicated too."

Margaret was aware that she was being slightly disingenuous. Her negative judgments of Dior were outweighed by her positive ones, and if Will had been in the audience, he would have raised his eyebrows in comic disbelief. She excused herself: her conclusion was rhetorical. And she felt certain that the students needed to hear that point of view.

After a pause, one student said, "You say constricting your waist in one of those corsets wasn't the worst thing. Have you ever worn one?"

That surprised Margaret. "No, I haven't. I wouldn't be allowed to wear any in the museum's collection, but you know, that's an interesting idea. Thank you for that. I'm going to think about it."

The discussion petered out after that. Rosie Tanaka, the professor, thanked Margaret for a stimulating presentation as the students gathered their coats and backpacks.

David Hillman had slipped in late. He and Jill, along with Léa and Margaret and Rosie Tanaka, were going to have a quick cup of tea. They invited Keitha, who was happy to come.

In the Director's sitting room, Margaret had a short aside with Rosie.

"I hope your students weren't too bored by the seminar."

"Don't worry. It's good to push them even a little outside their comfort zone."

Rosie looked to be her age and a kindred spirit.

Margaret said, "Do they ever get tired of seeing aesthetics in moral terms? I still think there's a place for just plain beauty."

"Is there any such thing as 'just plain beauty'? I wouldn't think fashion was a good place to advance that argument."

Perhaps Rosie was not the kindred spirit Margaret had imagined. Not for the first time, she saw herself as a rare remaining believer in art for art's sake. She searched for a response, but Rosie now turned her attention to Léa. Leaning toward the older woman on the couch, she looked like a fan who is hoping to charm. "Whenever I think of the seamstresses at Dior, a photograph comes to my mind, probably of the *atelier flou*, of all the women in white coats, bent over their work. Perhaps you are in that picture."

"No," Léa said. "In my day, Monsieur Dior always wore his white coat and carried a pointer so he could avoid touching the fabric. I see that the *petites mains* now also wear white coats, but we wore clean blouses and skirts."

"Did you ever sew one of those corsets?"

"We all hoped that we wouldn't have to, because in some ways they were more exacting than anything. I certainly sewed many channels into which we slid the bones and many hooks and eyes, but those were the easy parts, once the structure had been created."

Rosie pressed Léa for more details. Unlike the stylish showrooms on the first floor, the seamstresses worked in three overcrowded rooms under the eaves. Space was so tight that sometimes priceless brocades or hand-embroidered silks had to be cut on the carpet. At the end of the day, the *petites mains* swept up and stored any fragments of materials they found on the floor. They might come in handy for pockets, cuffs or other small details.

Léa sipped her tea and indulged Rosie with memories that were seventy years old.

"Everything demanded so many tiny stitches that we were always pricking ourselves. When blood got on our work, we chewed a piece of white cloth and dabbed the bloodstain with the saliva-soaked cloth. Voilà, the stain disappeared."

In the easy chairs across from the sofa, Jill was talking to Keitha, who looked determined to be a good sport. David left them and perched on a hassock near Léa.

"Did you miss being a *petite main*?"

"No, because I was to be married and move to America—two great adventures. But life in the atelier was like living in a village. We understood each other's fears and triumphs, which would have been laughable to other people. For example, we lived in terror of sweaty hands. If they perspired, that was no bad thing in the *tailleur*, where they worked with tweeds and flannels, but sweaty hands in the *flou* meant that chiffon 'cried' and lost its suppleness. When someone applied for a job, the *directrice* always felt their hands."

Rosie asked, "What was Dior like?"

As when Margaret had asked her the same question, Léa looked grave.

"I think we were a family for him. He always called the *petites mains* 'mes chères,' 'my dears.' He did little kindnesses for us, for example adjusting the price of lunch in the staff cafeteria according to your salary. So we *petites mains* paid very little. And he loved the feast of Saint Catherine, the patron saint of spinsters. Every year we competed for the best 'Catherine hat,' and there was a huge party where he was the master of ceremonies."

Her face was a mixture of sadness, affection and something else that Margaret could not define.

AUDACIEUSE

DIOR HAD AN ABIDING INTEREST in fashion history. A famous photograph taken in the Metropolitan Museum of Art's costume collection showed him with his head inside a nineteenth-century nightgown; he was investigating the way it was put together. He ransacked nineteenth-century portrait painters like Winterhalter for his swooping off-the-shoulder necklines. For the 1954 collection, when he flattened and pushed up breasts that appeared like two half mounds above straight-lined bodices, he knew enough about Tudor fashions to call it the Anne Boleyn bustline.

Interestingly for a man so dedicated to luxury, Dior admired the thrifty nineteenth-century habit of making two bodices for a single skirt. A long, full skirt required a shocking amount of fabric, so dressmakers optimized their investment with separate tops, usually a covered-up one for daytime and a more revealing one for evening. Dior followed this model several times. *Audacieuse*, from the 1955 collection, paired a black silk, box-pleated skirt with two tops that travelled a long, graceful line to below the hips.

Audacieuse has a fourth element, a separate one-piece corset with padded wire breast cups and three layers of crinoline and net that begin at the hip. Usually Dior built his corsets into his dresses, so providing a separate one looks like another nod to thrift.

Both tops are black silk, sleeveless and fitted. The difference between the day dress, suitable for tea and maybe a cocktail party, and the dressier one, meant for cocktails, the theatre or a nightclub, is more than subtle. The details are everything. The daytime dress, made from a slightly heavier silk, buttons up the side. It has a square neckline and a rounded mock pocket on one side. The side buttons and the fake pocket signal that this is for daytime. The dressier evening version has slimmer straps, a romantic sweetheart neckline rather than a square one, and a flowing silhouette with no buttons or pocket. Society women in the 1950s lived by these fine distinctions.

ELEVEN

Half a Dress

Margaret had a craving for honey cake. Not just any honey cake, but the dense, not too sweet loaf her grandmother Abrams had made. When the family visited her, she would give them one to take home, wrapped in waxed paper and tied with string. They sliced it thickly and spread cream cheese on it or ate it plain. Margaret had not thought of honey cake in years, but now she could not live without it.

She wrote to Lydia, "Do you have the recipe for Grandma's honey cake? And if so, can you send it? I want to make it this weekend with the girls."

Lydia sent a picture of the recipe, written in their grandmother's confident hand, adding, probably tongue-in-cheek, "Under no circumstances substitute a lesser kind for the buckwheat honey in the recipe. Grandma always mentioned that she sent away to Canada for the particular honey that made her cake what it was."

Margaret found a plausible-looking buckwheat honey in Wegmans, Rochester's fanciest supermarket. Probably not up to her grandmother's standards, but it would do. On Saturday afternoon, the girls read through the recipe and began collecting what they needed. Margaret had trained them to be more methodical than she was.

"Who was your favourite grandmother?" Bee asked, circling a bowl with cloves, allspice, ginger, whole wheat flour and the other dry ingredients.

"I was much closer to Marg, but Grandma Abrams was intriguing. She was so tiny that she wore a boy's knee-length knickers from the 1930s as full-length pants. But she had a big personality."

Nancy was reading the label on the honey jar. "This is the 'Guinness of honeys,' whatever that means. It has hints of malt and more antioxidants than normal honey."

"No wonder my grandmother swore by it. She was a health food pioneer."

Almost black and viscous, the honey clung stubbornly to the spatula. The batter was so heavy they had to take turns scraping it into the loaf pan.

"Your grandmother was mighty," Nancy said, carefully sliding the pan into the centre of the oven. "Did she make anything else for you?"

"The only other things I remember were individual sponge cakes she baked in cupcake pans. Each one had a spoonful of homemade strawberry or raspberry jam in the middle."

The honey cake lived up to its reputation, and they insisted that Will leave his murder and join them.

Over tea and cake, Nancy looked at her mother appraisingly and said to Bee, "I'm thinking of a messy bun."

"Yes!" Bee said. "That's perfect."

Here we go again, Margaret thought.

"Okay, what is a messy bun?"

"It's just a relaxed bun at the nape of the neck, but with a few tendrils left to hang down at the cheeks. You know, like Meghan Markle wore when she married Harry."

Margaret remembered Meghan's off-the-shoulder Givenchy

dress but not the details of her hair. The girls said there was plenty of time before dinner for them to show her how it would look, but Margaret remembered something pressing she had to do for work.

"Some other time, girls. I promise."

ON MONDAY, MARGARET had to meet with Dom and dial down his plans for the touch screens. Touch screens were labour-intensive but more fun than writing wall texts. Because the people who bothered to interact with the screen were more committed than the average visitor, Dom could write in greater detail about the fabric and the cut of the design. But probably not, as Margaret intended to remind him, about arcana like gores and the calculated tilt of a collar.

As she made her way to Dom's office, she collided gently with Padraig Heaney from Conservation.

He stepped back slightly and said, "I was just coming to talk to you about the stains and rents at the hem of the evening dress."

"The one that uses the wrong side of the material for more lustre?"

Padraig looked as if there were only one evening dress in the world, the one he was working on, so why was Margaret trying to clarify that?

"Of course. I've done a few tests and I think it's going to make things worse if we try to clean and repair it. The metallic threads in the silk have left it too fragile. I suggest this is the time for some artful lighting."

"That will mean taking it out of the magic circle in the centre. We can't light one dress differently from the others in the circle."

"No. But this one will hold its own off to the side, in a pool of the right light."

That ninety-second encounter left Margaret with two more things to do—consult with the lighting designers, and decide what should take the evening dress's place in the central circle.

She knocked on Dom's open door, and he beckoned her in to look at his laptop. Under the touch screen option "Dior's Pockets," he was writing what looked like an illustrated encyclopedia entry on set-in pockets, seam pockets, slash pockets, jetted pockets and more.

"Dom," Margaret said, trying to sound collegial and not harassed, "you know what I'm going to say. All this detail is fascinating, but you're not writing a scholarly paper in fashion history. The touch screens are background notes that inform, to a certain degree, and entertain."

Dom agreed, as usual, that he would moderate his wonkishness, and went back to writing about faux pockets. He was having a good time.

As she turned to leave, he said, "Margaret? I want to write the touch screen for the dress with two tops, and I need to have another look at its darts." Dom was a self-identified dart geek. "Can we meet tomorrow at the storage room?"

She agreed to be there at 2 p.m. on Tuesday.

Margaret found herself behind Alan Shea in the cafeteria line. He had been more than usually demoralizing lately, sending her each and every mention of Dior on Facebook, Instagram and Twitter—talks, courses, acquisitions and exhibits all over the world. Surely he realized that she got all these notices herself. This was his way of reinforcing how much competition a Dior specialist faced, crowding her with reminders of her rivals.

Picking up a Greek salad, he said, "Doesn't that Australian exhibit comparing Dior and Balenciaga sound absolutely glorious? Dior playing Mr. Nice Guy to everyone, and Balenciaga the haughty, unhelpful Basque. All they had in common was their wonderful clothes. Brilliant idea."

Leaving the unspoken suggestion that exhibits about the New Look were a dime a dozen, he took a bottle of San Pellegrino and moved even closer to home.

"I'm finding the revisionist exhibits cropping up now just fascinating, aren't you? The show in Marseille about Vuitton and his links to the Vichy regime and Pétain, the one in Stockholm that underlines the borderline pornography in Anders Zorn's late portraits, that kind of thing. They make the old straight-ahead shows we did look fawning and embarrassing. I can't wait to see the tricks you've got up your sleeve for *The New Look*."

Margaret was speechless with hatred. Alan put on a concerned face.

"I know what a tricky time it is to put on a Dior exhibit. And on top of everything else, I hear there are problems with the lighting people and the carpenters are being their truculent selves. And don't worry, they *always* mutter that the design hasn't been properly thought out."

Giving her a smile of dazzling insincerity, he paid his bill and left.

ON TUESDAY, SHE MET Dom outside the smaller storage hall after lunch. It was the evening bodice he wanted to see one more time, and she looked up its location in the register. She had every intention of connecting her computer to the register like Molly, but she hadn't gotten there yet.

"The skirt is hanging up, but the tops are in drawers 278 and 279. The evening one is 279."

For some satisfying minutes they perused the bodice's two long darts that ran from hem to bust.

"The back zipper doesn't come apart at the hem," Dom said, almost to himself, confirming what he had seen a dozen times. "So you had to step into it or pull it over your head."

"Leaving your maid or your husband or your mother to zip you up and do up all the hooks and eyes," Margaret said.

Dom asked if he could look at the daytime top for comparison, and she opened drawer 278.

It was empty.

The calm, coping Margaret surfaced first. "Someone has probably hung it up with the skirt."

But the skirt was hanging alone in its locker, looking pleased with its own fullness. And no one had signed out the bodice.

Cue the panic-stricken, hysterical Margaret. She called Conservation and demanded to know who was working on the bodice and had neglected to sign it out. No one was working on the bodice, so then she had to apologize to the conservator.

Losing the bodice was worse than the snakeskin belt. Two things missing was twice as many as one. Two things missing indicated a step-up in malice. And this was an important piece of the exhibition, illustrating a side of Dior that was not well-known.

Margaret felt on the verge of tears, like a child who has lost something important and needs absolution and comfort from her mother. In her office, after informing Claire, Gareth and Security, she put her head in her hands and whispered accusingly to herself, *Curator. Keeper. Custodian. You have failed.* She could not think how the new and severely restricted security code had fallen into enemy hands. The only people who knew it were Claire, Alan Shea in his position as a senior curator, the head of Conservation and herself.

She went to Claire's office for a brief meeting with Security. Unlike the surveillance cameras in the galleries, which were monitored around the clock, the cameras in the storage halls, where access was strictly limited, were only inspected in the case of an incident. Someone was looking through those tapes now. The top was probably still in the building, since Security looked through the contents of large bags and packages as visitors and staff left the building. Margaret hated to think of that silk faille being crushed into a cruelly small bundle.

While she was tormenting herself, a chiming sound told her she had a new email. It was from Patricia Bertelli, and it read:

Margaret, the second shoe after that anonymous message has dropped. The one where they threatened that I would hear more from the hat maker Fanny Berger. Today I received a radio script, taken from a diary Berger apparently kept during the German occupation. Presumably it was written in French, but I don't know who translated it or who edited it. And I can only reply to the message through a post office box. I'm writing to you again because it came with a note that says, "A companion piece to the New Look exhibit?" Could we talk?

TWELVE

A Handful of Brass Buttons

An alert about the missing top of *Audacieuse* had gone out through the museum that evening, sternly forbidding any leaks to the media or even discussion outside the museum. The examination of the security cameras had yielded nothing, except for a mysterious period of less than two minutes in darkness. Ordinarily, pressing in the security code turned on the lights in the room, but the perpetrator had apparently figured out a way to override that. Colleagues texted Margaret or stopped by her office to commiserate the next morning, which made her feel worse. Well, she reminded herself, that was what *commiserate* meant, to be miserable together. Luckily, Alan had flown to New York late on Monday, negotiating about a piece for his *Japonisme* exhibit. When she saw his name in her email, she pressed the trash can icon without reading the message.

After a brief conversation with Patricia Bertelli, Margaret agreed to read the hat maker's journal. She doubted that it would distract her from *Audacieuse*, but she felt too jumpy to attend to more pressing matters. Even so, once Nancy and Bee had gone to bed that evening, she delayed reading for a while, making dentist appointments for the girls, paying a library fine, looking through her agenda for a time she could get her hair cut and then deciding it wasn't necessary.

Finally, wondering why she had agreed, she clicked on the attachment Patricia had sent. The journal began in June 1940, shortly after the Germans occupied Paris. The woman writing was in the thick of busy, involving work. A shipment of straws from the Philippines had arrived, and she was experimenting with their rustic weaves. There was a particularly nubbly one she could see as a medium-brimmed hat with a striped ribbon around the crown. A summer straw, but citified.

Nor was Fanny Berger's life all work. She had recently gone with friends to a nightclub, aptly named Boîte à Sardines. While dancing in the crowd, she'd spotted a client wearing a cocktail hat she had designed. Triumphantly, she wrote, "That shiny black straw had resisted the mushroom shape I wanted it to take, but in the end I won. Mademoiselle LaForet looked charming."

Still, change was in the air. The Germans had barely arrived and already some of her suppliers were saying they would no longer be able to get certain velvets and silks. Fanny Berger had only a few metres of silk pongee left, and she planned to hoard it for the linings of her best hats. Even more alarming, one of her best saleswomen had left Paris for what she trusted would be the safety of the unoccupied south. Berger wondered if the saleswoman was worrying needlessly: France had surrendered, after all, so people hoped that that would be enough.

Although she was braced for the ending, reading the first few entries left Margaret less tense than she had expected to be. She understood the hat maker's absorption in her work, which made sense both for its own sake and as a measure of self-protection. Margaret was not ready to call it denial: in 1940, people genuinely did not know how things would turn out. Had Fanny Berger been writing in 1944, Margaret's reaction would have been different.

Life for Berger continued in the first summer and early fall of the occupation more or less as usual. There were a few ugly incidents, one very close to her premises. One day, a man in German uniform was driven along the Champs-Élysées where there was a string of smart dress shops owned by Jews. At each shop, he disembarked and threw a brick through the front window. Fanny Berger, Modes, was just around the corner, on rue Balzac, but on the second floor, so she was spared.

Margaret made herself read every word, but in the darker parts her eye leaped ahead, hoping for more millinery details. Berger did not disappoint her, whether she described designing a soft little winter hat with a few feathers that would appear in jewel colours or her struggles working with the new synthetics. The Germans had banned importing silks, straws and crepes from the Far East, so the textile manufacturers in Lyon were mixing small amounts of angora or silk into rayon to soften it, or blending hemp sacks and nylon stockings into more workaday fabrics. Whatever they did, the new fabrics rarely co-operated in taking or holding a shape.

But Frenchwomen still insisted on looking their best. One of Berger's favourite customers, Madame Duparc, had ordered a navy velvet suit from Nina Ricci, made from one of her last bolts of velvet. Madame Duparc wanted a hat to wear with it, but Berger had no velvet. Finally she settled on the tiniest of felt hats, almost hidden in a cloud of her best veiling. It was like a veil with a little hat attached, rather than a hat with a veil attached.

In the first months of the occupation, the Germans had concentrated on restrictions for foreign-born Jews, but in October they announced that French Jews must register at the police station. "Who is a Jew?" Berger wrote rhetorically in her journal. For the Germans, it was anyone who had three grandparents "of the Jewish race." Berger had four. Although not religious, her paternal grandparents, who had come from Belarus, had no trouble seeing themselves as Jewish. Her maternal grandparents, on the other hand, had lived in France for centuries and were ambivalent about their Jewishness. *Like my grandparents,* Margaret thought uneasily.

But the Germans were not interested in how connected people felt to their Jewishness. On October 4, Berger received the registration number of her Jewish dossier. What else, she wondered, would figure in that dossier? One answer came quickly: on October 18, she received word that she must put a yellow sign in the window of her atelier, saying in French and German that this was a Jewish business. *Entreprise Juive. Jüdisches Geschäft.* On peaceful rue Balzac, with its quiet stone buildings and wrought iron balconies, it looked very aggressive. The customers came anyway, even the Jewish ones—perhaps especially the Jewish ones—wanting festive evening hats for the holidays, with veils, winking rhinestone clips and the most convincing artificial silks Berger could find.

Margaret needed a glass of water. While she was in the kitchen, she overwatered the plants on the windowsill, whose names she did not know. Will had forbidden her to water them as she did not know when to stop, but she needed to do something, however destructive. She watched the saucers underneath the pots fill up with water. Dimly, she supposed she was drowning the plants, but another side of her brain hoped that she was helping them.

In the spring of 1941, the Germans enacted the first law that must have wounded Fanny Berger to the quick. She was not allowed to be seen by her clients, so she had to work behind a closed door that separated her from the reception area. With no idea she was on the premises, customers who came to browse or consult or be fitted were attended by the saleswomen. Berger recorded this development as matter-of-factly as she did most things. The solitude gave her more time for design, she wrote, and she was playing with some coarse straws that came in very small lots from Spain and Portugal. "That is the good side of the new law," she wrote. "The bad side is obvious."

Margaret thought she must have known then that things would only get worse. Will passed through the living room, where she was reading, and looked at her inquiringly. She did not meet his eyes. If she started talking about what she was reading, she was afraid she would put it down and never finish it. And, terrible as it was, she had to finish.

The situation within Berger's family was even worse than Fanny's own. Now that most professions were forbidden to Jews, her father's career as a paralegal was finished. He went into a kind of hiding with a false name, working as a travelling comb salesman. And because Fanny's brother was in the Resistance, his two young children were hidden with a Gentile family in the country.

The wall around Berger grew quickly in 1941. At the beginning of the year, she owned her own flourishing business. By the end, she could no longer access her bank account and, since Jews were no longer permitted to own property, she had been forced to watch a former employee buy her atelier from the Germans. Berger received nothing from the sale. There were two very small compensations. Although the Germans returned her to her birth name, Odette Bernstein, the salon would continue to be called Fanny Berger. And the new owner was allowing her to work behind closed doors.

Margaret was not reassured. Silently, she asked Fanny Berger, *How long do you think that arrangement will last?* Sure enough, by February 1942, Berger was forbidden entrance to the business she had founded. Late one evening, she walked through it one last time, beginning with the chic reception rooms with their padded chairs and flattering lights, where clients were offered tea and coffee after fittings or while they considered a hat. Berger thought back on a decade's worth of women turning their heads in the three-sided mirrors, often with a *vendeuse* holding up another mirror at the back.

Even more than the reception rooms, Berger had loved the supply of shapers, irons, hat stands and beret models that stood waiting in the stockroom and workroom. She ran her hand over the chassis of her Singer sewing machine, the way you would caress the flanks of your favourite horse. Even with all the problems of scarcity and difficult communications with Lyon, the inventory included twenty felt hats, eight Panama hats, eight Bangkok hats, five Italian straws, three fantasy straws, lengths of felt and muslin, as well as miscellaneous ribbons. From a drawer filled with small decorative pieces, Berger scooped up a handful of brass buttons and put them in her pocket. They were the only things she took away. "I will run them through my fingers for comfort," she wrote. "A Jewish rosary."

Margaret tried to imagine not being allowed to enter the museum, with her exhibit half finished. Her head hurt, but she went on reading. The world closed in on Fanny Berger more and more. Jews now had a curfew, so that she could not leave her room in the small hotel where she lived from 8 p.m. until 6 a.m. When sirens sent people running to the shelters, she watched from her window; Jews were not allowed in the shelters. Someone had denounced her brother and he had been arrested.

In June, all Jews were instructed to pick up three yellow Stars of David outlined in black from the police station and sew them firmly on the left side of their clothing. Beginning on June 7, they must never appear outside without them. For summer, Berger chose two blouses and a blue dress she wore often. When winter came, she would sew them on her coat and two sweaters.

June 7 was a beautiful, sunny Sunday. Hundreds of people gathered between the Place de la République and the Opéra to protest. Strangely enough, partly because of the weather and partly from the solidarity, it felt almost festive. Jews emblazoned with their new stars staked a defiant claim to seats in the outdoor cafés. Mothers pushed baby carriages and gathered in groups to chat. The flower prints of their light dresses and those bold yellow stars made an odd combination. Many Gentiles had homemade yellow stars and wore them in support. The Jewish veterans of the 1914–18 war promenaded slowly through the crowd in their uniforms, their Stars of David tucked in among their glittering, beribboned medals.

With no work and only walks for diversion, Berger's days were long. Department stores and boutiques were closed to Jews.

They could only shop for food between 3 and 4 p.m., when most food stores were shut. Jews could not own a telephone, nor use a phone booth. They were not allowed to have bicycles and could only board the last train wagon on the metro. Public gardens, pools, public showers, the cinema, theatres, concerts, museums and libraries were closed to Jews. So were sporting events, hotels and restaurants.

On September 8, 1942, Fanny Berger wrote, "Little by little we are being strangled and most of the time I no longer imagine that we will survive. Trying to escape into Vichy is filled with danger, and even if I succeeded there is no guarantee that I would be better treated there. But that is the only hope left."

Margaret's heart was pounding. She knew the large shape of Berger's life, but not the smaller twists and turns. Perhaps she had made it into Vichy and had at least a temporary respite.

But eleven days after she wrote that Vichy was the only hope, Berger was arrested on the Moulins bridge with eight other Jews as they tried to cross into the south. She thought she was resigned to whatever would happen, she wrote, but when the Germans surrounded them, she was so panic-stricken she almost fainted. Before she left Paris, she had entrusted her journal to her assistant Celestine Dandurand. From now on she would write very little, on scraps torn out from a sketchbook and then hidden. The guards who searched her wanted to confiscate the book, but she pleaded that she was a *modiste* and used it for new designs. She showed them a few sketches and to her surprise they agreed that she could keep it, but only to draw hats. They did not mention the obvious, that her designing days were over.

She wrote, "I feel quite numb. I am trying to crawl into a shell, to be as small and quiet as possible."

For nine months, Fanny Berger lived in a camp in Beaune-La-Rolande in the Loiret. Some things were strangely normal. The prisoners could receive mail and packages, including litres of wine. They could deposit a small amount of money with the guards, who noted it in their register with Germanic precision, and spend it for better food or the rare treat.

The women were allowed to go into the men's barracks for an hour in the evening, where they sang together—another odd piece of permissiveness on the part of the guards. There were three teenaged sisters in Fanny Berger's barrack—Flora, Raymonde and Suzanne. The sisters knew the words to all the songs, popular or classical. They told Berger their periods had stopped in the camp and what a good thing that was, because how would they clean themselves or their clothes? It was the same with Berger. The sisters were trying to keep their hairstyles exactly as they were when they last saw their parents, "so that they will recognize us."

In June 1943, Fanny Berger was transferred to Drancy, one of the staging posts for Auschwitz or another of the Polish camps.

On July 14, the prisoners were made to stand for a minute's silence in the main yard in honour of Bastille Day. *Liberté, Egalité, Fraternité.* Berger wrote, "Is there a god who smiles at these absurdities?"

The script concluded with a note from the editor.

Celestine Dandurand received an envelope with a note dated 18 July 1943. Fanny Berger wrote that she would be in a train headed for Poland in a few hours and was sending her the end of her journal. She had a ten-franc note left from her account, and she would pin it on the envelope and look for a likely place where she could throw it out of the train. She hoped someone would find it and buy a stamp. Her note ended, "You must be very busy getting the fall styles finished. Good luck. Goodbye, Fanny."

Although the postage cost only fifty centimes, whoever found the envelope covered it with ten francs' worth of stamps.

Fanny Berger arrived at Auschwitz on Convoy Number Fifty-Seven on 23 July 1943 and was immediately gassed.

The owner of 4 rue Balzac kept the nameplate, *Fanny Berger, Modes*, for the rest of his life.

THIRTEEN

Black Silk in a Bentwood Box

Will watched Margaret as she pushed her tablet slightly away from her on the coffee table.

"Are you okay? What are you reading?"

"Here. You can read it," she said, and stood up.

"Where are you going? Are you okay? You're pale."

"I'm always pale. I have to make a call."

But she did not make the call immediately. She sat on her bed for a while, staring at the fine black lines on the duvet cover. She had never noticed its resemblance to graph paper before. Finally, feeling that her arms and legs were very heavy, she took her notebook out of her purse. She had written down a few names and addresses from the cards and letters in her father's condo. She chose one, only because the man lived in the nearby suburb of Irondequoit, and found a phone number.

When a woman answered, Margaret asked if she could speak to Harold Abramson.

The man who came to the phone had an attractive, resonant voice with no familial echo that Margaret could hear.

"This is Margaret Abrams," she said. "My father was Michael Abrams." There was no response to that, so she added, "And my grandparents were Hester and Sol Abrams, or Abramson, depending on when you knew them."

Now he made the connection. "Moe Abramson. Your father is Moe?"

She said yes and explained that her father had died. Harold's and Moe's fathers had been brothers, and Harold had not seen his cousin in more than forty years. He said that he was sorry. Then he returned to the family tree, as if trying to situate Margaret on the right branch.

"So, Aunt Hester was your grandmother. She could be a pretty tough nut. You didn't want to mess with her. Somehow your dad . . . Well, Margaret, how nice to make your acquaintance. What can I do for you?"

She explained that, as was obvious, she didn't know much about her father's family. With his death, memories and a few facts had emerged, and she wanted to learn more. That sounded like a good idea to Harold Abramson, and he invited her to lunch a week from Saturday.

"Arlene," he called out, "my cousin Moe's daughter's coming to lunch next weekend."

Arlene said something indistinct, and he turned back to the phone.

"What about your family? Bring them too."

She thanked him, but for this first time she would rather come alone. After they hung up, she lay down and stared at the ceiling, thinking about the hat maker. Her question was similar to the one she had had when she finished reading about Catherine Dior: How could things ever return to normal after humans treated each other with such cruelty?

SOMETHING IN FANNY BERGER'S journal was niggling at Margaret. It was easier to focus on a detail than to think about the tragedy of her life. When Margaret thought she was approaching whatever it was that tapped at her brain, it vanished. Then, two days after reading the journal, she ambushed it. It was the nightclub where Fanny had gone to dance, the Boîte à Sardines. Something about that anecdote reminded her of Léa's story of the two men in the basement of the beauty salon powering the dryers with their bicycling. Léa had been having her hair done because she was going to a nightclub. But what was interesting about that? Untold numbers of Parisians in the 1940s went to nightclubs.

But—and here a more significant possible link between the two women clicked into focus, as if it had been waiting to be recognized—Léa had begun her working life as a hat maker. Paris probably had as many hat makers as it had nightclubs, so that was still a very long stretch. But it piqued Margaret's curiosity.

Meanwhile, the top of the dress had been missing for almost five days. Adding to Margaret's unhappiness, someone had leaked the story to the Rochester *Democrat and Chronicle*, known to the chattering classes as the *Demagogue and Comical*. The paper published a short article headed DIOR DRESS LEFT TOPLESS. The museum declined to comment.

Margaret was stubbornly refusing to choose a substitute outfit for the exhibit, insisting at the department meeting that the missing piece would return.

"Oh, I see!" Alan said roguishly. "You're going to do a Gardner." To the blank looks around him, he explained, "You know, the way the Gardner in Boston still hangs those empty frames in the places where the paintings were stolen in 1990. Margaret is planning to display a mount with nothing on it, next to the skirt and evening top. Brilliant."

She liked it when Alan acted out his cattiness in public because she could see from her colleagues' faces that they too found him insufferable.

As people scattered at the end of the meeting, Claire met her eye. "Do you have a minute? Let's go to my office."

Margaret assumed it was about the disappearance, but something else was on Claire's mind.

"I know you have more on your plate than you deserve, and I'm sorry to add to it. But I'm wondering if *The New Look* wouldn't benefit from some context. A slightly bigger picture. There was so much going on in the world when Dior began, and his clothes are still controversial. Not touching on one of the tender points—the traumatic postwar climate, say, or his attitude to women—feels like a missed opportunity."

Just what I need, Margaret thought. She couldn't see Keitha mentioning her idea for an alcove to Claire—that was unlike her. But Alan might well have made an apparently innocent remark or two. Or maybe it was such an obvious idea that Claire hadn't needed to be prompted.

"Of course, the subject is up to you. Something for you to think about, anyway," Claire said as Margaret remained silent.

"But quickly," Margaret said. They had two months before *The New Look* opened. How was that even possible?

"Yes, very quickly."

ALAN WAS GIVING A TALK at the museum co-hosted by the Japan Society, called "Reading Kimonos: Japanese Clothes and the Stories They Tell." Another step in his campaign to become Chief Curator. Claire had asked Margaret if she wanted to schedule a public lecture, but Margaret didn't see how she could fit it in before *The New Look* opened. Will said that was a mistake, but she could not face one more particle of stress.

Ordinarily, Margaret would have attended Alan's talk, if only because it would look strange if she didn't, but that evening she had a terrible headache. She sent her apologies to Alan and Claire, and was lying in bed in the dark when the phone rang. It was 10:20, late for a call.

Will appeared in the bedroom door. "Do you feel well enough to talk to Jill Hillman? She's found the top of the dress."

Margaret had never heard Jill so excited or happy. Come to think of it, she had never heard Jill at all excited or happy.

"It was in a bentwood box in the Pacific Northwest Gallery, of all things," Jill said, still sounding almost breathless. "And it doesn't seem to be harmed—whoever took it laid it on tissue paper."

Margaret's headache had disappeared, but she was confused. "A bentwood box with a cover?"

She knew very little about bentwood boxes, but she did know that not all of them had covers.

"This one has a cover, but it was propped up against the side of the box."

"Is that the way the box is normally displayed?"

"No, it always has its cover on. But the thief needed to remove the cover so that we could find the top."

"What were you doing in the Pacific Northwest Gallery in the evening?"

"David and I had been to Alan Shea's talk. And you know how boring the receptions afterwards are, so I just strolled over there for a break from all the chatter."

The Pacific Northwest Gallery was on the other side of the museum from Palmateer Hall, where the talk and reception had taken place.

Margaret said, "Right. Well, we're so lucky you chose that gallery for a break. Thanks so much, Jill. We'll talk tomorrow."

Margaret arranged to meet Gareth, Claire and Security at 9 a.m. in the Pacific Northwest Gallery. At eight o'clock she walked into the kitchen to make extra-strong coffee, but Will had anticipated that. He handed her a cup, and she sat down next to Nancy, who was writing in her "Mystery at the Museum" notebook.

"So, Jill is obviously the perp," Nancy said.

"Why do you say that?"

"The murderer often pretends to discover the dead guy, and he or she gets cut some slack because it seems their evidence is helping the investigation."

Any points Will might have gained with the cup of coffee were lost. Margaret rounded on him as he ate his Cheerios and tried to look innocent.

"What were you thinking, telling her all the details?"

Nancy removed herself from marital conflict by lowering her head and making some further notes.

Will spooned up the last few swallows of milk. "It's such a common trope, I thought it would be interesting for Nancy's notebook. Do you remember in *Murder Is Late for Vespers*, when the former nun claims to find the choirmaster stuffed into the cupboard with all the choir robes? That fooled Crispin into thinking she was innocent for quite a while."

Margaret glared at him, but she had no time to quarrel now. She wanted to see the top of *Audacieuse* before she met her colleagues. She said, icily, "We're not supposed to talk about this with anyone outside the museum. And that goes for you."

She left the coffee cup half full, to show Will the extent of her displeasure. Then, calling up the stairs, "Bye, Bee! Don't forget it's your day to be Daddy's sous-chef," she headed for the bus.

In the storage room, she handled *Audacieuse* as tenderly as you would a child or a pet who had been lost. Whispering to it, almost crooning, she patted it contritely and turned it over to make sure there was no damage. She even smelled it, at a safe distance. There was no hint of cedar. When she was satisfied that the top was fine, just needed a good rest in drawer 278, she went to the Pacific Northwest Gallery.

There she found Gareth and Claire, a man from Security and a World Cultures curator who seemed eager to be part of the drama. He demonstrated taking off and putting on the box's cover, which did not seem strictly necessary, but they watched respectfully. The box itself was a typical example of its genre, painted with enigmatic long eyes and curved rectangular shapes in black and red.

As with the Etruscan sarcophagus, the bentwood box had been chosen because it was just outside the security camera's reach. The duty sheet filled out by last night's guard told them that the gallery had been inspected at 6:17 p.m. and all was in order. The box had its cover on. Jill Hillman had notified Security at 8:46 p.m. that she had discovered the top.

"So, the top was put in the box between 6:17 and 8:46 last night?" Gareth asked.

"Not necessarily," Claire said. "The top might have been in the box before that. But someone came into the gallery between those two times and either deposited the dress top and removed the cover or just removed the cover."

Margaret calculated silently that Alan had had plenty of time to slip into the gallery before his lecture, which began at 7 p.m. He had gone to New York on the evening the top had been discovered missing, but only after Margaret and Dom had found the drawer empty. Another hundred or so people, who had come for the talk, would also have had access to the gallery. Normally the galleries were barred and locked in the evening, but the building's nineteenth-century configuration meant that some of them, including the Pacific Northwest Gallery, sprawled too much to make this feasible. The museum tried to make a virtue out of necessity by inviting people coming for talks and receptions to enjoy the galleries that stayed open. But how would a visitor have got hold of the top in the first place? Even Jill did not have that kind of access.

For a minute all five of them stared down into the bentwood box, where the white tissue paper still lay. Without it, the dark top would have been hard to spot in the dark box. Security had removed the dress top immediately and kept it locked up until someone from Conservation claimed it this morning. They knew better than to suggest dusting seventy-year-old silk for fingerprints, at least in this crowd. Most bad actors knew by now to wear gloves, but just in case, they would dust the tissue paper after they removed it from the box. Nobody expected much success from that.

Margaret noticed something about the tissue paper. When you lined a surface with paper that was longer than the surface, the normal practice was to make a fold in the paper and leave the fold on the underside. It looked neater that way. The fold on this tissue was on the top side.

Margaret was tired of things appearing, disappearing, reappearing. She wanted to get back to thinking about Dior and his designs. When she returned to her office, she called Léa and proposed lunch next week. After she accepted, Margaret said casually, as if she hadn't asked before, "I've been going over the hats for the exhibit and began thinking about your beginnings as a hat maker. What was the name of your atelier?"

"Le Chapeau Parfait. The Perfect Hat."

"Where was it?"

"Somewhere in the eighth. It was seventy years ago, I don't remember the street."

They arranged to lunch at the Middle Eastern restaurant where they had met before, on Tuesday.

After she hung up, Margaret searched online and in her databases but could not find any mention of an establishment called Le Chapeau Parfait. That didn't mean it didn't exist, of course. But if it had, it would have been a very small place.

Keitha appeared in her doorway and knocked on the frame, expressing jubilation that the dress top had been found. She also reported on her attempt to borrow one of Dior's sample pages from the Fashion Museum for the exhibit. These were stiff pages on which Dior sketched a few views of a particular design and wrote the name of the piece, the person in the *atelier flou* or *atelier tailleur* who was entrusted with its making, and the model on whom it was custom-made. Also pinned on the page were possible fabrics, colours, buttons and trims. The sample pages, all in museums or the Dior Foundation in France, were intimate, irreplaceable witnesses of Dior's design process. If one ever appeared on the auction market, it would probably fetch more than $100,000. Margaret had her heart set on the page for *Égypte*, a slim, strapless column of an evening dress. Keitha was making some slow progress, which was not her fault—it was the institutionalized reluctance with which museums parted with their treasures.

Margaret asked Keitha if she had been to Alan's lecture. She had, of course, and launched into what a revelation it had been, when Margaret cut her off.

"Did you see anyone or anything in the audience or at the reception afterward that struck you as at all strange or noteworthy? Anyone leaving the reception conspicuously early or arriving late?"

Margaret felt that Crispin Applegate couldn't have phrased that any better. But Keitha had noticed nothing remarkable. She recalled seeing David Hillman alone at the reception, but Jill's anti-social habits were well-known.

Margaret was finished with her questions, but Keitha lingered on the threshold. Usually she was so preoccupied with her work she wasted no time on farewells.

"Is there anything else?"

Keitha smoothed her hair, which did not need it. "It's probably nothing, but I noticed the name. The name Beyle, I mean."

Margaret took a few seconds to remember that Beyle was the last name of Alexander, the *Times* reporter.

"What about Beyle?"

"Well, it could be a coincidence, but I ran across an article in an academic journal about Dior's backer, Marcel Boussac, by an Anton Beyle. There wasn't any information that you hadn't already told me, I don't think, although it stressed the point that Boussac was a much richer man at the end of the occupation than he was at the start. And as we know, he was never questioned by the purification committees after the Liberation. The article contrasted his wartime experience with that of two people, one a young woman who had a baby with a German and the other a Jewish law student. The woman had her head shaved and was made to walk down the main street of her village, carrying her baby, while everyone jeered. She changed her name and moved to a new town. The law student died in a concentration camp."

Margaret put her hands in her pockets and nodded. She said, "And Boussac got off scot-free."

In her mind's eye she could see the woman with the shaved head and the law student bent over his books in happier days. In her imagination the student wore a Star of David on his sweater while he studied, but she corrected that. By the time the stars were compulsory, no Jew would have been allowed in law school.

"So, you think the author might be a relative of Alexander's."

"Well, judging by the date of the article, it could be a father or grandfather, but it's just a possibility. I googled Beyle a bit and it seems to be a fairly common French Jewish name."

"So maybe Alexander has a more personal interest in Dior's relationship with Boussac than we imagined," Margaret said. "Maybe Anton Beyle had some unfortunate dealings with Boussac. But it's a slim thread and doesn't help at all with the belt or the dress top, as Alexander wasn't even in Rochester at those points."

Keitha nodded, and Margaret thought again. "Unless he was here and we didn't know it. Or maybe there's an accomplice. Anyway, thank you, Keitha. Interesting."

We've all become detectives, she thought, a little amused.

When Keitha left, she texted Patricia Bertelli, thanking her for sending Fanny Berger's journal and asking if she planned to broadcast it. She did, Patricia wrote, sometime within the next month, but unless Margaret was aware of some connection between the hat maker and *The New Look*, she wouldn't tie the broadcast to the exhibit. Margaret assured her she knew of no connection.

Her phone rang, and she saw from the display that it was Gareth. Oh no, she prayed. But yes, there was another package. Gareth sounded as if he were trying not to blame Margaret, but without complete success.

"What is it?"

"Some wartime pamphlet." He added, "In French," in a way that made it clear he did not read French.

Unlike the first packages, which had had pride of place on Gareth's desk, this one was banished to a side table next to the door. It was as close as he could come to washing his hands of this infuriating campaign. Margaret turned the pamphlet's pages, printed in Vichy on cheap wartime paper, cautiously. It advertised a 1943 fair celebrating *"les produits artisanaux, les arts décoratifs et la haute couture de France."* The artisanal products ranged from wooden bowls to rustic pottery, and the decorative arts featured wall hangings emblazoned with General Pétain's face as well as fabrics printed with scenes of rural life or dancing lords and ladies. Haute couture was a strange addition to this mix of nostalgia and propaganda, but a suit by Lucien Lelong shared the cover with pictures of wooden spoons and a scarf honouring Jeanne d'Arc. The suit had a long, belted jacket in brave red, white and blue stripes, and a knife-pleated red skirt. The rest of the pamphlet elaborated on the skill and patriotism of French workers and invited visitors to the fair.

In the usual neat printing, the accompanying note said, "Strange bedfellows, or not?" Presumably, it referred to the coexistence of the sophisticated suit with the spoons and the scarf.

"I'm taking this to my office. It's four p.m. in London, and Deirdre Ferrar should still be in her office at the V&A. But first I want to ask your advice about something in my exhibit."

Gareth looked grateful that Margaret was taking the pamphlet out of his sight. If he was surprised to be consulted about a fashion exhibit, he didn't show it.

"I'm thinking about an addition that illustrates how Dior protected his designs while allowing manufacturers to adapt them to the American market. He presented himself as a man who sketched dresses in his garden and only involved himself in aesthetic decisions, but he was actually an entrepreneur who understood that even modestly priced copies could extend his brand."

Gareth looked attentive, so Margaret explained that luxury stores wanting to reproduce Dior's models were allowed to buy the piece itself, or a muslin version of the design called a *toile*, or a paper pattern. With the *toile* and the paper pattern came the all-important *référence*, which included all the directions for making the model, with sources for fabric, trims and accessories.

"Those stores were at the top of the pecking order for copying or adapting Dior designs. A dress made by Bergdorf Goodman, for example, using all the materials of the Paris model and faithfully following the *référence* instructions, could be described in the advertising copy as an 'exact copy,' although its price might be seventy percent lower than the dress made in France. Bergdorf relied on the prestige of scarcity, so they typically produced only about a dozen copies of one design, and would not produce more than thirty."

Gareth asked, "What if you couldn't afford Bergdorf's?"

"Lower down on the scale were copies, but not 'exact copies,' that still managed to be astonishingly faithful. Ohrbach's liked to parade the original and the copy together at their fashion shows and challenge the audience to say which was the imitation. Jacqueline Kennedy was one of their customers.

"Other stores substituted machine for hand sewing, changed the colour, the fabric or details of the style, often to suit American tastes. These were called 'line-for-line' copies or 'reproductions.' The further a dress was from the Paris original, the more the price fell. A genuine Dior could cost $1,000, and you could buy an exact copy for seven hundred. A line-for-line copy might sell for about $150 in a Fifth Avenue store and as low as $37 on Thirty-Fourth Street.

"For the exhibit, I'm imagining a spot in one of the smaller rooms, with a text panel and a few examples of original models standing next to two or three copies, each one more distant from the Paris model. Do you think that sounds useful?"

As Margaret expected, a flattered Gareth said that sounded like an extremely useful addition. He didn't think enough attention was paid to the business side of haute couture and was glad she had asked for his opinion. Margaret was prepared to justify this foray into the economics of couture as a response to Claire's request for more context, even though she knew this was not what Claire had in mind. But she felt too beleaguered and dispirited to venture onto more sensitive ground. She gave Gareth a smile she hoped was not too ingratiating and returned to her office with the pamphlet.

Deirdre was at her desk and happy to FaceTime. Today she was wearing a bustier topped with a shrug. The shrug was held in place by what looked like a vintage sweater guard, a chain with rosettes at its ends. She got up from her desk to close her door, and Margaret caught a glimpse of a felt circle skirt. Her own mother had made one like that for Margaret to wear skating when she was about the twins' age.

As soon as Margaret lifted the pamphlet to the screen, Deirdre was all business.

"Ah yes, one of the unholy alliances of the occupation. Pétain and the Fascists tried to unite the country around the idea of an old, rural France with happy peasants and charming aristocrats. Far from skinny clothes horses, their models were round symbols of fertility—the Pétainists despised haute couture. Too decadent. But Hitler hankered after its prestige, so designers like Lelong emphasized the continuity between the traditional crafts and couture. He frequently said that the clothes by Parisian designers depended on the age-old skills Pétain championed—everything from spinning and weaving to making the beads and ribbons that decorated evening dresses. As a result, Lelong got invited to craft fairs like the one advertised here."

"So it was a way for him to stay in business during the occupation."

"Not just for himself, but for couture as a whole. Which was his defence when the possibility of collaboration surfaced."

"Tell me how the suit plays into this."

"Well, first of all, it's a suit, something a woman might wear to work. Not a ball dress, which Vichy would have considered too frivolous. If we assume that Lelong chose it for the cover, the use of red, white and blue is canny because both sides, the Pétainists and the Resistance, used the colours of the French flag to symbolize their cause."

Dior was working at Lelong's house when this was made, Margaret thought. *Was it possible he had a hand in it?*

Deirdre's round head, seen from above as she looked closely at the suit, reminded Margaret of a late summer tomato bursting with flavour. Margaret, the natural redhead, wondered if she should colour her hair. *Then I wouldn't look so washed out and tense*, she thought. Intensify the red and maybe no one would notice its lack of style.

"By the way," Margaret said, "since I have you, does the name Le Chapeau Parfait ring any bells? It's the name of a millinery salon in Paris in the 1940s. In the eighth arrondissement."

Deirdre pushed her lips forward, as if to kiss. "Never heard of it." She thought a little further. "In the forties, you say? That doesn't sound like the forties. Their shops and ateliers had discreet, simple names, either women's first names, like Elodie, or sometimes British ones for snob appeal, like Cavendish. Something semi-ironic like Le Chapeau Parfait would be unusual."

FOURTEEN

A Long White Baby Dress

Margaret turned off St. Paul Boulevard onto Covington Drive. It was a pleasant street, with mid-twentieth-century houses planted well back on wide lawns. She guessed which house was the Abramsons' because it was the only one on the block not prefaced by a stroller, tricycle, bicycle or wagon. As Harold later confirmed, they had missed the memo about downsizing when their kids had grown up and now, in their seventies, they enjoyed all the life on the street. Harold in person was slightly smaller than his voice had led her to believe, but he was chatty and warm. Arlene was less chatty and more observant, and Margaret liked her too.

They sat down in a contemporary living room where the spotless windows made Margaret wonder how long it was since her own had been cleaned. Without any preamble Harold began, "I've made a little chart of the family for you, so you can see—"

"Stop it, Harold," Arlene said. "She doesn't want to look at that before she's even caught her breath. Let's get to know each other a little first." To Margaret, she said, "He loves charts. It's an engineer thing."

"I'd love to see your chart a little later," Margaret said. "But I think I need to start with the basics—you'll be surprised at my ignorance. So your father and my grandfather were brothers, and was your cousin Ruth the child of another brother?"

"Yes. There were three brothers—your grandfather Sol, my father Seymour and Ruth's father Morton. Those were their American names, of course. They had Jewish ones when they arrived at Ellis Island from Galicia in the early 1920s. I had two older sisters, one of whom is still living. She and your father were the same age, eight years older than I am. You remember these age differences forever when you're the younger one. I remember looking up to Moe—he played baseball, he caddied at a local golf club, I thought he was quite the guy. His mother, by the way, didn't approve of the baseball or the caddying, but Moe talked his way around her."

Margaret's grandfather and his brothers had settled in the Fifteenth Ward, which was where most of Syracuse's Jews lived when they first arrived. One by one, as they grew more comfortable in America, the brothers left the ward. Before the war, Margaret's grandfather moved to what was then a small country town called Manlius.

"That was Aunt Hester's doing, I'm sure," Harold said. "She was the engine in that couple. She was an early back-to-the-land type, and that went with her food fads and health gurus and things that people might have considered a little hippieish or even crackpot. Sorry, Margaret."

"No, that's fine," Margaret said. "Even as a child, I knew she was a bit strange. Coincidentally, my daughters and I just made her honey cake a few weeks ago."

"But it's not Rosh Hashanah," Arlene said, looking puzzled.

"Is honey cake a Rosh Hashanah tradition?"

"Of course, because you wish everyone a sweet new year."

"She also baked sponge cakes. Is that a Jewish dessert?"

"Yes. You can make a good sponge cake with vegetable oil and not butter, which means it can be eaten both at meat meals and dairy meals."

So, her grandmother's specialties were staples of the Jewish kitchen. While Margaret was absorbing that, Harold continued with his family history.

"Hester wanted chickens and a little piece of property in the country, and she got them. Sol got a long bus ride into town to his tailoring job at Gordon-Pinkney. We didn't see too much of them once they moved to the country, except for family celebrations like weddings and bar mitzvahs. Once your father finished school, he sort of disappeared as far as the family was concerned."

By that point, they had moved into the dining room. Arlene served salad and a quiche lorraine, and when Margaret complimented her, she said, "I used to make quiche, but now I'd rather read. We have quite a good French deli right at the corner."

They had reached a delicate point in the family story, with Margaret's father distancing himself from the Abramsons, so while they ate, Harold and Arlene asked Margaret about herself. She told them about leaving Syracuse to go to graduate school in Rochester and staying, about her work, her sisters, Will and the girls. They knew from Ruth Abramson that Moe had had three daughters, but not much else. Harold and Arlene had moved to Rochester for Harold's work at Xerox a generation before Margaret arrived and raised their two sons here.

A small silence descended, and Margaret decided to break it. "So, who was Moses?"

They looked blank.

"Moses who?"

Margaret laughed. "That's what I asked *you*. You know, 'Moses Michael Abramson.' Where did that come from?"

Now Harold laughed too. "Right, *that* Moses. He was your dad's and my great-grandfather, who never left Galicia. Our grandfather's father. Moe was the first male in the family born after he died, and it's the custom to name babies after dead relatives. As a matter of fact," he added, avoiding Arlene's eyes, "this could be the time for the chart."

Arlene did not protest, and he left briefly and returned with a drawing of a many-boughed family tree.

"This is yours to keep," he told Margaret, and pointed out Moses Abramson's place on the tree. Margaret caught a quick glimpse of people named Abraham, Selig, Zigmund, Rachel, Morris, Hannah and Golda. Imagine that—Golda. She wondered how Will's mother would have reacted if she had named one of the girls Golda.

She thanked him and promised to study it. "I have another question. Why did my grandparents shorten their name to Abrams?"

Harold and Arlene looked at each other.

"One of the great unsolved mysteries," Arlene said. "Not that we haven't talked it to death."

"It was during the war, wasn't it?" Harold said.

"It was sometime between 1935 and 1940," Margaret said.

"So, just before. And my parents always said that it was never formally announced, just something that appeared on their return address stickers. I was born in 1943, so I heard about it long after the fact. Maybe because the change was so low-key, most of the Abramsons never adopted the new version."

"Yes," Margaret said, "I noticed that Ruth addressed all her cards and letters to Sol and Hester Abramson."

Arlene said, "People wondered if they were trying to hide from Hitler, but that would have been a pretty feeble attempt. Sol and Hester weren't dummies, so I never bought that theory."

Margaret asked, "Is *Abrams* significantly less Jewish than *Abramson*?"

"I wouldn't have thought so," Harold said. "And a lot of immigrants changed their names, to sound more American. Dropping *-son* was neither here nor there, I couldn't see how it made any difference. But at the same time, I've always thought that that was the first sign that they were pulling back from the family and becoming less Jewish, or maybe not Jewish at all. Their distance from all that became even more noticeable after the war."

"What a strange time to move away from Judaism."

"Yes, on the face of it," Harold said. "And this is just speculation, but the effects of Hitler's Final Solution weren't always what you would expect. A lot of the Jews who came to America had either not been religiously observant in Europe or they saw America as a place where they could escape from all the rules of traditional Judaism. Maybe they were going to continue to think of themselves as Jews, but also as Americans and as secular people. Not all of them, of course. But I've had older Jews say to me, 'Hitler made me Jewish.' Meaning that because they didn't follow the Orthodox rules and regulations, they hadn't considered themselves Jewish. But Hitler wasn't interested in how they defined themselves. And they weren't necessarily happy about being 'made' to be Jewish. Many Jews did gather closer together in synagogues and communities after the war to prove Hitler's campaign a failure. Others seem not to have been swayed by that, and maybe—I don't know—that included your grandparents."

"I don't know either. But when we cleared out my father's condo, we saw that our grandmother had saved all Ruth's Passover and Rosh Hashanah cards."

Harold smiled. "Ruth just kept on being the family glue. I don't think she could have seriously contemplated her aunt and uncle leaving Judaism. And maybe the fact that your grandmother kept the cards shows she was partially right."

"But I wonder what my father thought about being Jewish."

"I don't know. It's funny, because I remember him trying to get away from his mother's rules. She wanted him to study, play the violin and not eat meat or any of the other foods that were forbidden in their household. He wanted to be a regular American boy. So, how do you rebel against a mother who doesn't want to be Jewish?"

Another silence, this time not from awkwardness but because no one knew.

"Well," Arlene said, "he didn't go the obvious route, of becoming Jewish."

"No," Margaret agreed. "There's something else I want to ask you," she said, taking out her phone. "When we were children and someone assumed we were Jewish, my sisters and I would say to each other, 'But Jews don't have a christening dress!' Because we had a baby dress, from my father's family, in which we were all baptized. To us it looks like the classic baptismal dress."

She showed them the photograph on her phone. The dress was intended for a young baby, made of fine white cotton batiste, with a multitude of tucks down its long length and a simple edging of lace around the neck and sleeves.

Harold raised his eyebrows and said, "No idea what that could be."

Arlene sighed in exasperation. "Sometimes your mind is like a sieve, Harold. Go and get that book I bought in Berlin at the Jewish Museum." To Margaret, she said, "His memory is still good when he's interested in the subject. That doesn't include clothes."

He returned with a book of portraits of Berlin families in the Jewish Museum's collection, taken around the turn of the twentieth century. Arlene riffled through the pages. The long white baby dresses stood out from the mostly dark clothes worn by the adults, so they were easy to spot.

"Here's one. And here's another. You look."

Margaret took the book. Surrounded by proud families, sometimes just the parents, sometimes including grandparents and older brothers and sisters, the babies wore dresses that looked identical to the one in which she and her sisters had been baptized in St. Stanislaus Church.

Arlene explained, "If the baby was a boy, he could be wearing it for the party after his circumcision, his bris. If it was a girl, it could be for her naming ceremony, although I'm not sure they did that a hundred years ago in Berlin. It could have been just a dress for family parties or for a photograph. And you see how common they were."

So, that mystery was cleared up. Margaret wondered for the first time if her grandmother or Aunt Dorothy knew how her family had used the baby dress.

She could not stop looking at the book. The grave fathers, the watchful mothers, the beautifully dressed children trying their best to hold their pose, transfixed her. Whenever possible, the fates of the people were noted underneath their names—who survived, who did not, the camp in which they had died.

The tears that had not come when she read Fanny Berger's journal came now.

Arlene patted her hand.

Margaret said, "I'm sorry."

"Absolutely nothing to be sorry for," Harold said.

They hugged goodbye, and Margaret said, "Next time you'll come to my house. I want you to meet Will and the girls."

ONE OF MARGARET'S UNEXPECTED talents was her skill at parallel parking. Their car was too old for parking-assist and she liked it that way. Her physical clumsiness ended when she was behind the wheel of a car and faced with a challenging parking space. But today, although the piece of road she settled on at the end of her block was a manageable length, as she was angling into it with her usual confidence, there was a thunk of metal meeting metal. Leaving the car pointing guiltily out into the road, she leaped out to inspect the damage and banged her shin on the fender. The scratches on the other car were minor, but Margaret left a note with her phone number under the car's windshield wiper just in case.

That never happened to her. Wondering who she would be if she couldn't parallel park, she entered the house in a bad mood. The girls' friend Amy had a puppy, so they were spending the afternoon at her house in an orgy of dog-love. There was no sign of Will, so she climbed the stairs to his third-floor office.

"How's it going?"

Will could make hunching over his screen look adversarial, so she guessed it was not a good day. Crispin Applegate was impatient with his bishop, as he kept scheduling meetings of the Church Building Society while Crispin had a particularly gruesome murder to disentangle. The idea of a Church Building Society in Tisdale was ludicrous, as they had barely any parishioners, much less a need for a new church, but the bishop had the soul of a developer. Will took his detective's problems personally.

"Crispin is so bad at confrontation. But he'll survive. How was your family reunion?"

"Nice. They're very nice people. They're going to come here and you'll make your famous chicken pie."

"But what did you learn?"

"Some details but nothing earth-shattering. They see my grandmother making the decisions and my grandfather doing as he was told."

"But what about the main event, 'Our Jewish Dad,' in Lydia's words?"

Margaret's shin where she had banged it was starting to hurt. "I bumped into someone's fender while I was parking down the street."

He gave her a look. "That's not like you. But I asked about your father."

"His parents didn't seem to want to be Jewish, maybe especially his mother. I remember her saying once, or maybe I just heard that she had said it, that people didn't need religion now that there was college. Which as a child I thought was funny, but she was saying that educated people didn't need what she saw as superstitious hooey."

"And how did your father fit into that?"

"I don't know. Maybe it hardly registered that his parents had been Jewish. They lived in a village with no Jewish people, so he had no experience of a community, and I don't think he knew very much about Judaism."

"Margaret, you can't grow up in New York State and not imbibe a lot of Jewish lore, even unconsciously. And do you really think he said no when Lydia asked him if he was Jewish because he hadn't noticed that his parents were Jewish?"

She turned away from the skepticism in his face. "You know what? Digging into his past like this doesn't feel good. It feels like a betrayal. He didn't want to go there or to have other people go there, and I'm trying to respect that."

She did appreciate that Will resisted asking the obvious question—then why had she gone to visit the Abramsons?

He nodded and turned back to his laptop. "Will you turn on the oven to four hundred? I'll put in the fish when the girls get home."

Margaret's shin throbbed, which could account for her testiness that evening. So could the possibility that she had lost her skill at parallel parking. She started whenever the phone rang, thinking it might be the owner of the car she had dinged.

Luckily, the girls were so enthralled by Amy's puppy and so crushed that their father's allergies condemned them to a dogless future that they asked few questions about Margaret's lunch.

In the middle of the after-dinner cleanup, Margaret left the kitchen abruptly.

"Mom, where are you going? We aren't done yet!"

"I'll be right back. I just thought of something I have to do."

Will, who did not do the dishes because he cooked, looked at her from his chair in the living room. She picked up her tablet and sat on the couch, googling "Berlin Jewish Museum Family Portraits." Instantly the cover of the book Arlene had shown her appeared, and she ordered a copy.

BAR

BAR WAS NAMED FOR A DESTINATION—the bar in the Hôtel Plaza Athénée, where women met for drinks in their best afternoon suits. The suit Dior called *Bar* was not the biggest-selling design in his first collection (that honour fell to a slim-skirted dress called *New York*). Seven private customers bought *Bar*, as well as fourteen stores whose price included the right to reproduce it. But from the moment the model Tania strutted through the crowded rooms of Dior's salon on February 12, 1947, overturning ashtrays with the amplitude of her pleated skirt, the white peplum jacket and the black skirt struck people as the quintessence of the New Look.

Ironically, Dior had been playing with *Bar*'s elements for eight years. In 1939, for Robert Piquet's salon, he topped a knee-length, black A-line skirt with a double-breasted white jacket that nipped in at the waist. Five years later, working for Lucien Lelong, the white jacket he designed was single-breasted and the waist significantly smaller; the black skirt was fuller but still knee-length.

In 1947, the conventional proportions of the first two ensembles gave way to something more remarkable. Normally, an open-necked jacket would have a blouse underneath, but, in a move considered radical, Dior dispensed with the blouse. Falling to mid-calf, the pleated skirt, which became a Dior hallmark, demanded five and a half metres of crepe—a breathtaking extravagance that contrasted with the tightly tailored silk shantung jacket. Usually Dior, who loved softly curvaceous lines, favoured shawl collars, but here he chose a strict notched collar whose slanted lines are echoed in the peplum that flared from Tania's waist.

A journalist wrote at the time that the peplum was "padded like a tea-cosy" to round out the model's hips. Wanting even more of an hourglass effect, Dior took desperate measures on the morning of the opening. Deciding that Tania's hips were still too narrow, he could find nothing in a salon full of fabrics for the effect he wanted. He dispatched his very young assistant, Pierre Cardin, to the nearest pharmacy for cotton wool to bulk up skinny Tania.

FIFTEEN

A Peplum Jacket and Miles of Pleats

Margaret arrived at the restaurant before Léa. The hostess seated her at the same table where she and Léa had eaten before, and Margaret accepted some mint tea while she waited.

She couldn't stop thinking about Léa's Diors. Knowing that not far from this restaurant there was a closet or a trunk that held the apparently simple summer dress whose pleats extended from the neckline to the hem, the navy afternoon dress with three-quarter sleeves from 1947, the *Zigomar* jacket with the *trompe l'oeil* pockets and, of course, the *crème de la crème*, the prototype of *Bar* made her feel as if her nerves were buzzing. Imagining Léa in *Bar*, she saw how the peplum jacket would flatter her long-waisted body. Plus, she was tall enough to wear the light jacket and dark skirt without looking as if she had been cut into two. Léa's pieces allowed her the fantasy of how they would light up and deepen her exhibit. At the same time, she was wretched because for some reason Léa was not going to allow that.

After Margaret mourned the Diors, she read the entire menu. She wondered if Will would ever be interested in making dolmades, although he favoured the Italian repertoire.

Margaret was trying to be mad at her father, so next she addressed herself to that. In fact, it was more complicated than mad; it was disconcerting. Although she had tried to downplay the effect of her visit to the Abramsons to Will, hearing their stories had aggravated her discomfort. Part of her still wanted to accept her father's reluctance to talk about his Judaism, but that was waning. Clearly, he knew that his family was Jewish, but he wouldn't talk about it. She didn't like to think of him cold-shouldering Judaism, but there it was. Or there it seemed to be, and it left her with a bad taste.

On the rare occasion when she would tell her father's fragmentary story to Jewish friends or acquaintances, they usually suggested that he just wanted to assimilate. Margaret rejected that: Why would her kind, tolerant father want to—ugly word—assimilate? In practical terms, his being Jewish would not have interfered with his education or his career as a teacher and principal. Or, Margaret believed, with his friendships or his happy marriage. Why would he pretend he was something he wasn't? She didn't know, but now she had to consider that disagreeable possibility.

The book of family portraits from the Jewish Museum had arrived yesterday, and she and the girls had spent an hour poring over it. Behind the carefully posed photographs there was a complex, teeming world that both beckoned and excluded her. Something rich and many-coloured and, yes, tragic, something she had known about from afar, now turned out to be an intimate part of who she was. Or perhaps who she could have been. She was working at blaming her father for her exile. Sometimes that felt fair and sometimes deeply unfair.

The waitress refilled her teapot. Margaret phoned Léa twice, as she didn't text or do email, and there was no answer. She put her thoughts of her father and Judaism aside and skimmed some boring memos from the museum that she had stuffed in her purse. She wished she had brought along the Henning Mankell mystery on her bedside table. She had read enough Mankell to know that the murderer was probably going to be one of Sweden's Nazi sympathizers, but she liked the graininess of the police procedural and the detective Wallander's dogged slowness.

This tardiness was very unlike Léa. After an hour, Margaret found her address on her phone and walked three blocks to a low-rise brick apartment building. She hoped Léa wouldn't consider this intrusive. There was no answer at Apartment 3B either, so Margaret supposed Léa had written down the wrong day.

BACK AT THE MUSEUM at the end of the afternoon, she was in a meeting with Learning. The young man in charge of the school tours for *The New Look* had just asked for help contextualizing Dior to a class of kids he was planning to bring to the exhibit. How to explain to children the fact that Dior's clothes were only available to the richest of the rich? Margaret was responding, not for the first time, that the museum was full of costly objects, often made from precious materials, like the Chinese jade vases or the art deco ebony furniture inlaid with mother-of-pearl. Part of her wondered how someone who seemed to hate luxury goods had ended up working in a museum, but more and more she understood the young man's dilemma.

"So how exactly would *you* talk to the kids?" he asked.

Margaret understood this to be a serious question that stretched beyond haute couture. One of her deepest beliefs was that the contemplation of artistry and beauty expanded everyone's life, no matter their experience, but she needed a minute to think how to connect that to Dior.

While she hesitated, Keitha opened the door without knocking. She looked distraught.

Margaret followed her into the corridor. Keitha said, "Léa is dead."

The parents of the cello player in Léa's building, Jane and Matt O'Connor, had discovered her body after they couldn't reach her for their weekly trip to the supermarket. The paramedics who'd attended the scene said she most likely had a massive heart attack. Keitha sang in a neighbourhood choir with Matt, and the O'Connors had run into her in the building several times when she drove Léa to the museum and occasional errands. They'd contacted her to pass along the news.

A shocked and horrified Margaret cut short her meeting and called Will.

"I feel terrible. I should have asked the super to enter Léa's apartment when she didn't show up."

"There was nothing to make you suspect anything serious, Margaret. Someone missing a lunch date is not a reason to call the super. It sounds very unlikely that anything could have saved her."

She hoped he was right. Mortified, she remembered the envious designs on Léa's Diors she had indulged in at the restaurant. She tried to keep them in a separate compartment in her mind from the scene in Léa's apartment, without much success.

THE O'CONNORS HAD ARRANGED a small reception in Léa's apartment the Sunday after her death. She had been cremated and when Margaret stepped into the living room, she was relieved to see that there was no urn or other receptacle prominently displayed. She doubted that Léa would have approved of that. The apartment was furnished from the more understated range of what Léa would probably have called Danish modern; now it would be described as Scandinavian mid-century modern. The understuffed couch and chairs and the beautiful, minimalist cabinets looked calm and almost timeless, and Margaret was grateful for that. She wasn't so much sad—in her experience, it took a while to understand a loss—as regretful that she hadn't had time to get to know Léa better. The older woman's reserve was beginning to melt, and Margaret had hoped for more revelations about her life as a *petite main*, and also about Léa herself.

There were a few modern paintings on the walls and some family photographs she wanted to look at, but first she had to greet people. Keitha was there, looking as if she had a bad cold, and David and Jill Hillman. Jane O'Connor introduced her to a few other neighbours, and an elderly student or two from Léa's years teaching at the Alliance Française. When you die in your nineties, most of your contemporaries have predeceased you. Other than a cousin of Stephen Slaney, Léa's late husband, there didn't seem to be any family.

Margaret was ravenous. She had read once that caterers budget twice as much food for a funeral as for a wedding. Apparently, death made you hungry, and she filled a small plate with cookies. When everyone seemed to be present, Jane O'Connor stood alone in front of the main window, announcing with her look of friendly tension that she intended to speak. Someone pressed a chair on Margaret, and she sat down.

Jane talked briefly about her neighbour, mostly about Léa's support of her son's cello playing. She had listened stoically to Liam's attempts at Leonard Cohen's "Hallelujah," which were perfectly audible in her apartment, but when it came to "Spring" from Vivaldi's *Four Seasons*, she offered the boy a deal. If he promised never again to play "Spring," she would pay for a better teacher for him. Margaret and David smiled faintly at each other: that was Léa's motive for taking the red silk dress to the consignment shop.

Liam, a sturdy twelve-year-old who looked as if he would be as at home on a soccer field as here tuning his cello, introduced his piece, the sarabande from Bach's Cello Suite No. 5. To

Margaret, it sounded like a repetition of the same simple phrase with small variations, as if a speaker were ruminating on a long-running sorrow, not at all embarrassed at saying the same thing over and over. Liam played well, and it was ineffably sad. Keitha, standing against the wall, lowered her head, putting her hands over her face, and David passed her a Kleenex.

One of Léa's students from the Alliance Française, looking older and frailer than Léa, spoke about her high standards, her patience, her happiness when the class was advanced enough to read and discuss a short story in French. All standard compliments for a teacher, but, without saying so, the woman gave the impression that there was a vein of disappointment or melancholy just below Léa's surface that had nothing to do with her students' shortcomings.

Stephen Slaney's cousin, Robert, talked about the arrival in the mid-1950s of "Stephen's French wife." The speaker had been only a boy, but he could remember how bewildering his family had found Léa's customs. She insisted on serving salad after the main course and not offering coffee with dessert, but separately, afterwards. And speaking of what Americans considered the sweet course, she seemed to think that a ripe pear or a slice of cheese was a dessert. Because she was European, the Slaneys had to assume that these were sophisticated practices rather than odd mistakes. Robert painted an amusing picture of two cultures, represented by Léa and the Slaneys, coming to a fondness that remained a little gingerly.

Liam played another Bach sarabande, this time from the Suite No. 2. In this one the melody struggled to stay aloft while the chords grated and sometimes groaned. There was little comfort here, and in spite of his youth, Liam seemed at one with its stoic, halting sorrow. Keitha was in tears again and others in the room were clearly melancholy. Margaret reflected that Fanny Berger, when she died, had been less than half Léa's age. The cliché "old age is a privilege" struck Margaret now with particular force.

Margaret looked at the photographs, ranged along the top of a teak bookcase. There were not many and there was only one of Léa's parents. Both wearing suits, they looked like serious people. Margaret wondered if the picture had been taken as they left Hungary or soon after their arrival in Paris, when Léa was ten. The hat maker mother wore what looked like a wool cloche, with a small nosegay stitched to the side. Léa stood between them, a gangly blonde whose braids were pinned to the top of her head. She did not smile either, but people in those days did not feel obliged to smile for a photograph. Perhaps she had an immigrant's wary look, but Margaret told herself not to overthink a casual snapshot.

The photographs that stopped Margaret's heart were two taken at the Slaneys' wedding, only recognizable as wedding pictures because Léa held a bouquet of lilies of the valley. The bride and groom stood in front of the *mairie*, and Léa wore street dress. But it was the most glorious street dress imaginable: it was *Bar*. Why had she not mentioned to Margaret that she wore it for her wedding? Inscrutable Léa.

Margaret's hunch was right: the flared peplum flattered her lanky body and made her hips look more curvaceous, and the calf-length skirt was perfectly proportioned to her long legs. Instead of the hat shaped like an overturned basket that the model wears in the famous photograph of *Bar*, Léa wore a clip-on style popular in the fifties, like a silk-covered comma that clasped her head. In addition to the picture taken from the front, the photographer had had the lucky inspiration to photograph the couple from behind as they left the *mairie* on their way to a celebratory breakfast or lunch. In the hand that was not tucked into her groom's arm, Léa flourished her bouquet high over her head, like a victory torch, and the pleats in her skirt flared with her purposeful stride. Margaret looked at the second photograph for some minutes, hoping that the optimism it promised had come true.

Standing by the door, Keitha had her coat on, and impulsively Margaret put her arm around her.

"Thank you so much for befriending Léa," she said, "and driving her to things at the museum."

Keitha nodded glumly. "It was a pleasure."

Making small talk with Jane O'Connor and drinking tea with the last of her cookies, Margaret thought of all the things she didn't know about Léa. Was she happily married? Why didn't she have children? Did she ever return to France and see her parents or colleagues from Dior? What were her parents like? But, as she stood here in Léa's living room, all those questions felt too inquisitive.

Instead, she asked Jane, "Did she stay interested in clothes? Did she sew?"

Jane laughed. "Well, she mended. Things of mine that I would have thrown out, she returned to new. It began when she noticed a hem I had turned up. To say it was beneath her standards was an understatement. She insisted that in return for the supermarket trips we took her on, she would repair what needed repairing in what passes for my wardrobe. As for being interested in clothes, I guess in some ways she was. She wasn't buying new things anymore, but the bones of her wardrobe were good. And she never missed an issue of French *Vogue*."

SIXTEEN

A Deco Bar Pin

The weeks after Léa's death were peaceful. There were no new packages sent to Margaret and Gareth and no pieces of the exhibit went missing. Was this the calm before the next storm, or was it possible that the disruptions were finished?

"So Léa was the perp," Bee said, doing a fairly good job of twisting her spaghetti carbonara around her fork.

Nancy was having more trouble with her pasta. "You're jumping to conclusions," she said. "There's still no explanation about how she could have gotten into the storage hall or the Etruscan or Pacific Northwest Galleries."

"That's what we're going to work on next," Bee said. "Where's your notebook?"

They had a small squabble about who was allowed to write in Nancy's notebook, Bee claiming that since they were working on the case together, they should both have access to the notebook, and Nancy pointing out that P. D. James's Detective Inspector Kate Miskin would not have dreamed of using Adam Dalgliesh's notebook. Rather than concede defeat, Bee asked her mother what she thought about the current calm.

"I'm assuming it will continue," Margaret said, "but that just means I hope it will. I can't see how or why Léa could have been responsible for the disappearances, and the timing of her death and this return to normal is just coincidental. But I'm too busy now to play detective."

Next morning, she and Gareth sat in his office, trying to make the numbers look less discouraging. They hadn't reached their donation goal and they needed to make one final push.

He said, "I think Rivkah Waldman is one of our best bets for a gift. Why don't we take her out for dinner and see if we can be persuasive?"

Naturally, the museum had a division of fundraisers. But sometimes, depending on the project and the possible donor, it was considered flattering if a curator or two intervened personally.

Margaret felt a pang of conscience. Not only had she not told Gareth that Rivkah had an idea for an alcove that came with a financial carrot, she hadn't given Rivkah a yes or no.

"I think that's a good idea," she said slowly. "But why don't I take her out by myself and see what I can do? You know, woman to woman."

Gareth was only too happy to reclaim an evening for his own life, and Margaret called Rivkah. They settled on a date for dinner and Margaret said, "You choose a restaurant you like."

"There's a fun little place on Sumner Park, called 23Sumner. Lots of small plates and you have almost no choice: they appear magically. The food is delicious, but after a day in the office, the biggest luxury for me is not having to make more decisions."

Margaret suspected that Rivkah's fun little place was going to cost the museum a pretty penny, but she had to trust it would be worth it.

A FEW DAYS LATER, an envelope from Sparshott, Whitehead and Goldman appeared on Margaret's desk, sandwiched between the usual announcements of gallery openings and couture auctions. The trio of names meant nothing to her, but something about the font—self-confident but too tasteful to swagger—made her open it first. As soon as she read the short letter, she started to dial Gareth's number and then stopped. He rarely answered his phone, even when he was in his office. She hurried there as mindfully as she could, and without waiting to be invited in, she stood almost breathlessly in front of Gareth's desk.

"Do you have one of these?" she asked, handing him the letter, and took a chair.

He held up his own copy. Gareth and Margaret were invited to a reading of the last will and testament of Mrs. Léa Slaney, to be held in the offices of Sparshott, Whitehead and Goldman, at 130 East Main Street, on the twenty-seventh of March.

Gareth's normally imperturbable face cracked into a wide grin. "Well, well. This is good news."

"Do you think so?" Margaret asked. She had never been invited to the reading of a will before and had not dared to think what it meant.

"Of course it's good news. Do you think they're inviting us to announce that Mrs. Slaney has left the museum nothing?"

Gareth must be right. This was good news, and perhaps great news.

THERE WAS MORE GOOD NEWS that week, when the Fashion Museum finally agreed to lend Dior's sample page for the strapless gown he called *Égypte*. It was so valuable that the Chicago museum sent it with its own escort, who cradled the package on his lap on the flight to Rochester. Margaret and Keitha watched solemnly as the escort unwrapped it, and Margaret signed something attesting to its good condition. Keitha and the escort took their own pictures of the page, and the escort left, leaving the two women, wearing latex gloves, to gloat over their treasure.

According to the sample page, the *première* in charge of translating Dior's sketches into *Égypte* was Christiane from the *atelier flou*. The mannequin on whom it was made was Lucky.

"Did either of these women have last names?" Keitha asked grumpily.

It seemed that black was often Dior's default assumption for the colour of a dress and later he thought better of it. He had pinned a piece of black silk on his sketch for *Zemire*, Léa's cocktail dress, but made up the dress in red as well. Something similar had happened with the sample page. The fabric attached to the page was black silk faille, while the museum's *Égypte* was a bright ruby red. Sometimes a sample page would have a few swatches of alternate colours, but not this one. A regular client or a luxury store that had paid for the licence to reproduce Dior's designs could petition for a different colour, and if it was approved, it could still wear the Dior label. That must have happened here, and Keitha and Margaret preferred the red. It gave the wrapped strapless top and the bow placed obliquely over the breast an insouciance that would have been missing in the black.

"Just imagine Dior securing that pin in place," Margaret murmured, as he was famous for his attention to the sample pages. Telling herself not to be fetishistic, she clasped her hands behind her back so she would not be tempted to touch the pin, even behind its thick plastic protection. She and Keitha put the page back into its foam-lined bag and locked it in the safe in the storage room.

IT WAS TRYING TO SNOW on the day the will was to be read, as if King Winter wheezed that just because it was the end of March, he had no plans to leave Rochester just yet. Margaret felt she should dress for the occasion, although her sense of the occasion came straight from Ngaio Marsh's mysteries from the 1930s. In a Marsh novel, the family, several of whose members detested other members and one of whom would eventually murder at least one of his relatives, gathered at their solicitor's office. The decor of the office, featuring oversized mahogany desks, Persian carpets and middling-to-bad portraits of dead partners, strove to reassure clients about the firm's longevity and success. In such a setting, Margaret would have been wearing a hat with a veil and perhaps one of those repulsive animal stoles that included a fox's head and tail. Since it was 2019, she had to settle for her black trouser suit. Maybe she could give it more oomph with her Stuart Weitzman heels, although her feet would hurt all day at work. The reading of the will was not until 4 p.m.

She was appraising the suit with heels when Nancy came into her bedroom.

"What do you think, maybe a scarf for some colour?"

"No," Nancy said. "You need the deco pin. You're an heiress now and you have to dress like one."

"Sweetheart, we hope that the museum will inherit some Diors, not me."

Nancy pinned the brooch onto her mother's lapel at just the right angle and it raised the suit to a new level. Will's mother had given Margaret the pin, a black onyx bar with chevron ends, a few oblique silver lines and a pavé stripe of small diamonds, for a wedding present. Helena had explained that nineteenth-century brides were typically given jewellery, not towels or champagne glasses. Why Will's feminist mother connected Margaret with Victorian brides was never made clear. Margaret knew about the custom of giving jewellery as a wedding present, but she was still trying to be a model daughter-in-law, so she looked interested, as if this were new information. She had yet to learn that Helena was so pleased with her own knowledge that she paid little attention to its effect on other people.

Sparshott, Whitehead and Goldman's office was in the Granite Building, a century-old tower as proud as the firm's stationery.

With its giddy twelve-storey height, it was said to be Rochester's first skyscraper, but on the inside Sparshott, Whitehead and Goldman parted company with the past. Unlike the law offices in Ngaio Marsh, these were pale, with unaggressive contemporary furniture and middling-to-bad abstract paintings. And Margaret was overdressed. Funny how one accessory could change a whole outfit. The O'Connors were there, taking time off from their tutoring jobs and dressed casually. Robert Slaney, Stephen's cousin, explained that he was there on behalf of his children, who lived on the west coast. Like Gareth, he wore a sports jacket. There were a few strangers and no sign of anyone else Margaret had met at Léa's apartment. Caroline Whitehead, who was Léa's lawyer, welcomed them wearing a sweater that was not stylishly baggy, just baggy. And pants that looked as if they had an elastic waist.

When everyone was seated, she read the will. Léa had left twenty thousand dollars to the O'Connors for Liam's cello lessons. She left one painting and one piece of furniture to each of Robert Slaney's two children, to be chosen by them. The rest of her belongings were to be sold and the proceeds were to be reserved, along with her savings and mutual funds, for an undisclosed project.

Margaret and Gareth, who were sitting side by side, did not look at each other. *What the hell,* Margaret thought, fingering her pin as if it would return her to her almost-heiress state. *Why are we here?*

Caroline Whitehead turned the page. "'There is one exception to the disposition of my belongings,'" she read. "'This refers to my Diors.'" Léa itemized them: The summer dress, the fall day dress, the two suits and of course *Bar*. Also, an afternoon dress with a boxy jacket from the mid-fifties named *Bambou*. Although the bamboo-printed silk was exquisite, the outfit was matronly and had never been one of Margaret's favourites. Perhaps Léa felt the same way, which was why she had never mentioned it to Margaret.

"I recognize the appropriateness of my collection going to the Harkness Museum," Léa had written, "and so I am giving the museum thirty days from the reading of the will to make an offer to buy the pieces. Caroline Whitehead will decide if the bid is fair, taking into account current estimates of their value. If she does not consider the offer reasonable, the collection will be offered for sale to other institutions, beginning with the Fashion Museum. If the Harkness Museum's bid is successful, I would add one caveat: none of my things shall be shown in the forthcoming New Look exhibition."

Caroline Whitehead thanked everyone for coming and said she would be available for any questions. The O'Connors and Robert Slaney nodded and smiled at Margaret, and the O'Connors left. Robert spoke briefly with the lawyer. The people Margaret did not know also left, looking satisfied. Perhaps they had some connection with Léa's unnamed project.

Margaret and Gareth still had not turned to each other. Margaret's first reaction to the will was an image of Alan Shea's smirking face. Damn him. This would send his *schadenfreude* skyrocketing. Why was Léa being so churlish about her exhibition? This was an undeserved slap on the wrist, and she felt bewildered and humiliated. Gareth recovered first.

"We need to make an appointment with Ms. Whitehead about how to proceed. I assume you'll need to assess the clothes' condition before we settle on a bid?"

"But how will we ever raise the money to pay for the clothes? We haven't even managed to cover the costs of *The New Look*."

"People are always more willing to donate money for objects that will go into the museum's permanent collection than for temporary exhibits."

He had a point. There was nothing to do but go forward.

Trying to look normal, Margaret introduced herself to Caroline Whitehead. They agreed to meet the following morning at Léa's apartment.

AT HOME, WILL WAS PUTTING the finishing touches on his spinach and ricotta lasagna. Seated at the kitchen table, the girls were writing up the latest development into their notebooks, called "The Mystery at the Museum (Nancy)" and "The Mystery at the Museum (Bee)." Will had given Bee one of the notebooks with marbled black-and-white covers he used for notes, saying, "Every detective needs her own."

Still with her coat on, depleted and yet nerve-racked, Margaret sat down heavily. "Why is Léa being so dog-in-the-mangerish about her Diors?"

Will said, "The villain's motivation is always in their backstory."

"I'm not agreed that Léa is the villain."

"No, but she's doing something irritating and mysterious."

"And now that she's dead, there's very little chance to learn her backstory."

Margaret moved to the hook on the wall where they kept the car keys, and then thought better of that. Her evening might require more than one glass of wine. She would Uber instead.

"Where are you going?" Will looked at the empty salad bowl, which she usually filled.

"I told you. I'm having dinner with Rivkah Waldman, hoping to get her to make a donation."

"You didn't tell me."

"Yes, I did."

Will was out of sorts too, which usually happened just before Crispin solved his case. She kissed the girls on their heads and Will on the cheek. She would walk to the corner and call an Uber from there.

Sumner Park angled off from Monroe Avenue's tattoo parlours and shops for vinyl and vintage. It was one of those streets that had balanced on the precipice of gentrification for thirty years but never quite tumbled over. 23Sumner was a brick row house that had probably been home to a nineteenth-century family with six or more children. The restaurant had preserved the original small rooms and painted them in various nuances of cream.

When Margaret relinquished her coat to a server and sat down, Rivka said, "But you look so nice!" She did not entirely mask her surprise, adding, "I love your pin."

"Thank you. It's from my mother-in-law."

She told her the story of the wedding present, which led to a digression about Helena's blithe lack of interest in the way she struck other people.

Rivka nodded. "I kind of know the type, but everybody in my family is all too interested in the impression they make on others. At least she has taste."

"Ferociously good taste," Margaret agreed. "But very trad."

Once they were sipping their wine, their server brought raw scallops in brown butter, garnished with shards of apples and radishes.

Rivka said, "Isn't this good? We don't even have to stop chatting to read the menu. There's no menu."

After that came two saucers with something yellow that, had they not been in a smart restaurant, almost looked like creamed corn. They began eating it and, lo and behold, it was creamed corn, but exalted to unheard-of heights that had nothing in common with the soupy canned vegetable their mothers had served. Once they had stopped exclaiming about the freshness of the al dente kernels and the way they were complemented by the minimal cream, roasted peppers and a few leaves of basil, Rivkah returned to how well Margaret was looking.

Maybe bad news becomes me, Margaret thought. She was not going to mention Léa's will.

"You know, with your height, you can wear anything," Rivkah continued. "My mother always told me to describe myself as petite, but let's face it, I'm short. And that limits your options considerably. I'd give a lot for your inches. Your skin is good, too. And I'm not saying 'good for a redhead.' It just looks like healthy skin."

Perversely, Margaret, who rarely thought about her skin, was now convinced that it was paper-thin, wrinkled and covered with freckles. She wondered if this was some sort of weird charm offensive on Rivkah's part, but it didn't feel that way.

"And I get it that you're too busy and possibly fashioned-out in your job to spend a lot of time thinking about your clothes. And here I am preaching to a fashion curator about her wardrobe—talk about taking coals to Newcastle. But whenever I see you, I think what fun it would be to be a tall redhead. Or even to go shopping with one."

She left that unexpected—and to Margaret alarming—thought hanging in the air. By now they were eating something wonderful the restaurant called "March parsnips."

"What is a March parsnip?" Margaret asked the server, thinking it was a rare variety.

No, it was just the parsnips that were still edible in March, treated with butter, breadcrumbs and the restaurant's own ranch dressing. Looking sadly at the few smears of dressing left in their saucers, Margaret and Rivkah agreed that they could spend hours working with those simple ingredients and it would never taste like this.

"Speaking of things that have their allotted time," Margaret said, knowing she needed to take control of the agenda, "we should talk about your idea for an alcove."

She had known before she came that she was going to agree to Rivkah's proposal, and she wasn't sure whether this made her a whore or simply a pragmatic curator. It seemed that Rivkah had also known or at least suspected the outcome, because she already had one of her clerks collecting photographs and articles and setting up appointments for interviews.

"Okay, it's not legal work," she said nonchalantly of the clerk, "but it's more interesting than mergers and acquisitions."

"That's great, Rivkah, and this is completely my fault because I was so slow making up my mind, but this is still an absurdly short amount of time to create even a fairly straightforward alcove. Aside from the actual components of the exhibit, the museum keeps adding more and more hoops we have to jump through before it gets okayed."

Margaret tried to imagine how Learning would react to these vignettes from wealthy women. From there her mind travelled to the fact that the donors to the museum's couture collection were disproportionately Jewish, and so were the women whose stories would be told in the alcove. Should she acknowledge that fact in the material? She had never had any reason to broach this topic with Rivkah before. But now there was no time for *politesse*.

Rivkah smiled. "I think the names will speak for themselves."

So that was that. They had accomplished the main business of the evening in under five minutes. They could go back to extolling their dinner, which now included a crispy-skinned cod filet with tiny, delectable Tokyo turnips, or, God forbid, return to Margaret's wardrobe. But having raised the Jewish connection, to her own surprise Margaret stayed with it. More than once in the past, Rivkah had hinted at an interest in the story of Margaret's family, but Margaret had resisted pursuing that conversation. Now Margaret found herself talking about her headstrong grandmother, who thought religion was for the uneducated, and her father, who when asked had always answered mildly that he was not Jewish. That looked like obedience to his mother's wishes, but was it more complicated than that? From a son who rebelled against her wishes whenever they clashed with his, was it an unusual example of filial piety?

Rivkah followed this twisting, half-understood, half-buried story with close attention. Margaret had the sense this was how she listened to her clients.

"Sounds like your father found the perfect, sneaky revenge," Rivkah said. "'Okay, Mom, you don't want me to be Jewish, so I'll choose the furthest thing from Jewish that I can think of. How about if I marry a nice German Catholic girl? And our three daughters will go to a Catholic school, and never suspect there's a Jewish side to the family. Now, are you happy? Not so much? What a shame.'"

Margaret laughed at this cartoon version of what was likely a many-layered and often unconscious set of decisions. And yet, maybe there was some truth to it. There might have been more ambivalence in her grandmother's un-Jewishness than even her grandmother knew. Perhaps her father suspected that, beyond a certain line, something of her Jewishness would resurface, and he challenged that. Although he unquestionably loved his wife and did not marry her to cross his mother, the fact was that his marriage and Catholic family life disappointed his mother. What Rivkah called his sneaky revenge was that he had obeyed his mother's wishes—at least the ones she verbalized, not the subterranean ones.

"But whatever his motives," Rivkah continued, "your father's exit from Judaism was relatively easy because he had very little to turn his back on. His parents' voluntary exile in the country accomplished that—he never knew a Jewish life or a Jewish community that he had to reject. As for you, it sounds as if you didn't have a complicated mother whom you had to alternately placate and defy. So you're free to claim your heritage. But only if you want to."

It had been far too demanding a day for Margaret to claim anything, much less her heritage.

"You're very matter-of-fact about this," she said. "I can't smell even a trace of partisanship."

"No? Well, Judaism can be a hard religion to belong to."

"I thought only Catholics felt that way about their religion."

They laughed and agreed that such unease was probably not limited to Catholics and Jews.

AT HOME, IN THE PADDED entrance, Margaret separated the girls' puffers ruthlessly and found a hook on which to hang her coat.

"Yes, stay awhile," Will said, in reference to her suppertime abandonment. "Was it worth it?"

"Yes, it was."

She was too tired to tell him Rivkah's theory about her father, but to make it sound like a full evening of business she expanded their talk about the alcove, Rivkah's advance planning and the possible minefields the museum might strew in their path.

"You lose some and you win some," she said of her day, "and this was the win."

She took an envelope out of her purse and handed it to him.

He opened it and said, "Wow." It was a cheque from Rivkah for fifty thousand dollars, made out to the museum with "The New Look" in the memo line.

"She was so sure of my decision that she wrote the cheque before she left for the restaurant."

He kissed her and said, "Well done, darling. Did she say anything else?"

"She said to make sure and insure my brooch if I hadn't already done that. Have I?"

He shrugged. They were both hopeless about things like that.

On top of Margaret's fatigue was a streak of euphoria. She turned to Will in bed, hooked a leg between his two and kissed his neck. He was reading an article in *The Atlantic* about Kodak's failure to embrace digital technology and its long, slow death. She bent her knee and raised her foot higher on his leg. Will put his hand in a friendly way on her foot, but held it so that she could not move it further. He kept on reading.

"Interesting article?"

"Depressing, but yes." He turned a page.

She gave up. "You're not in the mood."

"Sorry, sweetheart. Not tonight."

So, Crispin still had not solved his case.

SEVENTEEN

Twenty-Six Steel Bones

Will had an inner clock and was usually downstairs by seven, but Margaret relied on her alarm. When it went off at seven thirty the next morning, she thought, *I just need a few more days of sleep.* That was not an option: she had to start fast-forwarding Rivkah's alcove. And she must stop thinking of it as Rivkah's alcove, give it a less craven title, maybe "The Women Who Wore Dior." Actually, that wasn't bad, and Margaret was feeling quite reconciled to her decision, if you could call it that. But first she had to meet Caroline Whitehead at Léa's apartment and assess the condition of her Diors.

An hour later, Margaret was buzzed into Léa's building and she climbed the stairs to the third floor. No point wasting the chance for a little free exercise. When she pushed open the door to Léa's floor, the apartment door opposite the stairs flew open at exactly the same time. A boy emerged, slinging his backpack over one shoulder and looking startled at the sight of Margaret.

"Hello, Liam," she said. "We met when you played your cello at the gathering for Léa. I'm Margaret."

Liam looked as if he wanted to disappear back into the apartment. He ducked his head and mumbled, "Hi, how are you," while he brushed past Margaret into the stairwell.

Well, she thought, *a boy on the brink of puberty.* Caroline Whitehead, on the other hand, was delighted to see her.

"Margaret," she said, taking her hand firmly and not quite pulling her into Léa's apartment, "if I may call you Margaret, I'm so excited about seeing these Diors close up. Jane O'Connor has set it all up for us"—indicating five garment bags in Léa's otherwise empty closet—"and you just go ahead. This is a real privilege for me."

Round-faced, with sensible short hair and another pair of slacks that looked suspiciously elastic-waisted, Caroline Whitehead was not the most predictable Dior fan. But, as Margaret frequently told Will in their marriage-long discussion about the point of couture, beauty lifts the heart. There was no reason why Caroline would be exempt from that. She smiled at her soul sister and began patting the bags with a hand on each side.

To Caroline's inquisitive look, she said, "This isn't part of the assessment, just self-indulgence. I'm trying to save *Bar* for the last."

Not surprisingly, the clothes were mostly in good shape, especially given that they had survived seventy years, including fifteen or more years of wear in the case of the suits. Léa's alterations—she had first taken in the navy afternoon dress above the waist and later let it out—were beyond reproach, and she had known to keep the pieces out of light and excessive heat. The Conservation staff would sigh over the commercial dry cleaning they had "suffered," but except for some barely noticeable whiffs of chemicals, the clothes had escaped unscathed.

Once she unzipped the last bag, Margaret could not tear her eyes away from *Bar*. The five bound buttonholes with their oversized buttons, the long pockets, the military precision of the tailoring that managed to be ineffably feminine. Even sexy. Dior had probably been right: the steely elegance of the ivory jacket he'd finally settled on worked better with the black skirt than Léa's biscuit-coloured version. And yet this jacket had its own creamy allure.

"Can the museum bid on some but not all of the pieces?" Margaret asked. She was in favour of eliminating *Bambou*, the brown-and-white bamboo-printed dress with a matching jacket. She ran her gloved fingers over the jacket's portrait neckline.

"No, they are to be sold together or not at all."

That was Léa, all or nothing. It would never make Margaret's heart beat faster, but she supposed that *Bambou* was interesting in that it showed a rare susceptibility on Dior's part to 1950s matronliness.

When she had finished making notes and taking pictures, she and Caroline Whitehead shook hands. She explained that she would study the prices paid for similar pieces and make a bid once she had the museum's approval. Winning the museum's consent was where the process could shudder to a finicky, self-absorbed halt. She counted on Gareth to keep reminding the various bureaucratic levels of the thirty-day deadline. Which was now twenty-nine days.

"This has been a wonderful morning for me," Caroline said. "Far more fascinating than most of my mornings."

Her words reminded Margaret of Rivkah last night saying cavalierly of her clerk that being seconded to help out with a Dior alcove was more intriguing than mergers and acquisitions. Did every lawyer want to be a fashion curator? Or did Dior exert a special pull?

MARGARET CEREMONIOUSLY presented Gareth with Rivkah's cheque. Fifty thousand would pay many but not all the exhibit's outstanding expenses, and they enjoyed five minutes of relief tinged with elation. Just as they were coming down to earth, a security guard appeared in the door.

Together, Gareth and Margaret said, "NO."

If either of them was surprised by their unexpected unanimity, neither showed it.

The security guard, who had been on this errand before, looked alarmed.

Margaret added, pointing to the package he held, "We don't want any more of those."

But they had to accept it. Inside the wrappings that Security had loosened for inspection, there was a navy felt beret. A classic beret, with no distinguishing characteristics. The note ("the goddamn note," as Gareth called it, in a rare display of blasphemy) read in the usual printing, "Clothes tell many different stories, don't they?"

Margaret lifted the beret to her nose and inhaled. "It doesn't even smell old," she said disgustedly, as if its failure to be old added insult to injury. "It's brand new."

"What are the different stories a beret tells?" Gareth asked tiredly.

"Who cares?"

Judging by the look on Gareth's face, they were both tired of this silly cat-and-mouse game, and they weren't going to spend any more time on it. It led nowhere. Margaret didn't even want to ask Deirdre if she knew something about berets. Unfairly, she felt annoyed at Deirdre and her bottomless well of knowledge. It seemed to suggest there was meaning in these tidbits and souvenirs, when clearly there was none. Still, on the slim, slim chance that there was something even remotely relevant here, she took a picture and sent it to the V&A.

"What about this?" she texted almost rudely. "What stories do berets tell each other when they're alone?"

"You'd be surprised," the reply came about an hour later. "One beret would have to tiptoe around for a while trying to figure out what the other beret stood for. Because both sides in the Occupation claimed the beret as the symbol of true Frenchness. For the Vichy government and collaborators, it stood for moral rebirth and masculine strength; for the Resistance, it was a sign of the real *Liberté, Égalité, Fraternité*, not the bogus version Pétain was peddling."

Normally, Margaret would have considered that an interesting factoid. Today, she couldn't even summon enough energy to say "Hunh."

"I repeat, who cares?" she said, to Gareth's emphatic nod.

So much for their hopes that these packages would end with Léa.

MARGARET ASSUMED THAT Keitha must realize by now that an alcove dedicated to Dior's corsets was not going to happen. She hadn't told Keitha that in so many words—one of the slights, she thought ruefully, that interns must suffer regularly—but surely she could see that the time for designing and sourcing an alcove was gone. Yes, "The Women Who Wore Dior" alcove had begun crazily late in the game, but there was no arguing with fifty thousand dollars.

There would be another alcove dedicated to Dior's fabrics and his alliances with the premier French textile manufacturers. Molly Raines, the birdlike curator in the next office, had put aside her normal preoccupation with Hildegard of Bingen's sackcloth and fustian (Margaret was hazy about what twelfth-century nuns actually wore) and done a good job with that. Pride of place went to the custom-made silks, but she paid special attention to Dior's willingness to experiment with the new synthetics. In addition to the two alcoves, there was a long line of window boxes with seven pairs of shoes by Roger Vivier, Dior's anointed cobbler, and another window box with examples of the costume jewellery he favoured—one of his unexpected democratic tastes.

But Keitha asked anyway.

Opening her notebook as if their discussion might require making planning notes, she said, "Any decision about the corset alcove?"

"I'm afraid there won't be one, Keitha," Margaret said, trying to sound regretful. "There was so much uncertainty and interference with the exhibit, and that was one of the casualties. But Dom has written some fine pointers to the built-in lingerie for the touch screens, so interested visitors could learn a lot there."

"As long as they go to the touch screens in the first place and make the right choices when they get there. It's not the same thing as not even knowing about the corsets' existence and having your eyes opened by a whole alcove."

Keitha was not going to be assuaged.

Trying to shift the discussion a little, Margaret said, "You know, I keep thinking of the graduate student in the seminar we did who asked if I had ever worn one of those waist-strangling corsets myself."

"And you said you might try to find one. But you weren't serious, were you?" Keitha's tone was still cold, but she could not resist the subject.

"Well," Margaret said, "I keep thinking about it."

That evening, imagining mildly naughty Halloween costumes, she googled "corsets" and "bondage" and fell at once into a rabbit hole furnished with wrist and ankle restraints, arm binders, muzzles and nipple pinchers. Surprisingly wholesome-looking young women were shown frolicking with these devices. One model, dressed as a nun and doing something anatomically unlikely with a double-headed vibrator, reminded Margaret of her high school math teacher, Sister Aloysius. She did smile at the site's "Community Resources," which included Twitter,

Facebook and "Meet the Models," but looking up "bondage" had been a mistake.

She simplified her search to "corsets" and found what she was looking for. Although the site called *How to Self-Lace* sounded pornographic, it was simply practical. She flipped through "Anatomy of a Corset," "Novice Corsets" and "How to Get the Curves You Deserve." The corsets were for sale, not for rent, and once she saw the sweaty labour involved in getting into one, that made sense. The most credible-looking version had three layers of sturdy cloth, ultra-strong waist tape and twenty-six high-density steel bones. Twenty of the bones were spirals and six were flat. The spirals, which looked like chains that had been pressed down, were said to help flexibility and motion, and Dior had used them. Telling herself that wearing such a corset would make her a better curator of Dior's New Look, Margaret ordered it.

Even though she had used her personal credit card, Margaret needed to justify the purchase to herself. She felt battle-weary. Leaving aside Rivkah's donation, the fusillade of worries, large and small, was unrelenting—the disappearance of the belt and the dress top, Léa's death and her will, the mystery packages that kept on coming. The threat implied by the packages felt diluted now, but it still wasn't good. Margaret told herself, *You need some fun*. Will was always telling her she needed a hobby. Okay, she could see that this didn't quite fit the bill, but maybe it was a start?

For ninety-nine dollars, the company promised overnight delivery. Was it an emergency kind of product? Sure enough, the corset, in the proverbial plain brown-paper package, was waiting on the hall table when Margaret returned from work the next day. She stuffed it in the top drawer of her bureau and attended to family life for the next few hours.

Will was supervising the girls' first attempt at a niçoise salad. Although the finished dish looked casual, the recipe they were using was rigorous. This made Nancy happy and Bee impatient.

"Really?" Bee mimicked incredulity. "We have to boil the potatoes for eight or nine minutes, until 'the thin tip of a knife pierces a potato as if going into soft wax'?"

Nancy stood by with the spider to capture the waxy potatoes.

"Isn't that poetic? And then we boil the beans for four to five minutes until they transform 'from raw and dusty to saturated deep green.'"

Bee was temporarily mollified by the drama of throwing the boiled eggs (eight minutes from refrigerator to cooked) into the sink with some force, so that the shells cracked and they could be peeled under cold running water with ease. Now that the calculated boiling was over, she was ready to scatter the remaining ingredients "artfully," as directed. But no, first the beans had to be split in half crosswise, the artichokes, cherry tomatoes and radishes into quarters and the eggs into wedges.

"I'll do that," Nancy said. "You wash and dry the lettuce and then tear it."

Once the platter was lined with lettuce, Will began to strew chunks of tuna over it.

"No, Daddy, you're throwing it. You have to 'nestle' the pieces."

"Who is this poet laureate of the niçoise salad?" Margaret asked.

Will, trying to scatter more delicately, said, "Gabrielle Hamilton." She was one of his favourite food writers.

They all admired the finished product, laid out on a carpet of lettuce—the red-and-white commas of the sliced onions, the creamy yellows of the potatoes and the intense yellows of the yolks, the occasional pop of a cherry tomato. When it came to the dressing, Gabrielle Hamilton suddenly changed tack. "Toss to dress," she wrote breezily, "and don't worry about messing up the beauty."

Bee, her mouth full of tuna, asked, "So why did she make us work so hard to create the beauty?"

"For the joy of the work," Will suggested from his Zen side. Bee looked scornful.

The girls changed the subject to *The Chestnut Man*, a Danish mystery they had just read.

"Have you noticed," Nancy asked, "that a lot of detectives are workaholics and neglect their families?"

Bee nodded. "It's a trope."

Margaret thought, *They haven't even got their periods, but they know what a trope is, and especially a mystery trope.* Occasionally she tried to broaden their reading, and had semi-successfully sold Jane Austen's *Emma* to them as a mystery, but she knew they were indulging her. A real mystery had a murder, not just a secret romance and some hurt feelings.

Nancy continued, "But when the detective is a woman and obsessed with her case, it feels like everybody gets to be more judgy. A woman who misses her kid's Halloween party, like the detective in *The Chestnut Man*, loses more points than a male detective."

Will nodded. "Society blames distracted mothers a lot more harshly than it does the distracted fathers."

Margaret was happy to let Will be the more vocally feminist parent. As for her own work-life balance, he had met her when she was a driven graduate student and he took her intensity for granted. Maybe he even liked it.

While Will and the girls talked, Margaret's mind was on the package in her bureau. Will was going to his writers' group tonight. The group had begun long ago, when he was a high school teacher trying to finish *Murder in the Vestry*. Now that he was successful, his modesty would not let him quit—otherwise he would look full of himself. And he genuinely liked his group. Once Will had left and the girls were in bed, that would be an ideal time to try on the corset.

Unfortunately, the girls went to bed late, stymied by math homework that was beyond Margaret's ability to help.

Nancy went first and finally Bee stood up and intoned, "My work is done. Why wait?"

She was quoting George Eastman's suicide note, which every Rochester child knew by heart, from numerous school trips to his Museum of Photography. The note was displayed in a room on the second floor with other personal effects, including, weirdly, some bits of metal from his coffin that had escaped burning in the cremation.

Once the house was quiet, feeling embarrassed and guilty, Margaret took out the print instructions that came with the corset and was immediately lost. They ordered her not to start with the busk, but what was that? She resorted to the YouTube guide to self-lacing and saw from the voluptuous, businesslike woman doing the demonstration that it was the rigid front of the corset, which fastened with loops and posts. But first she had to loosen the laces at the back, and then fasten the busk, starting with either the second post from the top or the second from the bottom. The instructions were as precise as Gabrielle Hamilton's for niçoise salad. Once the busk was fastened, she located the two pull tabs at the waist and gave each one a brisk tug.

Then came the hard part, which was to start at the top and pull each X of the laces as tightly as possible while trying not to get it tangled in the previous X. When she reached the waist, after multiple tangles, she had to pull on the waist loop while remembering that the above-the-waist ribbons were controlled by the bottom waist loop, and vice versa. The matter-of-fact guide, who assured her audience that self-lacing was "an important skill to have," suggested taking a break of between fifteen and thirty minutes after the first lacing. Then, once the wearer's body had become accustomed to that level of constriction, the laces could be tightened further. How much leisure time did these corset-wearers have, Margaret wondered, and in what universe would self-lacing count as an "important skill"?

When she had been struggling with the thing for perhaps half an hour, her cheeks were pink with exertion and her arms ached with the effort of pulling and disentangling laces at her back. She was wearing panties, but, uncertain about a bra, she had left it off until the corset was in place. Her breasts were hanging out from the top of the corset like invitations. She realized, not completely reluctantly, that the getup was sexy. *Duh*, she told herself.

But before she could enjoy it, she heard the front door open. Oh my God, why was Will home so early? She hurried to the closet to put on her robe, but the robe wasn't there. She must have left it in the bathroom this morning. Counting on Will's usual deliberate pacing through the first floor, she ran down the hall to the bathroom, which faced the stairway. But before she got there, she heard his tread on the stairs. He could see his wife of fifteen years, dressed for a bordello and cowering, and his eyes widened.

Before he reached her, she began explaining, "Will, this is just... I was just..."

But he ushered her back into the bedroom, saying, "Let's keep the girls out of this."

Good point. Once he had closed the bedroom door, he seemed remarkably incurious about what was going on, putting his hand gently over her mouth to forestall any more explanations. Then he spanned her corseted waist experimentally with his hands and she thought, *When was the last time Will held me around the waist?* Come to think of it, when had she ever had a waist like this?

"It isn't quite finished," she said apologetically, as if this were an assignment he had given her. "The laces are supposed to be even tighter, but it's hard to pull them."

"Let me see what I can do."

He had her kneel with one knee on the bed, which was both erotic, because as he leaned against her she could feel his arousal, and comic, because as he pulled she frequently fell over. As he righted her, he would cup her breasts tentatively, as if to make sure they were still there. After several tries, he had laced her as tightly as possible and she said, into the pillow he had provided, "That's enough."

"Not quite enough."

Dexterously he slipped underneath her, holding on to the waist he had called into being. Will was not much of a breast man; the part of Margaret he found most irresistible was her inner thighs. But now, with Margaret on top and her breasts floating free from the corset, it seemed he was intent on making up for his failure to appreciate them.

Margaret was beside herself with lust and something that was not so agreeable. It seemed ungrateful to the corset, but her waist hurt and maybe even her lower back. She could see a line in the instructions that was in bold and said, "If you feel pain in your lower back, loosen the laces immediately."

"Can you loosen the laces?" she asked.

Not seeming to feel there was any hurry, Will fumbled with the bow that she had instructed him to tuck under the corset.

"I mean NOW!" she hissed, but he could not extract the bow.

"Take it off!" she screamed. "Or I'll never come!"

In an instant, he was out of bed and searching for the manicure scissors on the top of the bureau.

"It seems a shame . . ." he began, looking sadly at the corset that had brought him so much pleasure.

"NOW!" she screamed, and he cut the laces.

Then he was on top and put his hand on Margaret's mouth, not at all gently this time. He knew what was coming. When it was over, Margaret lay in his arms, her ruined corset rucked up on one side and falling to her hip on the other. Will tried to reconstitute what was left of it, at least provisionally, and then gave up.

"Mary Margaret, Mary Margaret," he said, resting his hand on her uncorseted, undefined waist, "what has come over you?"

"'Toss to dress,'" she said, "'and don't worry about messing up the beauty.'"

"Huh?"

"I'm just quoting Gabrielle Hamilton."

He laughed, and after a pause he said, "I'm sure we could find some new laces."

She moved closer to him. "This might be a one-time thing."

They didn't finish that discussion because they made love again. In the morning there was a scramble to hide the abused corset and its wrappings in case one of the girls came in.

At breakfast, Will kept smiling at her idiotically. She kicked him under the table and said, "Stop it."

"Stop what?" Bee asked.

"He's bumping my knee."

KEITHA HAD BEEN EDITING the texts for the vitrines of Roger Vivier shoes, and they met in mid-morning to go over her work. Positioned for side and front views, the shoes were lined up on a table in Conservation.

"Their elegance is just so understated," Margaret said, looking fondly at her favourite. It had a high throat and a slightly rounded toe.

"And look at that middling, slightly chunky heel that flares a little at the bottom," Keitha said. "So much easier to walk and stand in than stilettos."

The curator in Margaret had to correct that. "Vivier wasn't actually against the stiletto, he just hadn't invented it yet. In the mid-fifties, he inserted a metal rod in a wooden heel, and the rest has been unspeakable discomfort. But these human-scale shoes were perfect for Dior's *soigné* suits and dresses." She hesitated for a second. "Speaking of discomfort, I actually spent some time last night in a corset with twenty-six steel bones."

"You didn't! What was it like?"

"It was astonishingly effective. I would even say transformative. But also torture."

Keitha only paid attention to her last point. "You see? That's what I keep telling you. Could you bring the corset in? I'd love to see it."

"Yeah, someday," Margaret said vaguely.

EIGHTEEN

Red Silk for Cocktails Once More

When Gareth called her and said, "There's another," Margaret said without thinking, "But it's too soon." It was only four days since the arrival of the beret. The other parcels had all arrived at intervals of a week or more.

In Gareth's office, she watched as he extracted a pamphlet from the wrappings. It was a program for a Paris fashion show in October 1941, when gasoline shortages were already making bicycles the preferred means of transport. Prizes would be awarded at the fashion show for the best cycling outfits worn by members of the audience. The enclosed note said, "For the vast majority who were not wearing couture."

She said to Gareth, "As if we didn't know that most French women couldn't wear couture. This hand is all played out. And no, I'm not going to contact Deirdre. There's nothing new here."

But Nancy and Bee, when they heard about the package that evening, saw something new, at least in the timing of the package.

"This is too soon," Bee said, echoing her mother but with more significance. "The perp is losing the plot. He or she is emptying their drawer, willy-nilly."

Nancy agreed. "They're losing their nerve."

"What do you think?" Margaret asked Will.

"Could be. If the latest deliveries added something to their campaign, I might feel differently, but the timing, added to the blandness of the pieces, makes me think someone just wants to get this over with."

Margaret liked the sound of that. If the sender had run out of gas, then maybe everyone could forget these offerings with their holier-than-thou messages and get on with the work at hand.

Ostensibly watching a documentary about John le Carré with Will that evening, her mind wandered to *Égypte*, the strapless evening gown, and its sample page. Dom had written a good touch screen about Dior's design methods, and the spotlit dress would stand on a small pedestal. The sample page had its own little glass shrine, next to the dress but protected from thieves and too much light: you had to press a button for the precious page to emerge from semi-darkness.

When her phone rang, Margaret was annoyed to have to put away her daydream. She moved out of the living room so Will would not be disturbed. It was Alan Shea, sounding genuinely upset.

"Margaret, I'm sorry to have to tell you this, but I was just depositing some contemporary netsuke in the safe and it was obvious that the bag with the Dior sample page is empty. Maybe you've cached it somewhere else. There're so few of us who know the combination that I can't imagine . . ."

Margaret's first thought was, *Oh my God, the Fashion Museum will never forgive us.* Her second thought was for *The New Look*. She stared at the phone as if it could transmit the horrible news to the Fashion Museum, and she became aware that she was moaning softly.

"I'll be right down."

"Margaret, there's no point in that. Security is here, and there's nothing for you to do that can't be done in the morning."

She saw that it was after eleven. But the hour didn't matter now. "I'll be right down," she repeated.

Margaret went alone. When she got to the storage hall, she wanted to ransack everything. In the safe, where Alan had deposited the netsuke for his *Japonisme* exhibit, the foam-lined bag for the sample page was indeed empty and nothing else had been touched. She searched the compartment where *Égypte* hung, and not surprisingly there was no sign of the page. It was the same for her office and Keitha's cubbyhole.

In the morning, she cared about nothing except the sample page. Since everything had gone to rat shit, confidentiality was the least of her concerns. When Bee asked her at breakfast about the swollen, purply-grey circles under her eyes, she told the truth.

Nancy said, "So, it's Alan who is the thief. He has motive and opportunity and he's just pretending to have discovered the missing page. You should have searched his office."

"I can't just go in and search offices," Margaret said, ignoring the fact that she had done that with Keitha's. "And besides, he sounded really shocked and even a bit sorry for me."

"And that's an acting job," Bee said. She had been googling something on her phone. On his Facebook page Alan Shea mentioned having done quite a bit of drama in high school and briefly in college. "There, you see?" Bee said conclusively.

Nancy regarded her twin approvingly. "She's right, Mom. In Agatha Christie, one of the ways to spot the villain is to suspect anyone who's been an actor. Dead giveaway."

Will looked torn between concern for Margaret and pride in his daughters' perspicacity.

MARGARET MOVED THROUGH the next days in a state of high-functioning misery. Security had dismantled the work-around the perpetrator had used to turn out the lights when *Audacieuse* was taken, but with the theft of the sample page there had been a piece of luck for the perpetrator that worked as well as darkness: a new shelving unit, waiting to be permanently installed, temporarily stood between the security camera and the safe where the page was kept.

In addition to making sure that the lighting design and the Learning outcomes were on schedule and that "The Women Who Wore Dior" alcove was proceeding at its breakneck pace, she had to research the current prices for Diors and make a reasoned case for the offer she was proposing for Léa's clothes. Then she had to calm Gareth down over what he saw as an outrageous figure that the museum could never afford and to coach him on how to present it to the finance committee. And, of course, she had to break the news about the sample page to the curator at the Fashion Museum, who was understandably upset. She promised with much more certainty than she felt that the page would be found unharmed.

In her numbness, she noticed her colleagues only dimly. Claire was her motherly self, but there was nothing she could do. Jill Hillman dropped by her office regularly, to indicate that Margaret was silly to be surprised at another disaster in such an incompetent organization. Jill sighed frequently, always with a hint of gloating. Keitha did not sigh but had a permanent wrinkle between her brows. She searched the Textile department high and low, and then went to the galleries. She could not touch the exhibits themselves but buttonholed the increasingly irritable security staff to ask if they had opened and looked inside that Renaissance strongbox or that Victorian sewing cabinet for the missing sample page. They always had done these checks, with no success.

Then the NPR program on Fanny Berger was announced, with the sensationalist teaser, "Christian Dior had great good luck and some dubious friends. Will the Harkness Museum's long-awaited exhibition shed new light on his legend? Listen to a story about the other side of French fashion in the 1940s. It's called 'The Killing of a Hat Maker.'"

That was worse than misleading, since Dior was never mentioned in Fanny Berger's diary. Patricia Bertelli had promised Margaret that she wouldn't fabricate any connection between the radio program and the exhibition. It was a small kick, but Margaret was already down so it felt doubly unfair.

She said to Gareth, "Can any more bad things happen?"

He responded, "Don't ask that." And he was right.

The *Times* article about Dior appeared online the next day, with Alexander Beyle's byline. It was a coup for an intern, and had Margaret been an objective reader, she would have admitted that the piece was a workmanlike job of assembling a significant amount of information about Dior's connections during and after the occupation. Almost all of it was already known and there was no proof that Dior had done anything approaching direct collaboration, but the cumulative effect left Margaret feeling even more battered. Alexander had called her for a comment a few weeks ago, and she had repeated her usual response: neither Lucien Lelong nor Marcel Boussac had been convicted of any wrongdoing, and the obscure and inexperienced Christian Dior had never been accused of collaboration.

The strongest part of the article was the inclusion of two historians who told a convincing tale about the malleable standards of the purification committee. As they noted, Lelong's championing of French couture might well have tempted the committee to ignore any unnecessary co-operation with the Germans. And although Boussac's business collaborations with the Germans were well-known, he was so important to the shattered postwar economy that the committee bypassed him completely.

"So the purification committee charged smaller offenders and left big guns like Lelong and Boussac untouched," Gareth said. "And now Dior is guilty by association."

"My least favourite line," Margaret said, "is the first historian saying, 'Dior was a lucky guy, with powerful and possibly shady friends.' It says nothing but implies so much."

Something about that line seemed familiar, but she couldn't think what it was.

"And this is going to make it even harder to get the committee's approval to buy Léa's collection," Gareth added gloomily.

Three days after its online publication, the article appeared in the front section of the print *New York Times*. That was still the way Margaret's mother-in-law got her news, and she called to sympathize. *Sympathize* was perhaps not the right word, since she sounded her usual complacent self.

"This is going to test your mettle, Margaret."

Helena's tone implied that, until now, Margaret had squeaked through school and work thanks to a series of flukes. Finally, she was going to be held accountable.

Margaret murmured something about sensational journalism and added, in a way she hoped sounded credible, that neither she nor Dior had anything to worry about.

As she was saying goodbye, Helena added, "I'll see you tomorrow night."

"Tomorrow night?"

The Abramsons, whom they had invited for dinner before everything started going to hell, were coming tomorrow night. Hadn't Will invited his mother for dinner the following Thursday?

"Yes, Will asked me for next week, but my book club is reading Virginia Woolf's *The Waves* that night, so we settled on tomorrow."

"Right, see you tomorrow."

Why had she married a dolt who refused to use a calendar? She could hardly uninvite Helena, but she couldn't think of anyone worse to pair with the Abramsons. And trust her mother-in-law to belong to the only book club in the world that was pretentious enough to read the impenetrable *Waves*. She wished them all a horrible evening.

Will did not even have the grace to be properly ashamed. "Yeah, I forgot about the Abramsons, but you're overthinking this. Things are awful for you at work and this is probably a spillover. Don't look at me like that, Margaret. I'm sure my mother will be charmed by your cousins. I'm wondering about dessert, after the chicken pie. Do you feel like making the Guinness chocolate cake or is that one carb too many?"

Now she really hated him. How could he refer to things being "awful at work," as if it were some picayune detail in her life, something she could tuck away in a drawer, when it was everything? (Except of course for her family.) And she had never seen Helena remotely close to being charmed by anyone.

Recklessly, she moved to the hook with the car keys, banging into the table where glasses stood waiting to be re-shelved. They trembled at her unexpressed fury.

"Where are you going?"

"Out to get fruit for tomorrow's dessert."

Another thing she could hold against him was that although he cooked well, he had no sense of how to put together a menu. She would make a winter compote of dried fruits and, if she had time, the Viennese crescents everyone liked. Guinness chocolate cake indeed. She slammed the door.

ON TUESDAY NIGHT, peace was restored. The chicken pie was bubbling merrily. Bee was acting as if Harold and Arlene were going to be new-found grandparents, and she had set out a few albums where she could show them family pictures. Refusing to wear all black, Margaret found an old green sweater that looked surprisingly good on her. Why didn't she wear more green? The sweater didn't work with the deco pin that Helena had given her, but she had given up trying to show her what a grateful daughter-in-law she was.

Margaret still felt a little awkward being around the Abramsons. She liked them and she liked the idea of getting to know her father's family, but once again she felt uncertain about the Jewish side of her heritage. It was as if a penny had dropped for her, but then landed prematurely on a ledge, where it was stuck.

When she entered the living room, Nancy and Bee were sitting on the couch on either side of Harold, as they showed him pictures of the cousin he called Moe. On chairs in front of the fire, Arlene and Helena were disagreeing about *The Waves*. Oh dear, Margaret thought, but Arlene was holding her own.

"I just read a little bit," she said, "before I decided life was too short and took it back to the library. I liked *Mrs. Dalloway*, so I gave it a try. But there are no characters, no dialogue, no psychology—not my cup of tea."

"You're looking for the wrong things," Helena said equably. "It's a long poem really, about elemental things like life and death. And it's told entirely in soliloquies."

Margaret, who had never been tempted by *The Waves*, thought how appropriate a novel full of soliloquies was for Helena.

"As I say," Arlene returned, also peacefully, "not my cup of tea."

When they assembled at the table, Harold thanked the girls for showing him the pictures of their grandfather. "I rarely saw him once I was a teenager, so that was a real pleasure. As he got older, he looked a lot like our uncle Morton. At the same time, it made me sad that he and Dorothy and his parents sort of left the family."

He and Arlene talked about their four grandchildren, all of whom Harold described as brilliant. Arlene corrected him, saying they were "nice kids and smart enough." Harold asked Nancy and Bee if they knew what they wanted to be when they grew up.

"Maybe a veterinarian," Nancy said. "Specializing in dogs," she added, with an ambiguous look at her allergic father.

Bee wanted to own an independent bookstore.

Nancy asked, "Specializing in mysteries?"

Bee shook her head. "Not necessarily."

Lifting a forkful of lethally hot chicken pie, Nancy asked Will abruptly, "Was Agatha Christie an anti-Semite?"

Later, Will would describe her question as more of a semi-sequitur than a non sequitur.

"Why do you ask?" he asked.

"Because whenever she has a character with a Jewish name, she goes on about how exotic or foreign they seem, even if they were born in England. Sometimes she even says they have hooked noses and are always thinking about money."

"The short answer is yes," Will said. "She was part of the careless and stupid anti-Semitism of the English upper classes of her day. Some people say it was more obvious in her early books and she either smartened up herself or was told to stop it. I don't know about that, but you're right to notice it."

"She always makes the Jewish character seem very suspicious," Bee said.

"Yes," Will said. "To Christie and her class, their differentness made Jews funny or maybe slightly sinister, but rarely evil. Still, it's anti-Semitic."

"They never do turn out to be the murderer," Nancy said. "It's more like a tease."

Harold, who had been silent during this exchange, murmured, "Very observant."

They might have moved from that to something easier, but Helena was not one to let a possibly thorny subject slip away. She said to Margaret, "The twins tell me you're looking into your Jewishness."

"Looking into your Jewishness," which sounded like looking into your stock portfolio or the causes of the Franco-Prussian War, struck Margaret as slightly odd phrasing, but she supposed there was nothing really wrong with it.

"When my sisters and I started clearing out my father's condo, we found Jewish holiday cards and lots of addresses of people named Abramson. Which is how I met Harold and Arlene." She smiled at them. "I hadn't expected there would be such a clear paper trail back to my father's Jewish family."

"You should have asked me," Helena said, rotating her stack of Mexican silver bracelets. "When you and Will decided to get married, I told my family and all my friends that you must be Jewish."

Gee, how did I pass up that golden opportunity to find out who I was? Margaret thought. *Remind me to ask you about any other uncertainties that cross my path.*

Helena persisted. "So your father didn't want to be Jewish?"

"I can't see any sign that he did, no."

"Then I suppose you aren't really Jewish either." Helena said this neither happily nor regretfully, but simply as a matter of fact.

"I don't know. I might decide that I am."

She saw that she now had the full attention of Will and the girls.

"Why would you decide that?" Helena asked.

"I'm not sure. And I'm not saying that is what I'll do. It seems my father chose to look the other way and not to be curious. Much as his parents tried to distance themselves from Judaism, I think he sensed that it was still part of their package. He didn't want the package—I think because he resented his controlling mother—and he couldn't or wouldn't disentangle the Jewishness from it, so he left it all behind. That's my theory, anyway."

Mentally, she left Rivkah's more devious theory aside for the moment.

"And if my hunch is true," she continued, "nothing ever shifted that for him—not lifelong Jewish friends or Abe Solloway, his first principal and mentor in the school system. When you keep on denying something, I can imagine that you start to believe it. A Jewish friend says I am free to claim my heritage. That sounds like a story about a princess with a locked chest and a magic formula, and I don't know about my heritage. But I don't want to avert my eyes anymore."

Well. It seemed that the penny had suddenly left the ledge and was dropping again. Harold and Arlene, who had not said a word throughout this exchange, gave her a sympathetic smile.

In the silence that followed, Helena said, "What about the girls?"

"The girls? This isn't about the girls. It's about me."

Bee opened her mouth, but Nancy eyed her fiercely. Margaret heard her whisper, "Don't."

Margaret suspected Bee had been about to bring up the subject of the bat mitzvah Diors.

The rest of the evening passed without more revelations. Like Rivkah, Harold and Arlene treated Margaret's possible interest in her Jewish heritage calmly and without much outward curiosity, for which she was grateful. The chicken pie and Viennese crescents were duly admired, everyone said they enjoyed meeting the new people, and by ten thirty Margaret and Will were left with the dishes.

"Just promise me one thing," Will said. He turned to smile at her, running hot, soapy water into the pie pan. "You won't wear a wig."

Sometimes he baffled her. "I thought this was something you wanted."

"I wanted you to stop being wilfully blind about something that was obvious. And I'm glad that's over. I'm kidding. Except it feels a bit . . . unclear where you and your heritage are headed. And it would be a shame to cover up that red hair."

He was facing the sink, and she stood behind him and rested her head for a minute on his.

"Very funny. I'm not planning on becoming Orthodox. I promise, no wig."

IT HAD BEEN TWO WEEKS since the sample page had disappeared. Intensive searches had turned up nothing and one horrid possibility was that it had vanished forever into the bin for non-recyclables. Once a week, Margaret forced herself to send reports of their lack of progress to the Fashion Museum curator who had arranged the loan. Curtly, he acknowledged receipt of the messages, but in the past week he had sent an ominous reply in which he raised the question of the Harkness Museum's financial obligation. The Fashion Museum had taken out insurance on the page years before, but its value had skyrocketed since then. It seemed obvious to him that Harkness would have to make up the difference.

Margaret thought about that in the middle of the night, when she could not sleep for worrying about the exhibit and everything in it that was misunderstood, besmirched, jeopardized and stolen. In the daytime, the opening was so close and she had so much to do that there were times when she simply forgot about the missing page. But that was temporary, a brief glimpse of sun permitted by a sullen grey cloud that never really left the sky. The empty glass shrine that had been designed to hold the page haunted her.

The morning after Helena and the Abramsons came to dinner, Munro Lesniak, one of the mannequin makers, knocked on Margaret's open door.

"I think I've finally gotten the shoulders for Red right. Shall we take a look?"

He meant the shoulders on the mannequin for the red cocktail dress, officially *Zemire* but known as Red to the conservators and mannequin makers. The dress was verging toward off-the-shoulder, so the mannequin had been sent back a few times to get the exact shoulder breadth it required.

Margaret followed Munro to the storage hall, where the headless mannequin, sheathed in a stretchy off-white fabric, stood waiting. With Munro looking away, she entered the combination and went to the locker that housed *Zemire*. It was empty.

Without thinking, Margaret immediately called Conservation and asked if anyone was working on *Zemire*. She knew the answer because the dress had been in perfect condition for weeks. Then, without saying a word to Munro, who still stood with his hand on the mannequin's back—the mannequin that was not going to be wearing *Zemire* any time soon, if ever—she ran to her office. Anyone she collided with on her way got a whispered "Sorry." She closed her door and looked for a lock. Although she had never wanted one before, she wondered, *Why don't I have a lock?* For a mad moment, she thought of putting a heavy chair against the door so that no one could come in.

Instead, she called Will.

"What's wrong?" he said immediately. She almost never called him from the office.

At the sound of his voice, she began sobbing. "They've taken it," she said, crying harder.

"Taken what?"

She noticed that he didn't ask who "they" were, just what was taken.

"The red cocktail dress. The one that belonged to Léa."

"Do you want me to come down?"

"No, what could you do? This is a complete nightmare. The exhibition will never happen."

She knew that wasn't true. The exhibition was long past the point of no return. The show would go on, diminished and disfigured.

"Is the dress the one with a very full skirt? With net or something inside to make it stand out?"

Even after all these years, Will's understanding of Dior's clothes remained basic.

She whispered, "Yes."

"That's going to be very hard to get out of the building, so don't lose heart. Someone is going to find it. Just don't stay until the evening. Once you get the search under way, it's better if you leave Security to do its job."

When they hung up, she put her head down on her desk and wept some more.

Why did someone hate her, or Dior, or maybe both of them? Why were all these terrible things happening? Why had she ever imagined that Léa might be behind the disappearances? She thought of Nancy and Bee peppering their texts with KMN, "Kill Me Now." Her sentiments exactly. She could not imagine lifting one more finger to advance *The New Look*. But of course she would.

First she needed to salute the dress, its vibrancy, its red, the V at the neck and the Y at the waist, its mixture of sauciness and tact. The way you would salute the endearing qualities of a parent or a friend at their funeral. Even if she never saw it again, it had been an honour to know *Zemire* at close quarters. But the dress was probably not dead. More likely, it was in danger.

She did not know how long she stayed like that, resting her face on its left side, letting the warm tears from the right eye fall over the bridge of her nose and join the tears from her left eye.

She remembered seeing desks with blotters in old movies. One would have come in handy today.

There was a knock at her door and she heard Claire saying, "Margaret, it's me."

Once inside, Claire hugged her, said how sorry she was and dialed Gareth. "You can come over now," Margaret heard her say.

If Gareth was coming to her office, this was officially a catastrophe.

They went through the now-familiar questions with the head of Security. Someone was beginning to look at the surveillance tapes, which led Margaret to ask angrily why they had not posted a guard permanently in the smaller storage hall as soon as the top of *Audacieuse* had been stolen. They didn't have the resources for that, Security told her, and then pointed out that the new shelving unit should either have been installed permanently or removed from the hall, where it still partially interfered with the security camera. That was embarrassingly correct: Claire and Margaret had been too distracted and too used to seeing the shelves standing semi-orphaned in the storage hall. Margaret had last seen the dress two days ago, and Munro had measured it yesterday once Thelma Davies, the head of Conservation, released it to him. Alan and Claire had no reason to visit the dress and said they could not remember the last time they had seen it. The usual impossible riddle. Security was already checking every imaginable hiding place, including the staff lockers. There would be extra inspections of everyone leaving the building.

Once everyone had left her alone, with a flat feeling of déjà vu, Margaret thought through her list of suspects. Alan still had motive and opportunity. Would he go so far as to steal a dress? She could imagine him taking a malicious pleasure in sending the packages or even lifting the snakeskin belt, but taking the sample page or *Zemire* seemed outside his repertoire. Margaret didn't like him, but he was a curator. His vocation was to safeguard things, not maraud them. Was she being naive?

Léa's motive had always been vague and questionable, and she'd had no opportunity. Plus: she was dead. As for Jill Hillman, the only thing that seemed to raise her spirits was trouble at the museum, so she had greeted each recent disaster with a dank burst of satisfaction. But that was hardly a motive, and she didn't have opportunity. Although, if she set her mind to it, Margaret supposed, Jill might have found a way around that. Perhaps a security guard was bribable. If a guard could be corrupted, that would also make it easier for an outsider like Alexander Beyle to be the perp. But what would be Alexander's motive? A relative who had suffered in the occupation while Boussac prospered?

She was getting nowhere with these stabs in the dark, so she decided to go home. Running into Claire in the hall, she remembered something.

"Have you seen Keitha?"

"I forgot to tell you. She was in early this morning but looking quite grey. After that, she had an urgent appointment with her dentist."

On the bus, Margaret got a text from Keitha. "Sorry about my absence today. It turned out to be a root canal and my jaw is sore but otherwise I feel a lot better than I did. I'm tracking down some press clippings of National Council of Jewish Women fundraisers for Rivkah, so I'll see you on Monday."

So, Keitha did not know about today's disaster yet. She didn't seem to be close with anyone in the department, so that made sense. As the bus lumbered up Goodman Street, Margaret returned to her bereavement. Will was right that the dress would be difficult to hide, but that might mean that the perp would resort to violence. She shuddered at the thought of someone taking a scissors to those five layers of tulle, the crinoline and the silk lining.

A PINK HAT WITH A SLOUCHY BRIM

A HAT CAN LOOK SO hopeful. This one, made of felt in the colour of strawberry ice cream, in the collection of Paris's Fashion Museum, is optimistic but not innocent. It has a high, sugarloaf crown and a rolled brim that comes to a gentle point at the back. It's urbane, without trim except for a black ribbon, the kind of hat that pulls an outfit together. The label says *FANNY BERGER* in oversized capitals in a modern font.

The museum dates it to 1940–41, very probably after the start of the German occupation. As the occupation wore on, materials became scarce, frustration grew, and hats became increasingly bizarre and towering. When Berger designed this one, felt was readily available and elegance, not exaggeration, was still the norm.

There are only three known surviving hats with Fanny Berger labels. Besides the pink felt, the Fashion Museum has a similar model in fawn, and a private collector owns a fine-grained black straw trimmed with feathers. Any comparison with Dior's huge oeuvre is meaningless, first because he began after the chaos of war, second because he was instantly famous, starting in 1947, while Berger's creations travelled beyond her clientele only by word of mouth. But the contrast between their fates is remarkable.

NINETEEN

The Killing of a Hat Maker

When Margaret got out of bed the next morning—because she was tired of trying to sleep—she moved toward the closet with eyes only half open. Should it be the unstructured black trouser suit or the black sweater dress with tights? Then she remembered it was Saturday. Oh God, even worse than going to work and having to face everyone's condolences was not going to work. At least in the museum she might distract herself briefly with carpenters, lighting people and printers.

At breakfast her family looked at her sadly.

"I don't think we've pursued the idea of Jill Hillman enough," Nancy said. "She did 'find,' or she *said* she found, the half dress, which is suspicious."

Margaret smiled faintly, but said to Will, "I'll take Bee to pottery."

Nancy spent Saturday mornings at her Irish dancing class, but she could walk there.

In the car, Bee asked something that had clearly been on her mind. "The other night, why did you say that your becoming Jewish wasn't about Nancy and me?"

"Because you can make up your own mind about that. And you don't have to do it this year or any time soon. Just when you're ready."

"So, now that you're Jewish or probably Jewish, what are *you* going to do?"

"I don't know. Maybe nothing except say that I'm Jewish."

"Why did it take you so long to accept Grandpa was Jewish?"

"Because I wanted him to be perfect, and I thought a perfect person wouldn't deny that his family was Jewish."

Margaret pulled in at the back of the art gallery, at the door where students entered for painting, sculpture and pottery classes. She asked, "What are you working on now?"

"A head. Kind of like the Wizard of Oz," Bee said, and kissed her goodbye.

Margaret stayed in the car for a minute, going over their conversation. She wanted to think of her father and Dior like a Dior dress—finished and flawless, with the lining as impeccable as the outside. Ideally, they did not cut corners or avert their eyes from things that were awkward or worse. And yet good people did turn away from things they preferred to ignore. It's not what you want from them, but it happens.

Since her lunch with Léa, she had returned again and again to Léa's description of Catherine Dior as "a ghost at the banquet." At the openings, in the pale-grey-and-white elegance of her brother's premises, she was a dark reminder of France's recent past and humanity's capacity for evil. One side of Dior was devoted to his stoic, private sister, but another side had curious words of praise for the two women who were most important to his business. Of the technical director, Marguerite Carré, he wrote in his memoir, "If the world came to an end while she was poring over a dress, I really did not believe she would notice it." He lauded his muse, the ultra-glamorous Mizza

Bricard, for being "superbly indifferent to politics, finance, or social change."

Sitting in the car, Margaret thought, *How could Catherine Dior's brother celebrate those women in those silly terms? Oh my.* That was the first time she had used the word *silly* in relation to Dior. She tried to soften it, imagining him torn and veering between his sister's principles and the aesthetic tunnel vision of his colleagues.

It reminded her of her conversation with Rosie Tanaka, the fashion history professor, after the lingerie seminar, when she had championed the idea of "just plain beauty" unmoored from social issues, and Rosie countered, "Is there any such thing?"

Now Margaret would answer, "I guess not."

She thought of Will's question again, and amplified it: What would you lose if you accepted that Dior might be even the tiniest bit compromised or that your father lied about being Jewish? Well, she'd have to accept that some people she called beloved might be morally untidier and more complex than a perfectly tailored suit, and that their imperfection didn't necessarily make them less lovable or their work less admirable. Put that way, it sounded like something she could work on. She didn't look forward to it, but at least it made sense.

Margaret couldn't decide whether to take a stroll and come back in time to pick Bee up, or to go in the gallery and visit her favourite paintings, which she sometimes did during Bee's class. Nancy and Bee loved the soaring Fountain Court, with its intricate medieval sculptures and tapestries. Nancy would stand for long minutes looking at the high-strung, tightly collared dogs raking the ground in the tapestries. For Margaret, the gallery was a series of faces—the profile of a Renaissance Venetian, for one, wearing a hat like a Jackie Kennedy pillbox over his pageboy hairstyle, or *Tom Cafferty*, Robert Henri's alert little boy with the visor of his cap turned rakishly to the side.

But today she needed to walk. She set off on University Avenue and went west. Thinking she would have a coffee, she turned onto Gibbs Street and headed for Ludwig's café. It was usually full of students from the Eastman School of Music, so she was surprised when, on the other side of the window, she caught sight of Patricia Bertelli. Patricia's younger daughter was in Bee's pottery class; she must be killing time too. She was facing Margaret, who could only see the back of the man who was with her. She waved at Patricia and two things happened instantly: Patricia looked startled, even slightly alarmed, while the man turned around to face Margaret.

Then it was Margaret's turn to be startled. How did Patricia and Alexander Beyle know each other? And why was he in Rochester, when all was apparently quiet with the *New Look* story? Why did they look so guilty? Normally, she would have gone inside, and today she would have said something to Patricia about her Fanny Berger program, which was to be broadcast that evening, but the scene on the other side of the glass looked strangely tense.

Margaret decided she did not need a coffee after all, and continued walking toward what had been the confluence of the downtown department stores, when Rochester had a downtown and department stores that weren't in malls. It was a melancholy pilgrimage that suited her, and as she walked, something that had been bothering her clarified. She had wondered why the academic in Alexander's article who mentioned Dior having luck as well as some dodgy friends had sounded familiar. Now, seeing Patricia with Alexander, she remembered the promo on the radio for Patricia's feature, which used almost those exact words about Dior. Something about Dior's "luck and some dubious friends." Alexander's piece had not been published when the promo was broadcast, so Alexander must have shown it to Patricia in advance. Were they plotting something, or—horrible thought—had they already done something? And why?

Her phone buzzed and she saw that it was a text from Rivkah. Oh no. She had completely forgotten that Rivkah had browbeaten her into going shopping that afternoon. She wanted to show Margaret some unintimidating places, including some "hole-in-the-wall joints," where she might find some clothes that were a bit more interesting than her usual fare. Even at the end of a good week, that would be Margaret's idea of a thoroughly bad time, and now it was impossible. Out of the question. Without mentioning the red dress, she wrote as forcefully as she could that it had been a harrowing week and she absolutely could not go shopping. She was so sorry and she promised there would be a better time.

Now her phone was ringing. Rivkah was not deterred.

"Margaret, honestly, this is going to be way easier than you think. Our mothers did this all the time, for entertainment. Your and my generation work too hard, and we've lost the habit. And shopping online is no substitute. I'll pick you up at two."

It was true, Margaret's mother had enjoyed shopping, which she thought of as hunting and gathering. On second thought, Margaret didn't suppose shopping with Rivkah would make her feel any worse. She decided to go through the motions and get it over with later that afternoon, after picking Bee up and dropping her home.

When Rivkah's car appeared, Nancy and Bee stood at the front window and waved their mother off as if she were going to war. They loved shopping, but they knew how she felt about it.

In the car, Rivkah asked, "What was the last outfit you wore where you felt absolutely fantastic?"

At first Margaret said, "That never happened." Then she amended it. "When I was about six, my mother made me a dress in a very pale grey cotton with red smocking. It had a white Peter Pan collar and puffed sleeves, but what made it for me was the combination of the grey and the red. Grey wasn't a usual colour for a child, and although I didn't know the word, I felt it was sophisticated."

Rivkah stopped the car at Sibley Place, just off Park. "Interesting. I'm not promising we'll find the adult equivalent of that today, but it's good to have a marker."

Unsurprisingly, Rivkah's behaviour was pitch perfect. She seemed to know what Margaret could afford and took her to a few shops on Park Avenue and a few more in Brighton. She made a beeline for things that Margaret had to admit were smart and sometimes even stunning but that of course she could never wear. Rivkah did not press her.

"This is just to let you know what's out there," she said. "And I get to fantasize about things I could never carry off but you could." She had only a few directions: "Asymmetrical hems are over. Think colour. Green. Red. Wasn't Moira Shearer famous for breaking the rule that redheads couldn't wear red?"

At Dado, on Park Avenue, she pulled out a pantsuit in a subtle check of two shades of grey. "With a crisp white shirt or black turtleneck, perfect for work."

In theory, Margaret could see that, but it was so *tailored*. She loved Dior's tailored suits and dresses, but wearing one herself was a different matter. Tailoring meant you were trying, and Margaret was at pains to indicate she was not. A few doors down from Dado there was a shop called Statement, an unfortunate name as far as she was concerned. Rivkah found a single-breasted camel's hair coat with a long shawl collar and held it up against Margaret.

"Puffers are going to be old very soon," she prophesied.

At least they agreed on that, but Margaret already had a good wool coat. Next Rivkah detached a green plaid flannel shirtwaist from the rod and held out its full, mid-calf skirt. Margaret petted the flannel, which was meltingly soft. But something with a waist? Given her commitment to slouchy, unconstructed clothes, that felt transgressive.

"It's the waist," she murmured, as if that explained everything.

"Excuse me, but didn't I hear that you're a Dior expert? He was pretty high on waists."

"I can see Deirdre Ferrar in this," Margaret said. "With clunky black Doc Martens and athletic socks."

"And I can see *you* in this," Rivkah said, "with black tights and flats."

Attempting to sound credible as well as retreating to her comfort zone, Margaret said, "There's an Eileen Fisher store in Brighton."

"I know, but this little excursion is about showing you that there's more to life than Eileen Fisher. Or COS."

Rivkah drove them to a shop called Peppermint near Cobbs Hill. There, riffling through the racks, Rivkah took a deep breath. "Oh my God," she said. "This is fabulous."

It was a royal-blue sheath with red felt roses—bold and three-dimensional—appliquéd on a stem that stretched from the dress's hem to its jewel neck.

"That *is* fabulous," Margaret agreed.

"The changing room is down the hall to the left."

"I didn't mean I would try it on. I have no place to wear that."

"Don't you ever have to go to some museum event in the evening? How about the opening of *The New Look*?"

But Margaret would not admit that she ever had occasion to wear such a dress. And she could not think about the opening of *The New Look*.

After that, Margaret thought they would be finished. It had not been as much of a trial as she had feared, and if she ever survived the next few weeks, she could even imagine—maybe—coming back to a few of these shops. But Rivkah was not done.

"I just want to take you to one more place."

It was in a wooden house on Thayer Street, marked by the most discreet of signs that said, *T. Rowley. Dressmaking*. An arrow pointed to the second floor.

"There's no need to look like that, Margaret. He can copy anything—a picture in a magazine, a dress you'd like in another colour, whatever. Or you could, for example, take a top you like to him, and he would suggest the right skirt or pants and make it for you. He's brilliant, and not scary."

Trudging up the narrow stairs, Margaret imagined that T. Rowley would resemble D.H. Lawrence, spindly and tubercular. But he was burly, a gentle giant with a bald head circled by a silvery fringe. Judging by the mannequins that crowded the studio, wearing semi-finished or finished pieces, his meaty hands could conjure up a slinky wedding dress cut on the bias, a poufy party dress and a coat of dazzling severity. The coat's set-in pockets looked worthy of an *atelier tailleur* and Margaret resisted the urge to slip a hand inside one of them.

Rivkah and T. Rowley, whom she called Tom, were chatting about projects past and present, and Margaret joined them at the cutting table. Rivkah told him about the New Look exhibit, and he began rooting among the bolts of material on the table.

"I just saw something about the New Look," he said. "Where did I put that . . . oh, here it is."

He extracted a copy of *Vogue* underneath a bolt of apple-green velvet and paged through it until he found what he wanted.

"Look what's happened to *Bar*."

Wearing a suit from the latest Dior collection, a model posed in front of a Greek temple. There was no peplum jacket, no padded hips or cinched-in waist, but this was recognizably *Bar* for the twenty-first century. The filmy chiffon pleated skirt was white, not black, and the model wore high-heeled white boots over crew socks that said *Christian Dior*. But the loveliest thing was the jacket. Hip-length with two flap pockets, buttoned up to a softly pointed collar at the neck, it had the gentlest indentation at the waist—just enough to suggest the natural shape of a woman's body.

"This would make my intern happy," Margaret said. "She thinks the New Look was cruel and unusual punishment for women."

Rivkah straightened herself on her stool. "Which it was, in spite of your views, Margaret. Maybe it took a woman creative director to design this."

Margaret nodded in deference to Maria Grazia Chiuri, the firm's first female director. "She brings out a different incarnation of *Bar* for every collection."

Bent over the picture, the three agreed that, had Dior not been dead already, the model's laced-up boots and the Christian Dior crew socks would have killed him. Margaret shook hands with Tom Rowley and made a vague promise about seeing him again. He seemed pleasant and his work was excellent, but she doubted she would return to Thayer Street.

ONCE MARGARET WAS HOME, she asked the girls if they wanted to listen to the NPR feature about Fanny Berger.

Bee asked, "Is this part of our new Jewish education?"

"I'm not in charge of Jewish education," Margaret said. "I'm going to listen and I thought you might find it interesting. I warn you, there's no happy ending."

Since its title was "The Killing of a Hat Maker," Nancy asked if it was a mystery.

"No. The murderers are all too obvious."

Will joined them and sat in an armchair while the girls sat on either side of Margaret on the couch. As the noose around Fanny Berger tightened, they took hold of her hands. She wasn't sure who was comforting whom. Patricia Bertelli had done a good job, and Margaret appreciated that the actress playing Fanny spoke an unaccented English. She loathed movies or plays or podcasts where a French or Turkish character was supposed to be speaking in their own language but was unaccountably burdened with an accent—as if the English-speaking audience needed a constant reminder that the character really spoke a foreign language. There were very few sound effects, except for the occasional turn of a page or German singing or soldiers marching in the streets.

Berger's unvarnished words were enough. Occasionally she brought a scene to life—the demonstration against the wearing of yellow stars, for example, with the young mothers in their flowered dresses and Stars of David and the Jewish veterans of the First World War, walking deliberately through the crowd in uniform, their medals cheek by jowl with their Stars of David.

Sometimes but rarely, she could not resist a terse conclusion. About the teenagers in the camp who kept their old hairstyles so their parents would recognize them, Berger wrote, "This would be heartbreaking, if I had a heart to break." Faced with the order to return to the police prefecture for yet another identity card, she wrote, "I must, I must, I must. Where is the young woman who defied her culture to leave home unmarried and start her own successful business? She has become a person who must return to the commissariat on short notice and subject herself to another humiliating procedure." But mostly, she let the events speak for themselves.

When the feature was over, there was a surprise. To finish the hour, Patricia did a short interview about millinery in the occupation with the "renowned fashion historian" Deirdre Ferrar. Margaret wondered crossly, had everyone who met on the night of Deirdre's talk become friends? Deirdre was talking in her usual bright-as-a-button style about advertisements for hats in the occupation with the models posed against slanting views of the Eiffel Tower and other landmarks to suggest uncertainty and danger, when Margaret turned the radio off.

"Mom!" the girls protested in unison.

"You can listen to it any time, on the NPR website. I've had enough."

They looked at her closely.

Finally, Nancy said, "What happened to your people was terrible."

Margaret almost smiled. "If you're going to say that, maybe you should say 'our people.'"

They talked about what they had found most poignant. For Margaret it was the thought of Fanny walking past her tools and materials for the last time and scooping up that handful of brass buttons.

Will, who had been silent through the program, said, "I won't forget the image of the Jewish veterans, who had risked their lives for France and were now condemned to wear what the Germans considered an emblem of shame. But more than that, what hit me was the sense of Fanny Berger being trapped in a machine that was systematically robbing her of her rights, and worse."

The girls both found the teenage sisters who shared a barracks with Berger the saddest, especially their hope that they would reunite with their parents.

Bee asked, "Do you think they ever saw them again?"

"Probably not," Will said.

TWENTY

A Patchwork Coat

On Monday morning, Margaret gritted her teeth. She was scheduled to present the exhibition, or the parts of it that were ready, to the docents who would lead the tours. Each docent would receive a full set of notes about the exhibit's individual pieces, and Margaret and Keitha would talk about Dior's early collections in general. Margaret admired these keen volunteers—about fifty women and two men—and she usually looked forward to this first audience. Not today.

She got to the museum early, having bought coffee at a dive on South Clinton. The fewer people she had to see and the more she could avoid the cafeteria, the better. Unfortunately, Jill Hillman would be there with the docents, wearing her I-told-you-so face, but what had she ever actually told Margaret that could have prevented this disaster?

Almost as soon as Margaret had hung up her coat, there was a condolence-level knock on the half-open door. It was Alan Shea.

"Margaret," he said, stepping inside, "I'm so awfully sorry. You've had the most rotten time with this exhibit, and no one can understand why."

She stared at him, too taken aback to speak. Was he reviving his acting career, or how had he managed to cast off his *schadenfreude* and impersonate a sympathetic human being?

"I'm sure you're crazy busy," he went on, "but I just wanted to say one thing. You feel that the whole exhibit is damaged beyond repair with the loss of the cocktail dress, but trust me, the audience will never miss it. There will be so much for them to see and think about, they'll be dazzled. I predict a great hit."

And with that, he left. No doubt this was a ploy designed to lower her suspicions of her rival. She was not going to fall for it, but he had been weirdly disarming.

She needed to pick up the notes for the docents at the printers, and as soon as she remembered that, she thought, *Oh no*. The notes included a fine description and assessment of *Zemire*, which the docents must not see. The theft must remain a secret. She flew out of her office and collided with Keitha, who burst into tears at the sight of Margaret.

"Oh Margaret, this is so awful. Why didn't you call me? It's horrible, just horrible."

She was carrying a big bundle of files, and Margaret asked, "Are those the docents' files? Because we have to—"

"No, they're okay," Keitha said, with tears still running down her face. "I deleted the stuff on *Zemire*, and we reprinted them."

Blessed Keitha.

Together they went to the exhibition hall to move the mannequins on either side of where *Zemire* would have stood, pulling them closer together. It felt like a mourning ritual. After the sample page from the Fashion Museum had been gone for a week, its glass shrine had been taken away, so she didn't need to worry about that. Margaret stifled the melodramatic thought that the exhibit was going to diminish piece by piece until there was nothing left.

In fact, just as Alan had predicted of the audience at large, the docents were enchanted. They marvelled at the clothes, from the most dated to the timeless, they listened attentively to Margaret's and Keitha's remarks, and they asked smart, pertinent questions. Margaret had urged moderation on her intern, but Keitha could not resist noting the unreasonable demands, physical and psychological, that Dior's designs imposed on their wearers, and the docents nodded sympathetically. Margaret wondered if Keitha was becoming more temperate, or was she herself coming closer to her intern's position? Keitha's position did make sense, it was just a question of emphasis. Also as Alan had predicted, no docent inquired about a certain red cocktail dress that had been touted in recent museum newsletters as a prized new acquisition.

Afterwards, Margaret went into Keitha's office to debrief and go over the guest lists for the press opening and the VIP opening and reception. While they talked, Keitha wrapped some jewellery and accessories they didn't have room for in the "Women Who Wore Dior" alcove, to be couriered back to Rivkah's office. The necklaces, pins and bracelets would travel in their carefully kept original boxes, and she folded a cashmere scarf in tissue paper. Tacitly, the two women had decided not to discuss *Zemire* but to concentrate on more mundane things. When Margaret stood up to leave, without a word, they embraced.

THE DAY FINALLY ENDED, about five hours after Margaret felt it should have. When she was at home, she wanted to be at work, and when she was at the museum, she wanted to go home. Nothing felt right.

Now she counted the hours until she could go to bed. Dinner, dishes, reading and doing some light editing on Bee's essay about microaggressions would occupy her for the next few hours.

When Bee stood up, quoting George Eastman's suicide note as usual, Margaret was disappointed to see that it was only eight thirty. She gave in and watched a far-fetched German mystery involving murderous nurses at two rival hospitals. When Nancy had asked for a subscription to the mystery streaming service, MHz, for Christmas, her parents tried unsuccessfully to talk her out of it. Now they watched it much more than Nancy, absorbed in mysteries from Iceland, Luxembourg, Sicily and farther afield.

When it was finally a reasonable bedtime, she remembered that she had to mail a birthday present for Constance tomorrow. Lydia disliked getting gifts and Margaret was neutral, but Constance craved them. When the subject came up, her sisters would chime in with Constance as she explained each time, "It's because I'm the BABY." Margaret had a good present for her this year, a 1960s or '70s cardigan studded with pearls that the girls had spotted while the three of them trawled through the vintage shops on Monroe Avenue. It was a shade Margaret and her sisters called Blessed Mother Blue. Trying to make the wrapping an end in itself, she enclosed the sweater first in tissue paper, then in a box and finally wrapping paper.

She woke at five, and although she tried to persuade herself that she would return to sleep, she knew she wouldn't. Will found her in the kitchen at six, languidly stirring honey into her tea.

He asked, "What are you doing up?"

"I don't know. What are you doing up?"

"There was someone in my bed tossing and turning."

"Sorry. It feels as if I almost have something—there are two things that need to touch or come close, to cause a spark. But I don't know what the two things are, or how to bring them together."

They talked a little about what Margaret had to do in the dwindling weeks before the exhibit opened. Will had finished a draft of his mystery, and his agent was reading it. This was the fallow period in which he threw himself into home repairs that far exceeded his skill level, and that remained unfinished as soon as his agent got back to him. They discussed how he might avoid that predictable pitfall this time around, without much hope that it would happen.

On her way upstairs, Margaret caught sight of Constance's gift on the hall table, waiting to go to the post office. The two elusive things she had been trying to identify suddenly surfaced and made contact with each other. From a faraway science class, she dimly remembered something about an object with a surfeit of negative electrons coming close to an object with a smaller negative charge, and the combination of electrons made them jump. But the scientific details did not interest her. What did was the coming together of the two things, and the resulting spark. She raced upstairs and dressed.

Will came out into the hall as she was struggling into her coat. "Why are you leaving so early? I just started the coffee."

"I'll tell you later."

She knew she would not be able to withstand Will's conviction that what she was about to do was idiotic. If she was wrong, it would do some considerable damage, but she did not think she was wrong.

Half an hour later, she was standing at the staff entrance, just inside the point at which Security was inspecting large bags and packages. It was only seven thirty, and few people came in. Those who did looked at Margaret quizzically.

"I'm just waiting for an early bird," was all she said to them.

The early bird arrived at 7:45, wearing her patchwork coat. Obligingly, Keitha opened her bag and took out a book. Security nodded at the big book and waved her through.

"Margaret," she said when she was through the turnstile and saw her. "Fancy meeting you here."

It was a tired greeting, and Keitha did look a bit wan.

They got into the elevator and Margaret said, "Come along to my office for a minute."

"Of course. Is it something about the publicity announcement? Just let me drop my coat and things in my office first."

"You and your smashing coat. No, come with me. This will be very quick."

When they got out of the elevator, Keitha stood still. "I need to use the bathroom. Right away, I'm afraid. I'll be back in two minutes."

At that point, Margaret took Keitha firmly by the elbow and half pulled, half pushed her into her office. "Let me help you with your coat."

Ashen-faced, Keitha clutched it tightly around herself and said, "I'm quite embarrassed. I'm going out after work and I'm wearing a very inappropriate outfit that I wouldn't like you to see. Just let me get into my work clothes."

"No." Margaret was stern. "I'd very much like to see what you consider an inappropriate outfit."

She grabbed Keitha, who tried at the same time to wriggle free and to wrap her coat even more tightly around herself, but it was hopeless. Margaret wrenched the top button open and Keitha crumbled. With no more fight in her, she let Margaret take off the big, cape-y coat as if she were a child or a doll. Underneath was *Zemire*, admittedly not looking its best. Keitha was too short and narrow-shouldered for the dress, and her dark cotton work shirt wrinkled above *Zemire*'s dramatic V-neck. Nor did Keitha's expression match the brio of the dress. She had begun taking deep gulps, and at the sight of them Margaret shouted.

"No! You cannot cry in that dress! Stop!"

Margaret whirled Keitha around and something in her brain keep repeating *three hooks and eyes, three hooks and eyes*. She meant, undo these in addition to the zipper. But the reminder was unnecessary because Keitha, dressing alone, had been unable to use the hooks. Margaret freed the dress from Keitha and the threatening salt water, and threw her own coat on the floor in order to use its hanger. For a few minutes, before she realized Keitha was in no state to do any damage, she interposed her body between the dress and the soon-to-be-former intern.

"Why? WHY?" she yelled at Keitha, who was crying too hard to answer.

While Margaret waited for her to compose herself, she remembered the book that Keitha, apparently all innocence and co-operation, had shown to the bored security guard. It had looked familiar, and Margaret recognized it as soon as she began to extract it from Keitha's bag. Called *I Brought the World Home*, it was the self-congratulatory memoir of Robinson Harkness, the museum's first director, and his unabashed quest to buy, barter and sometimes pilfer treasures from every continent for the museum. Copies were regularly given on significant work anniversaries to staff members, who tried to look grateful. Later, when Margaret had recovered her sense of humour, she would find Keitha's choice of that book funny, probably unintentionally. And Robinson Harkness, reposing under an imposing headstone in Mount Hope Cemetery, would never know.

The book looked and felt normal and its pages riffled convincingly at the edges. But in the centre of the book there was a cavity, a skilfully cut pocket made to transport Dior's sample page for *Égypte*.

Keitha's sobs were slowing, and she registered no new misery at the sight of the sample page. *In for a penny, in for a pound,* Margaret thought. *Might as well be hanged for a sheep as for a lamb.* Although the sodden Keitha did not look like a cynical criminal.

Staring at the sample page nestled in its customized carrying case, Margaret remembered an afternoon in the library when she'd found Keitha poring over a bound volume of eighteenth-century fashion journals.

"Your mother was a bookbinder!" she cried accusingly, as if that were guilty in itself. "That's how you learned how to do this!"

Keitha, who had sunk onto a chair and was looking smaller and smaller, nodded. "She hated destroying books, but every bookbinder has customers who see books as luxury boxes."

Hold on, Margaret told herself. *This is a side issue. You're getting ahead of yourself, or beside yourself.* More than anything, she wanted to know why Keitha had done this. And next, how she had done it. But first—was it first?—the perpetrator was sitting here in her office, with the two most precious things that had disappeared. Should she call the police? Security? Instead, she called Gareth, who was always in early, and told him there was something he urgently needed to see in her office. But she also asked him not to arrive for ten minutes. She texted Claire at home, asking her to get to the museum as soon as humanly possible.

Then she moved her chair out from behind the desk and placed it close to Keitha. "Just tell me why." With an effort, she kept her voice neutral, although her head was bursting with what felt like a three-note ostinato—shock, anger and relief.

Wiping a hand across her nose and eyes in an unladylike but deliberate way, Keitha seemed surprisingly eager to answer.

"Because Dior was part of that whole . . . that whole thing, that mindset, that sensibility, that arrogance, I don't know what to call it, that made women feel their bodies were never good enough. He chose models most women could never dream of looking like, and then he made the models' bodies even more impossibly unrealistic. The corsets, the bones, the padding. He wasn't the first or the last, but this show is going to celebrate something that shouldn't be uncritically celebrated. Do you know how many women die or have lifetimes of poor health from anorexia? I kept trying to get you to connect the dots between the New Look and women's bad feelings about their bodies, but you weren't interested. You didn't care."

None of this was new, coming from Keitha, but now her words had a new clout.

She added, with a truculent twist, as if this would make it all right, "We wanted to wake you up."

"Who is 'we'?"

Keitha, who had been looking down at her clasped hands and rubbing first one thumb and then the other, looked up in surprise. "Why, Léa and me. Of course."

"Léa." That partly made sense, but partly didn't. "Was she concerned about what Dior did to women's bodies?"

Keitha looked uncertain. "Probably not as much as I was. She had some other concerns."

"What brought you two together, then?"

Her wording made what they'd done sound harmless, as if they had started a dog-walking business or a catering company, but Margaret couldn't think of another way to put it.

"When I drove her home from Deirdre Ferrar's talk, she asked me about my family. I told her my mother has never recovered from the anorexia that began when she was a teenager, that often she isn't able to work. I guess that led to my feelings about Dior. Léa said we could work together to restore some balance. Everybody worshipped Dior, but we thought the time had come for some criticism."

"So you sent the packages too? Or at least, after Léa died."

"No. I swear, I never sent any packages. I heard rumours that you were getting odd things in the mail, but I don't know anything about them." Keitha began crying again. "Mostly we gave each other moral support. We were tired of the canonization of Dior, and we worked on the logistics together. Taking the belt was Léa's idea, and she regretted it almost instantly. She couldn't bear the thought of it being hurt or lost, but I convinced her that it would be perfectly safe in the cavity I had made in *I Brought the World Home*. She went through the same worries when I took the top half of *Audacieuse*, and when I spirited it home, under cover of my coat, she felt even worse. By the time *Zemire* and the sample page went missing, Léa had died. I don't think she would ever have agreed to those"—a fresh gale of tears—"but I never would have harmed any of the pieces. Never. I took very good care of them. I started here wanting to be a conservator, and I take that seriously. I know that sounds crazy, but I do."

If Margaret had known where to find a Kleenex in the catastrophe that was her desk, she might have handed one to Keitha. There was no stopping the snot and tears she was rubbing away.

"I had to get the dress and the sample page out of the building," she continued. "The dress was too big and the sample page too precious for me to hide them in the museum, but I was so careful. You have to believe that."

"Oh right, hats off to you and your duty of care," Margaret said. "What world are you living in? You sabotaged the exhibition, demoralized the staff, jeopardized priceless pieces of the collection, ruined our relationship with a sister museum, threw your scruffy coat—which, by the way, doesn't suit you—over *Zemire* getting it in and out of the building . . . Don't talk to me about being careful!"

She was winding herself up into the rage this deserved when she heard a gentle knock on the door. She pulled it open and almost shouted at Gareth, as if he were the perp, "Come in!"

Gareth advanced slowly, probably trying to make sense of the miserable young woman huddled over her chair and a furious Margaret. He seemed oddly fascinated by *I Brought the World Home*, which was lying closed on Margaret's desk, but when he noticed that *Zemire* was hanging on Margaret's door, he brightened.

Briefly, Margaret explained. She put a speechless Gareth in her chair and, sitting on the edge of her desk, continued her interrogation.

"How did you do it?"

The question seemed to perk Keitha up and she explained almost brightly, rather as if she were reporting on some research Margaret had requested. Impersonating someone from Conservation and taking the belt had required a wig—a bob with bangs à la Anna Wintour, but black—and a pair of big glasses. Luckily, both Jill Hillman and the docent were keen to put away the accessories on their cart quickly and accepted her help without paying much attention to her. (So, Jill herself was guilty of the negligence for which she criticized the museum, Margaret thought with a grim satisfaction.) The belt fitted neatly into the cavity Keitha had made in *I Brought the World Home*, which no one searching her office had thought to open. When it was time to return the belt, she located a statue outside the reach of the security camera, satisfied herself that the security guard had just left the Etruscan Gallery, slipped the belt out from the book she was carrying and looped it over the statue's neck.

"That was the most frightening part," she added, as if she expected congratulations.

"What about the top half of the dress?"

To Margaret's chagrin, Keitha explained that it had not been difficult to glimpse someone keying in the combination for the smaller storage hall while she pretended to be absorbed in some nearby task. In the days before the belt was taken, no one expected any trouble and those who knew the combination made little attempt to hide the keypad with their other hand. Keitha had learned the combination before the belt was taken and security heightened. She experimented with the lights and found that if you pressed the light switch three times once you were in, you could override the connection between the code and the lights. That allowed her the precious minute or so to take the bodice in darkness. As she did with *Zemire*, she wore the top out of the building, underneath the patchwork coat. (While Margaret shuddered at the thought of the black silk top worn with Keitha's ubiquitous jeans, she recognized that *Vogue* would consider it a very cool outfit.)

"And what about the sample page—how did you know the combination for the safe?" Gareth asked.

It was his first question. Keitha looked almost sorry for him.

"I didn't expect it to work, but I started out by just reversing the numbers of the combination for the storage hall. And there it was."

Margaret avoided looking at Gareth. What a bunch of amateurs she, Claire, Alan and the head of Conservation had been. In their defence, combinations and codes were not their area of expertise, but why hadn't they at least consulted Security? The guard monitoring the security tape was used to seeing Keitha in the storage hall at various times, going about what looked like her normal duties, and he assumed that one of the curators or conservators had buzzed her in. And of course, taking the sample sheet and *Zemire* had been done using the shelving unit as a cover.

Margaret was saved from further self-loathing by the appearance of Claire, who looked as if she had dressed in the dark. One sock was black, one brown, and her long black pullover was inside out. Margaret gave her an outline of the morning's discovery and Claire immediately took charge.

"We need to talk in private," she said, and dialed Thelma in Conservation. "Come to Margaret's office, and bring someone with you."

When they arrived, she put *Zemire* into the arms of a happily flabbergasted Thelma and handed the sample page to Thelma's colleague. "Check out the dress and the sample page and put both of them back where they belong. Put Keitha in my office, close the door, and you, Thelma, please sit outside with something you've been meaning to read while we decide what to do.

Everyone will know the dress and page are back, but don't discuss the perpetrator. They'll know soon enough."

A frightened-looking Keitha was led out. What was next, Margaret wondered, an arrest? Tarring and feathering her on her way out of the museum? Whatever happened, it was bliss having Claire in charge.

As soon as the door closed, Claire asked, "How did you figure out that it was Keitha?"

"It was just a little thing. When we found the top of the dress in the bentwood box, I noticed in passing that the tissue paper on which the top had been laid was too big for the box, and the surplus tissue had a fold that was placed on the top of the paper, so that it touched the dress. Most people put the fold on the underside of the paper. A few days ago Keitha was packing a scarf to return to Rivkah Waldman and I saw her arranging the tissue with the surplus fold on the top, as with the dress in the bentwood box. Consciously I didn't put those two things together, but something was on the verge of clicking for me, I just didn't know what it was. Last night I had a gift to wrap myself, and as usual I put the fold of the extra tissue paper on the bottom. But the light bulb didn't go on until this morning when I passed the wrapped package on the hall table and it all fell into place. Eureka. Or so I hoped. Actually catching Keitha red-handed with the dress and the sample sheet was luck—I was just planning to take her by surprise and accuse her."

While she basked in Claire's and Gareth's admiration, Margaret thought about her deduction. It wasn't rational and logical like Hercule Poirot's use of his little grey cells, she decided. It was more like Miss Marple's intuition, coupled with her attention to the trivial details of everyday life in St. Mary Mead. Whatever it was, she looked forward to telling Will and the girls.

"I wonder when she smuggled *Zemire* out," Margaret said to Claire.

"I'm guessing it was the morning when she pleaded a dental emergency. She did look quite miserable, perhaps from nerves, and she could have worn it under that coat before anyone was checking everything. You and Munro discovered the dress was missing that afternoon. She'd already taken the sample page home, of course."

Gareth assumed it was a matter for the police, but Margaret asked, "Does it count as theft if you return the pieces, or just move them, as in the case of the belt and the black silk top?"

"Technically, she's guilty of mischief in that she rendered something useless or unable to operate as designed," Claire said.

Margaret remembered something about Claire's partner being a lawyer, and this had a nice ring of authority.

Thinking out loud, Gareth was changing his mind. "But do we want to press charges? The publicity won't be happy, and we'll look incompetent in that we allowed an intern to crack the codes. I don't see the Fashion Museum or any museum being keen to lend things to us after that."

Claire and Margaret agreed, he was right. Suspicion would obviously land on Keitha, who would be escorted out of the premises forever within the hour, and the museum would hum with baroque rumours. But there would be no charges and no formal statement to the staff except a useless appeal for discretion.

TWENTY-ONE

Encore: A Scarf, a Brooch, a Handkerchief, a Corsage and a Beret

K eitha sent Margaret a note.

I trust that you will come to see that most of my motives were pure. I hoped that the disappearances would show you some of the anger that Dior inspires and you would have to look at his legacy more seriously. *The New Look* was a golden opportunity to make women see that the image of the female body he foisted on us was a kind of abuse. Sometimes a beautiful abuse, if such a thing is possible, and even more dangerous because of its beauty . . .

But you weren't interested, and that led to a feeling that was not so pure. The more you refused to take my concerns seriously, the angrier I became. Léa wasn't angry. She just wanted you to stop treating Dior like a demigod. But I wanted to punish you, Margaret, and what better way than to sabotage your precious exhibition? That was why the top to *Audacieuse* had to be removed, as well as *Zemire* and the sample page. I enjoyed watching your panic and misery.

Of course, I understand that the idea of any recommendation from you is ridiculous. Luckily, I was accepted into law school last month, so that won't be necessary.

Keitha in law school. Of course. It was to laugh, but Margaret could only rouse a tight smile.

"I SUPPOSE IT WAS LÉA who sent the letters to the news editor at the *Times*," Margaret said to Will. "But who sent those mysterious packages and notes to us? When I knew Keitha and Léa were in it together, I assumed Léa began that campaign before she met Keitha and Keitha carried it on after she died. I still think Léa was behind the packages, but I believed Keitha when she said she knew nothing about them."

She and Will were walking with the girls in Mount Hope Cemetery, over hills and dales busy with angels, soldiers, obelisks, symbolically broken columns and more straightforward nineteenth-century gravestones. Keitha's deformation of Robinson Harkness's memoir had intrigued Nancy and Bee, and they were looking for his tomb.

It was April 20 and still miserably cold. *The New Look* was to open on May 13, the same week as the annual Lilac Festival in Highland Park. On this mean, grey day, blooming lilacs and a polished exhibit seemed equally unlikely in a little more than three weeks. Margaret wound her scarf around her neck more tightly, to the height of a turtleneck.

She had told Will about the possible link Keitha had discovered between Alexander Beyle and the article about Boussac. "Do you think Alexander could have had anything to do with the packages?"

"That would mean he's more than an ambitious intern," Will said. "If he sent the packages, before or after Léa's death, or both, he must have a personal axe to grind. I guess that could be some family grudge about Boussac and the couturier he backed."

He looked dubious. Margaret remembered happening upon Alexander and Patricia Bertelli drinking coffee in Ludwig's. The two looked so disconcerted and, at least in the case of Patricia, downright guilty. When she told Will about their reaction, he laughed.

"Darling, they're having a flirtation, if not a full-blown affair. That's why they looked embarrassed."

Margaret found that almost as hard to believe as the idea that Patricia was part of the sabotage plot. For starters, Alexander was probably fifteen years younger than Patricia. No doubt Will would think that was another example of his wife's naiveté.

The girls had learned to ride their bikes on Mount Hope's spooling paths, and their parents trailed behind them as they visited their favourite graves. As usual, they paid a duty call at Susan B. Anthony's simple marble headstone and tossed an even more cursory look at Frederick Douglass's flush-to-the-ground stone. They preferred the heart-rending statues and inscriptions on children's graves. They stood now at one of their favourites, a family group of three with headstones and footstones designed to look like beds. The grave of eight-year-old Wilhelmine Bembel, who died in 1860, was tucked protectively between that of her parents.

"Thank heavens they've stopped asking us if we would do that for them if they died," Margaret said.

Next, the girls headed for the statue they called "the schoolboy." It commemorated Henry Selden, who died at twelve in 1858, holding a book and leaning against a pillar draped with morning glories. The inscription read,

> *He is not dead, this child of our affection,*
> *But gone unto that school,*

> *Where he no longer needs our poor protection*
> *And Christ himself doth rule.*

"That's pretty cool," Bee said, "the way they rhymed *affection* and *protection.*"

When will they start to realize the unbearable sadness of these children's deaths? Margaret wondered. *Right now they're intrigued by all the accessories and codes, like the fact that morning glories symbolize an early death, but when will that fascination turn to empathy?*

Leaving the schoolboy, the twins listened to their parents talking about the mystery packages. They agreed with Margaret that the first ones were sent by Léa.

"She believed in dividing and conquering," Bee said. "When it came to her accomplices, she diversified. So her collaborator could be someone we've never thought of."

Nancy said, "Keitha was definitely an accomplice, but maybe the package mailer wasn't." She thought for a minute and continued, "It was someone Léa trusted. It was a small job, really, since the packages were probably all wrapped and addressed. The sender rushed the last one out, as if they wanted to get rid of it. Could be they lost their nerve, or had never been all that keen on the assignment. Maybe the sender owed Léa something."

Margaret stared at Nancy. "Yes, of course. Thank you, sweetheart. You're brilliant."

Unlike Margaret's affiliation with Miss Marple, Nancy and her little grey cells were on the Hercule Poirot side of the ledger.

They never happened on Harkness's grave, so Bee took out her phone and looked up its location on the cemetery website, leaving Margaret to wonder why she and Will hadn't thought of that. Under a bas-relief of a globe, they read of Harkness's exemplary citizenship, philanthropy and curiosity—far less interesting that no one in the throng of kids walking to school on Winton Road was paying attention to them.

"About a month before she died. She showed me a drawer in her desk that had three or four wrapped packages in it. She said that these were things she was mailing to the museum. Things that would help them with some exhibit they were getting ready. She said that she wasn't well, and she wanted to ask me a favour. If she died before all the packages had been sent, she wanted me to mail them, a week apart, and she gave me the money for the postage. There were two packages left in the drawer after she died. I felt weird about it. I mailed the first one, but the whole thing was kind of creepy, and I didn't want to wait a whole week to send the second one. So I sent it sooner than she wanted." He hung his head.

"That's all right, Liam. You did what Léa asked and now everything is signed, sealed and delivered."

For the first time, he risked a small smile. "Not quite."

"What do you mean?"

"There was a letter I was supposed to mail to you three weeks after Mrs. Slaney died. I sent it yesterday."

She left a relieved Liam a block from his school, repeating that she would be happy to fill in the context for his parents after he told them. There was no letter at the museum or at home that day, and Margaret wished she had asked Liam what time he had mailed it. Well, it would arrive tomorrow.

She spent most of the next day with the alcoves and window boxes. Like the exhibit as a whole, they were close to completion and awaiting final touches and panicky, last-minute fixes. "The Women Who Wore Dior" brimmed with life. Rivkah had thrown herself into it, and it showed. There were pictures of Rivkah's mother and her friends attending committee meetings in couture suits, going to synagogue in very dressy outfits that sometimes to the twins than gravestones shaped like beds or the schoolboy statue. But for Margaret the excursion had been a success.

NEXT MORNING, SHE ARRIVED at Léa's apartment building at the same time as, weeks before, she'd arranged to go over Léa's Diors with Caroline Whitehead. This time there was no one to buzz her in, so she waited at the front door until Liam O'Connor emerged on his way to school. The look on his face when he saw her was identical to the dismayed one he had worn on that earlier morning, when he flung open his apartment door and found her in the hall.

Margaret had had enough of tearful culprits, so she grabbed his arm and talked fast to fend that off. "No, stay here, Liam. I'll walk you to school and we can talk as we go. I promise, no one is going to blame you. You were doing a favour for a friend, and you had no idea what it was all about. And really, no harm was done. I don't think your parents will be cross either, when I explain—"

"But I don't know what to do with the money!" Liam interrupted.

Margaret was still holding tight to his sleeve and trying to slow his walking. He looked distressed, but at least he wasn't crying. Was he talking about the inheritance Léa had left for his cello lessons?

"What money?"

"The money Mrs. Slaney gave me for the postage," he said, as if that were obvious. "I still have about four dollars left, and there are no more packages."

"I'm certain that Mrs. Slaney would be more than happy to consider that a tip. When did she ask you to take over the packages?"

Liam pulled his arm away from her, and Margaret accepted that he was not going to run away. He looked around to make sure required the addition of straps or a modesty panel at the breast, dancing at fundraisers for Israel in splendid gowns. Margaret had supplemented that with photographs of WASPs doing similar things, also stunningly dressed. The touch screens filled in their lives, including a few audiotapes of women reminiscing about their landmark clothes and a virtual album of society columns from the *Democrat and Chronicle*.

At the end there was a nook with six chairs and a video where Rivkah interviewed women from three generations about what clothes had meant in their lives. She began with women in their seventies and eighties who apparently set their clocks according to the fall and spring couture showings, and went on to their daughters and even to a few grandchildren. Both Rivkah's daughters appeared in the tape. The elder was interested in fashion, but she picked and chose from outlets, garage sales and high-end shops. The younger, an economist who specialized in women's start-ups in the Third World, seemed to regard fashion as Will would have done, had Margaret left him alone. She dressed like a soccer mom on an off day. When Rivkah and Margaret watched the video and the younger daughter came on, Rivkah shook her head.

"And she could look so good, with that face and figure. Where did I go wrong?" And then she smiled, because she was proud of her daughter.

Compared with "The Women Who Wore Dior," the alcove on the design and making of Dior's textiles, although admirable in every curatorial sense, now struck Margaret as possibly too specialist. And definitely a bit airless.

At the costume jewellery vitrine, Margaret found Claire in front of a picture of Dior pointing his baton at something in the pieces of jewellery laid out on a long table. Dressed in his usual white coat, he looked like a doctor whose patients were necklaces, earrings and bracelets.

"My grandmother had some like those," Claire said, pointing to a triple strand of irregularly shaped, iridescent beads. "Looks great, Margaret."

She was less enthusiastic when it came to the sidebar about the American copies of Dior. Margaret had made it the story of two designs that travelled from couture to department stores. One was a ball dress that dropped several of its luxury touches as it travelled down the food chain—a satin edging on the neckline, bows at the dropped waist—but its smart festivity remained intact. The other was a suit that became more conventional in successive adaptations, as outsize buttons on the jacket became smaller and pockets on the skirt moved to the jacket.

Gareth had taken more interest in the sidebar than in anything else in the exhibit, and when Margaret expressed worry about Claire's reaction, he assured her he would put in a good word for it. Watching Claire as she viewed the finished display, Margaret murmured that she hoped this filled in some of the "bigger picture" Claire had wanted.

"A bit," Claire said faintly.

Margaret told herself that she was offering a little-understood window into the economics of fashion but she knew she should probably have tried to illuminate something more gnarly. Once again, she had brushed aside Dior's connections with prominent figures in the occupation and his controlling ways with the female body. Nor was she proud of her deviousness in using Gareth for an end run around Claire. It was not her finest hour, but there it was.

Other than that, Claire had high praise for the exhibit—and then she left, rather abruptly. After her admiration of Margaret's role in the unmasking of Keitha, she almost seemed to be avoiding her. Likewise with Alan—after his apparently kind behaviour when the dress was stolen, he was also steering clear of her.

Margaret was too busy to take it seriously, and she was probably imagining it, but it registered.

SHE FOUND LÉA'S LETTER at home and took it to her bedroom. She moved several changes of clothing from the easy chair that functioned as a second closet and sat down to read.

> Dear Margaret,
> I have no way of knowing whether your exhibit is in the last stages of preparation or has already opened as you read this. But my cardiologist and I know my body rather well by now, and we both feel that my time is drawing to a close.
> My behaviour has been intemperate. I do not apologize for that, because I wanted to wake you up. I've spent my life obeying the rules, so this has been a departure for me.
> You mustn't think that I see Dior as evil. He was generous, sympathetic. Modest, even. If his horizon was narrow, his sister's fate would have made it impossible to ignore what people in the Resistance had gone through. But everything I read about your exhibit said celebration, celebration, celebration. Of his rounded shoulders, his gores and faux pockets. All of which deserve praise, but that's not the whole story.
> Dior flourished in a world where people close to him probably cut some ethical corners. Not that he himself did, as far as we know, but does it lessen his greatness if you let him stand where he was? Not a bad man, but not a hero either. He lucked out, as you say in English. A bystander. He lived between two very different figures—his sister who refused to name her fellow

Resistance workers under torture and Marcel Boussac, who profited enormously from the war but did some good things too.

Dior loses nothing if you open the doors and allow in the complications of his time and, perhaps, his personality. Seeing only the bouquets and the Louis Seize moldings of his showroom while ignoring the chaos just outside feels like another blow to those who suffered so much in the war and its aftermath.

Perhaps that reality undercuts the elegance. Or perhaps it gives the beauty of his clothes more depth, more *gravitas*. I don't know. I do sometimes wonder if the New Look's reliance on a glamorous, outmoded past was a way to forget the Occupation when so many had made deals with the devil.

One photograph that Deirdre Ferrar showed during her talk, taken soon after the Liberation, has stayed with me. The one where, on a desolate street, a model places her gloved hand on the battered gun of a tank as if it were a side table. Her hat is atrocious, as befits 1944, but her coat dress still looks chic and the leather of her beautiful pumps and bag is polished to a high gloss. In the background, a man sits on the sidewalk, his worldly goods in bags. From one point of view, the photograph is monstrously insensitive, a fashion version of Marie Antoinette's "Let them eat cake." From another point of view, it is ... realistic? Even optimistic, as in the "life goes on" cliché?

Whatever it was, that rawness and incongruity was the ground in which the house of Dior grew. How fitting that the Dior family fortune came from manure. Not from lilies of the valley, his favourite flower, but something more pungent, which in its turn allows flowers to thrive.

    The intensity of the war, when we seemed to live on secret symbols and adrenalin, made it impossible for me to leave behind my little cache of souvenirs—the scarf, the pin and so forth—when I came to America. I hoped they would fill out your idea of Dior's world, and perhaps they have. Or perhaps they will.

    Dior had lots of good fortune—the artistry he was born with, his training in Lelong's house, Boussac's financial backing. But his greatest luck was that he was a Gentile. And Fanny Berger was fatally unlucky in that she was a Jew.

    You probably suspected that I worked in Fanny Berger's atelier. I saw the misgiving on your face when you asked the name of the millinery studio where I worked and I made one up. Just before Fanny was forced out, I found a job in Lucien Lelong's house. I stayed in touch with Fanny's assistant Celestine, and she gave me Fanny's diary.

    (Here I permit myself a personal digression and even a pat on the back. Of all my little attempts to make you think again about Dior and his legacy, I was most proud of the radio script I created from Fanny's diary.)

    Like Dior but not so spectacularly, I too had luck. My doctored papers were good, and I was fair enough that no one suspected I was Jewish. My parents were not so fortunate. By the time I began working for Lelong, they had vanished into the camps.

    Mary Margaret Abrams. Your name splits into two, Christian and Jewish. When we first met, I said there must be a story behind that name. You answered that someday, when we didn't have dresses to look at, you would tell it to me. Isn't it time you gave some thought to that story?

I wish you luck with that.

Don't be too hard on Keitha. She has a good heart and a good brain—she's maybe a bit over-passionate. I couldn't join her in her horror of Dior's body shaping. No doubt we accepted his impossible standards too easily, I see that now. As a *petite main*, I also saw how his designs could be adjusted for women of many sizes and shapes, but if Keitha were here, she would tell me that is beside the point.

For what it's worth, I feel sure your exhibition will be a good one. You have lots of wonderful pieces and you don't need mine. I think I told you that I have a rather strict personality. Keeping my things from the exhibit is my small and I hope not too mean-spirited refusal to add to Dior's glory. He has enough.

All the best,
Léa Slaney

MARGARET SAT SMOOTHING the sheets of paper, closely filled with Léa's shapely French cursive. Léa called herself intemperate, and Margaret thought: *So am I. And so is Keitha. If we were pieces of fabric, they would not have much give.*

Léa and Keitha had used the same phrase, that they wanted to wake her up. Probably part of waking up meant accepting that Dior was what Léa called him, a bystander. But what would Dior have done if he declined to be a bystander? Leave Lelong? Refuse Boussac's financial support? That would have been silly. Dior did what he could do, and did it sublimely. She remembered the theory Lydia had mentioned about family being the handful of stories we never tell. Postwar France was also buttressed by deliberate forgetting and untold stories. Dior must have known his share of those, and very possibly played a part in some of them. One of the fortunate few in a horrific time, he remained a complicated onlooker, from one side admiring his heroic sister and from the other exalting his colleagues who lived only for fashion.

Still sitting in her bedroom, Margaret wondered what had happened to the family tree Harold Abramson had made for her. She wanted to show it to Nancy and Bee, but she had mislaid it. She had a thought and went to her unloved closet. There, in the pocket of the jacket she had worn to the Abramsons', was the missing piece of paper.

There was much more information there than she'd had time to absorb when Harold gave it to her. Unknown places, like Biały Potok and Czernowitz, in what was then the Austrian province of Galicia, were carefully noted. In a quick glance at Wikipedia, Margaret read that Galicia now spanned western Ukraine and southeastern Poland. From there, in the first decade of the twentieth century, Abramsons, with their relatives the Rosenstocks and Saltzes, travelled to Syracuse. That answered the question of her grandparents' origins, but Margaret still didn't know what language they spoke. She stared at their names—Selig, Machla, Ester, Meyer, among others—wishing she had a picture of each one of them.

She called Harold before supper that evening, and after exchanging brief pleasantries, she thanked him for the family tree and asked, "What about the Abramsons, Rosenstocks and Saltzes who stayed behind in Galicia? There must have been some contact, at least at the beginning, between those who emigrated to America and those who didn't."

"I've wondered about that too," Harold said. "If anyone knew, it would have been my cousin Ruth. But second best would be my sister June, the one who's your father's age. Not that she knows much about that generation, but she knows how to find out things. There are all kinds of guides and people who help with researching your Jewish ancestors, and that kind of thing is catnip to June."

They agreed to have lunch with June once *The New Look* had opened. Léa had prodded her about her Jewish/Christian origins, and Margaret agreed: it was time she gave some thought to that story.

After supper, she said to Will, "I'm just going back to the museum for a while. I haven't heard any cries for help with homework, so I think you're safe."

"What is it that can't wait until morning?"

"I just need to look at something in peace and quiet. I won't be long."

What she needed to look at was the whole exhibit, the clothes first of all, arranged around the central circle or in companionable small groups elsewhere in the main rooms, the sidebars including the one on the Dior copies, Rivkah's alcove and the one featuring Dior's use of textiles, the vitrines that showcased his use of costume jewellery and Roger Vivier's shoes. Dior the artist, the tastemaker, the businessman, the benefactor and beneficiary of an army of associated trades.

She ended at the seven window boxes that held Vivier's shoes. Once she had read Léa's letter, she had known that would be her final stop. Oh, how she loved those shoes, their modesty, their refinement, the way they welcomed the foot and the leg into the whole outfit. The fact that, unlike the vulgar, vertiginous stilettos of today, they allowed women to walk normally. *Touché, Keitha,* she thought, and almost smiled.

"I'm sorry," she whispered to the shoes. "You're beautiful."

But there was nothing to be done. She went backstage, knowing perfectly well that the backs of the boxes were screwed on, but she needed to run her hands over them. It was as close as she could come to patting the shoes.

"YOU WANT TO *WHAT*?"

It was early the next morning, and she was talking to James Delgado, the Senior Designer, who was ordinarily famous for his calm. He was a bluff, good-looking man with a great head of white hair and aviator glasses, which he was now pushing into the bridge of his nose as if he couldn't believe what he was seeing. They were standing in front of the vitrines with the shoes.

"It's, what, two weeks until the exhibit opens?"

"Nineteen days," Margaret said.

"That's completely impossible, and you know that."

"James, I'm not saying it's going to be easy, and if I didn't know that you could do it, I wouldn't be here. But look"—she gestured toward the boxes—"the main work is done. We have the boxes, and the new things are just going to fit inside."

"But what are these 'new things'? You say they're coded messages and keepsakes and mementoes, but what are they? Are they shoes, that stand up by themselves? Or jewellery, that needs custom-made supports? Or what?"

Margaret mumbled something about him having to see them.

James was not done. "You realize my staff is finished with *The New Look*, or they thought they were. They're busy with the dinosaur show, which is *really* big." (As if *The New Look* were tiny.) "And who's going to write the panel? And the texts? And when will that be ready?"

At least he sounded resigned, which was a relief.

"I'm doing all the writing, and you'll have it very quickly."

Fifteen minutes later, Margaret and an even more incredulous James stood in his studio. She had brought the items destined for the boxes and James had spread them out on his drafting table.

"*Seriously?* You seriously thought this was just a matter of dropping these things into the boxes? You know better than that, Margaret. How do you think we're going to display the scarf and the handkerchief? This brooch is so small it's going to get lost in the box. The corsage is going to need some kind of custom support, and the beret needs a mannequin head. As for the pamphlet and the photographs . . ." He shook his head as if to indicate that the task was not only hopeless but possibly malicious.

Margaret did feel contrite. She knew it was a lot to ask, and she also knew that with much whining and perhaps a little drama it was going to get done, and done well. She noticed that James hadn't asked her why she was insisting on an eleventh-hour change. Curators sometimes said that designers were visual people and that was all the content they needed, but Margaret didn't believe it. James was smart and he deserved to know why this was important. So she told him, and then she went back to her office to start writing before she forgot what she had just said.

She began with something Léa had written: that the mysterious things she sent were meant to fill out the picture of Dior's world. Not the world of the perfumed rooms and formal chairs at 30 avenue Montaigne—that was well-known—but another world that was still in the foreground in France in 1947, much as people tried to forget or deny it. The occupation, a place and time where the French grappled with shame, treachery, cynicism, hope, camaraderie and making-do, was the period in which Dior learned his trade. It was also when he attracted the attention of a man skilled at coexisting with the Nazis, his mentor Lucien Lelong, and when his sister was betrayed and imprisoned in a series of brutal work camps. Incongruous as it sounded, this was the shallow, meagre soil in which the house of Dior was planted. The glamour and the luxury of the clothes were an attempt to annul the recent past, a fact that attracted some and repelled others.

Margaret cobbled all this into a draft and sent it off to James with a note.

"Sorry, James, this is rough, but I hope it gives you an idea of the Introductory Panel and what we're trying to create here.

Think of the artifacts as silent witnesses to that world. I have some display ideas and I'll send them with the texts for the individual vitrines. More soon."

She had left the artifacts with James, but she knew them by heart. The tartan handkerchief and the saccharine scarf with its flowers, clasped hands and Staffordshire dogs suggested a single word: *lonely*. How isolated the French in the occupied zone must have felt, with England their only hope for rescue until 1942. No wonder they clung to their symbols of connection with their allies across the Channel. No wonder a stranger sporting a plaid handkerchief in his pocket could rouse a conspiratorial flicker of a smile.

As for the vitrines, the scarf should almost fill the box. James would devise some sort of frame to support it. The handkerchief was more tricky, as it was small. Margaret could search for some pictures of other wartime tartans, perhaps in clothes, as a background. Or should she fill in the other side of the picture, with the reminders of Old France that decorated the Pétainists' fabrics—rural idylls, folkloric prints, portraits of Louis XIV?

Undecided, she moved to the tiniest piece, the knock-off of the Cartier pin of the bird in the gilded cage. The bird facing downward, sticking his head out of the cage as if he were trying to escape, suggested a stifled people. But how to fill the rest of the box? She could find a picture of the original Cartier design, its gold and real gems contrasting with this cheap imitation. Maybe, for contrast, a picture of the pin Cartier designed after the Liberation, of a fat bird sitting at the open door of his cage? She was floundering. Keitha would have made short work of this research and probably found the perfect images to accompany the pin.

Sadly, the felt corsage with a Star of David in the middle of each flower was all too easy to illustrate. The archives were full of haunting pictures of Jewish people wearing the official sign of their misfortune. Many of them, especially those photographed in 1940, looked cheerful, or perhaps defiant. One that came to Margaret's mind showed two young women friends, or sisters, wearing their stars on handsome coats with nipped-in waists. They held hands and smiled at the camera.

She was drowning in images, not sure if she had too many or not enough or the right ones. She sent them all on to James, along with a few stabs at the texts for the vitrines.

He wrote back, "Stop. You're overwhelming me. Meet me in my studio at 8:30 tomorrow morning. Calm down."

That seemed to help. She didn't stop, although she was frequently interrupted by questions from the staff about other parts of the exhibit. Everyone was so fixated on their particular detail that no one noticed what Margaret was doing. She thought for a while about the beret, the double-faced symbol that each side wore to communicate their indisputable Frenchness—traditional and rooted in the countryside for the Pétainists, sympathetic to if not actually a member of the Resistance in the occupied zone. She would have no trouble finding pictures of beret-wearing Frenchmen of all stripes, but for the time being she would not send anything more to James.

She toyed for a while with writing the text for the Vichy pamphlet that advertised a strange array of French products on its cover, from wooden spoons to a couture suit by Lucien Lelong. It was a good example of the canny way Lelong worked to position couture at the heart of French culture, but she was tired. That text would write itself in the morning, she told herself. She sent a mental *merci* to Léa for keeping these mementoes and realized for the first time that the acknowledgement at the end of each descriptive text would read "Collection of Léa Slaney." Would she have hated that or would it have pleased her?

There was only one of the souvenirs that bored Margaret, the program for the fashion show of bicycling clothes. Léa was scraping the bottom of the barrel by the time she had chosen that, and Margaret would not waste one of her precious boxes on it. For the final vitrine, she wanted to move to 1947 and the opening of the house of Dior. There would be one or maybe two photographs of the actual opening—of the crowd, the sashaying models whose big skirts threatened cigarettes and drinks, the feeling of something unexpectedly exciting in the air. (She hoped there would not be expensive rights to pay for those famous pictures.) Accompanying them, in an abrupt change of mood, there would be a photograph taken under the eaves at the top of the building. There, under neon lights and a tightly packed shelf of headless, armless mannequins custom-made for regular customers, an army of *petites mains* bent over their sewing. Signs warned *Copier est Voler* (Copying Is Stealing). The luxury and the drudgery. The show-off fashion show and the patient, anonymous work. A tribute to the clothes and to the women who made them.

When she and James met in the morning, without any more communication, they had both come to the same general conclusion. The walls of each box would be lined with a collage of images from the period—coded jewellery, examples of anglophilia, protests against the Star of David edict, whatever underlined the artifact in the box. In addition, James was planning some modifications to showcase the smallest pieces. For the tartan handkerchief, he would design a headless white bust with a caricature of 1940s lapels drawn on in a bold black outline and a real pocket so the handkerchief could be tucked in. For the vitrine with the caged bird, the box would shrink a bit and another headless bust would have a simple dress top drawn on it, on which the brooch would be pinned. The head he was planning for the beret would have no features except a bushy Gallic moustache made from a clothes brush. Although he would not admit it, James looked as if he was having fun. Margaret let out a big breath. She felt like she had been holding it ever since reading Léa's letter.

TWENTY-TWO

Margaret's New Look

Two days before the launch of the exhibit, Claire asked Margaret to come to her office.

Margaret's heart skipped a beat. Was she going to congratulate Margaret on becoming the new Chief Curator? On her way there, she passed Alan. For the first time in weeks, he looked her full in the face and nodded hello. There was something else in his look that she couldn't translate. Had Claire told him that *he* was the new Chief Curator?

Almost as soon as she took the chair that faced Claire's tidy desk, Margaret knew that things were not going her way. Something about Claire's speech, which was slightly speedier than usual, or the way she kept fussing with her yellow chignon, prepared her for bad news. Claire began by praising *The New Look*.

"Even taking your Sherlock Holmes skills out of the equation, you've done a wonderful job. It's an exhibition the museum will be proud of and that will have a long life touring to other museums. And the way you grounded and enriched our sense of Dior with the new window boxes . . . well, my congratulations again."

That all sounded rehearsed. Then she took a breath.

"I wanted to wait until after the opening to tell you this,

but there's going to be a scoop in the *Times*' Museum Notes for tomorrow. The scoop has Alexander Beyle's footprints all over it and I wish I knew how he found out, but that's not the point. You were an excellent candidate for Chief Curator, Margaret. But the job has so many demands, including a lot of administration and liaising with the academic community, and we've settled on a candidate we think can wear all those hats. To use a fashion metaphor, ha ha. What the *Times* is going to announce is that Deirdre Ferrar is going to succeed me as Chief Curator."

Deirdre Ferrar. Why had that never occurred to her? Deirdre with her PhD, her Leeds accent (far more on-trend than fusty old BBC English), her speaking ability and, it must be admitted, her formidable knowledge.

Margaret managed to say that Deirdre was a fine choice, and mean it. Even though her heart felt more than a little broken. She went to Alan's office and stood in the door.

He looked wearier than Margaret had ever seen him. Maybe even shaken.

"Yes," he said, although so far Margaret had not spoken. "I should have thought of Deirdre. It sounds silly now, but I overheard Claire a few weeks ago talking on the phone with someone and saying that a doctorate was really essential for the Chief Curator. So I thought that meant me."

"And that's why you were avoiding me," Margaret said.

"Yes. I felt sorry for you, so it was easier not to engage."

THAT NIGHT, AFTER THE girls went to bed, Margaret ran a bath. She rarely took one because the tub was too short for her legs, but tonight she was willing to run the water as high as possible in a vain attempt to cover her bent knees. She lay back and let her hair float in the water.

Will knocked on the door. "Do you want company?"

"Yes."

He came in and sat on the stool. The girls had used it to brush their teeth when they were small and they had never removed it.

"You look like that Pre-Raphaelite painting of red-headed Ophelia in her watery grave. Except for the knees, of course. Who painted that?"

"Millais."

"Did the model really have red hair?"

"Lizzie Siddal. Yes." She moved some of her hair off her shoulders. "Speaking of hair and water, did you know that when a Jewish woman goes to the mikvah, the ritual bath after her period, she has to submerge herself so that every single hair on her head is completely under the water?"

He gave her a look. "Mary Margaret. You've been studying the law of your fathers."

"A little. Why not?"

"Absolutely no reason not to. I just wondered. How are you feeling about Deirdre?"

"Well, it smarts. But when I think of all the administration Claire has to do, that part of the job probably wasn't going to be my jam." She had an image of Claire's orderly office and the epic mess in hers. "Alan is consoling himself by saying not getting the job will give him the chance to write a book based on his *Japonisme* exhibit."

"What about you? Would you think of a book about Dior?"

"I don't think so. But now that you mention a book, I'm wondering about maybe editing Fanny Berger's diary. It might ultimately lead to an exhibit about Jews who worked in couture in the occupation, but the diary itself is such a priceless witness to those times."

She had no idea where that had come from. Until she heard herself say those words, the thought had never crossed her conscious mind. But she would let it run around in her head. She could see a cover, with the pink felt hat and Fanny Berger's assured label used for the title.

"But not right now. I'm going to wallow for a while."

AS IT HAPPENED, THERE wasn't much time for wallowing. The museum had agreed at the last minute to Margaret's estimate of the value of Léa's Diors, and Sparshott, Whitehead and Goldman accepted their bid. As Gareth had predicted, it was easier to raise money for additions to the permanent collection than it had been to support *The New Look*, but Margaret was still busy negotiating with the donors.

She submitted to several feature interviews about the exhibit, the most important of which was by the *Times*'s Vanessa Friedman, who actually understood fashion. It amused Margaret to hear herself inserting some historical and even political context into her answers to Friedman's questions. She and Alexander Beyle both came for the press opening. Friedman inspected the front, back and sides of each piece, read every bit of the touch screens and took copious notes. Her review would appear the Sunday after the opening. Alexander looked bored, but his assignment was over. Judging by their body language at the press opening, Alexander and Patricia Bertelli were not as close as they had been that morning in Ludwig's café.

Deirdre FaceTimed with Margaret, and after assuring her that she would have been a "brilliant" choice as Chief Curator but that there was no accounting for taste, she announced she would be in Rochester in a few weeks to see what she was sure was a genius exhibit.

"And I hear you're a dab hand at detection too, good on you. Thanks for clearing up the recent unpleasantness before I take over. It's going to be such fun working with you!"

Margaret rather thought it would be fun working with Deirdre.

The night before the opening for donors and special guests, Margaret dreamed of her mother. By the time she awoke in the thick darkness, the content of the dream had vanished, but she knew it was something about sewing. Even before she went to school, Margaret had seen sewing as a comfort and a permanence. As she grew, it became something outside of and more reliable than the ordinary world where Margaret was too red-headed and too tall, taller than her teacher by the time she was eleven. Now here she was, about to celebrate the apotheosis of sewing. It was normal to feel anxious about the exhibit—she could not remember a time when she hadn't felt anxious about it—but underneath, was she satisfied? She couldn't answer that yet.

In the afternoon, Margaret walked slowly through *The New Look*. Everything was ready for the 7 p.m. opening, from the flowers to the Prosecco chilling in the museum's refrigerator. Alan and Léa were right, the audience wouldn't miss the summer dress that was all pleats, or *Zigomar*. Nor, since they didn't know how close they had come to seeing it, would they miss *Bar*, although it still hurt Margaret to think about it. The presence of *Bar* would have raised the exhibit to a whole new level, but it was not to be. And yet, there was so much beauty and information artfully on display here that *The New Look* was going to be a success.

But not perfect. It would have been more perfect if she had agreed to Keitha's corsetry alcove. But it was still very good. Now that she had walked through it, she was sure of that.

THE WEATHER GODS HAD PULLED themselves together for the Lilac Festival. As Margaret rounded the corner of Rockingham, it was as if the fragrance of more than a thousand lilac bushes had wafted down from the park. At home, her sisters had arrived. Constance, who had the waist and hips to pull it off, was wearing a tuxedo. Lydia, who was petite, looked more vulnerable than usual in a flowered slip of a dress, with a short black jacket. Nancy and Bee were wearing their only dresses and needed to have a brief argument with their mother about her refusal to let them wear lipstick. Will insisted that the grown-ups have a glass of real champagne before descending to the museum's Prosecco, so Margaret went upstairs to change first.

Will came into the bedroom bearing a small, gift-wrapped box. "I wanted to give you this in private. A small token of my admiration."

Inside was a pair of long white laces.

"Will. You are sweet."

On second thought, that wasn't the right word. *Sweet* was probably not the effect he was going for. That was the thing about lust: until it seized you, it could be hard to remember its power, especially when your exhibit was about to open.

"But where is the rest of it?"

Remembering his morning-after rush to hide the mistreated corset, she realized she did not know where it had gone.

"I hid it in the bottom drawer of my desk, underneath the drafts of *The Mystery of the Chalice and Paten*."

She kissed him then, seriously, by way of a promise.

"Now go. I have to dress and the girls have to do my hair."

THE RECEPTION AREA OUTSIDE the exhibit was full of guests and the heady scent of lilacs.

"I know you asked for lilies of the valley," the event planner whispered to Margaret, "but it's early for them and they're too small to make much of a statement."

Margaret was fine with that. The extra-large bouquets on tall stands looked very Dior-like. She could imagine his mother growing them in her Normandy garden.

More than one person said, "Margaret, you look absolutely wonderful. This is a new look."

The more discerning of her well-wishers knew that it was, in fact, an old look. Rivkah's friend Tom Rowley had taken Dior's *Pondichéry* evening jacket and made it his own. Or Margaret's own. She considered it more a homage than a knock-off. Originally Tom had thought of a green fabric, but Margaret wanted something closer to the heavy, off-white linen Dior had used. Together they had scoured Rochester's yard goods shops, and in a vast brick warehouse on Anderson Avenue, not far from the art gallery, they found an upholstery fabric that was almost canvas-like in its heft. It was machine-embroidered with drooping blossoms and Tom himself added another layer of birds and flowers with iridescent thread and green sequins. Margaret wished she had taken a picture of oversized Tom embroidering his delicate, meandering vines. Dior had lined his jacket with emerald silk, and to highlight Margaret's hair, Tom had extended the silk to include generous cuffs and lapels.

"Swirl as much as you can," Tom told her, "to show off the lining."

Margaret was not much for swirling, but she loved the swing of the jacket. She remembered Léa talking about working on *Pondichéry* and saying that she was "rather known" for the back pleat that gave the jacket its swing. As she used to imagine when she fantasized about buying *Pondichéry*, Margaret wore her version over a black cashmere sweater, tight black slacks and ballet flats. The girls had made her a messy bun, with just the right number of tendrils, and Margaret had to admit it suited her.

Rivkah approached, resplendent in the blue sheath with the red roses they had seen in Peppermint. The long line of the rose stem gave her the illusion of more height, helped by scarily high heels.

She widened her eyes in admiration at Margaret and said, "I guess the grey smocked dress has fallen to Number Two."

Margaret laughed in agreement.

The guests could drink and nibble in the reception area but not in the exhibition hall itself. Margaret had not been able to pry herself from well-wishers when Helena returned from walking through the exhibit and actually told Margaret it looked very good. Then she reverted to type.

"What a disappointment being passed over for Chief Curator must be, Margaret. Do you have any plans for the future?"

Avoiding the implication that she had no future, Margaret said that she was going to be busy with *The New Look* for a time, while she organized its tour to other museums. Then she began talking, almost thinking out loud, about what she called "the faintest glimmer in my mind," editing Fanny Berger's diary. Caroline Whitehead had told her the profits from the sale of Léa's Diors and her other assets would go to a permanent exhibit in Washington's Holocaust Museum about the German occupation of France. She assumed that Léa had left the diary to the Holocaust Museum, so that would involve negotiations and perhaps a co-publication. Rather than frustrating, she found the potential complications absorbing.

Helena lost interest in these details rapidly and left to greet Constance and Lydia. Margaret was almost amused that her newborn idea had acquired considerably more heft since she had first mentioned it to Will. Today she was thinking of a cover that featured the photograph of a relaxed, happy Fanny Berger in her late thirties.

Rivkah took her over to meet several of the women whose mothers and grandmothers figured in her alcove. A tiny woman with bright-red hair was motoring her wheelchair around the central circle of outfits. When Rivkah introduced her, she nodded at Margaret's jacket and emitted a short guffaw.

"Well, they say imitation is the sincerest form of flattery."

Astonishingly, this was Barbara Halprin, the original owner of the museum's *Pondichéry*. Margaret stared at her, calculating that she must be in her mid-nineties. The old woman knew exactly what she was thinking.

"Yes, I was a child bride," she said coquettishly. "I bought it soon after I was married."

She must have been using the child bride line for more than half a century, probably as long as she had been dyeing her hair.

One redhead to another, she eyed Margaret's jacket more closely. "That was a good idea, to use the green for the cuffs and collar. In my day, redheads weren't supposed to wear green, so I was being a bit rebellious even to choose something with a green lining."

Claire was gesturing to Margaret, so it was almost time for her to welcome people and make a few acknowledgements. While Claire made her way through an overlong and over-flattering introduction, Margaret picked out Gareth, Alan, the Hillmans, the O'Connors, the Abramsons, Helena and her sisters in the crowd. Will had positioned Nancy, Bee and himself at the front. Léa and Keitha were not there, of course, and she still had to reckon with their impact.

She had had a plan for her remarks, but now she struggled to corral her scattering thoughts. What she wanted to do was to acknowledge her muses for *The New Look*, other than Dior—her grandmother and her mother. That would involve summoning up her grandmother's dining room table, where as a child she watched Marg and her mother flashing their scissors through fabric, taking a chance on a new style, debating the placement of a dart or finessing a shortcut that was not part of the pattern. Their seriousness, their skill and something about the look on their faces as they worked, concentrated and serene, had prepared her for Dior. Two modest women, one an immigrant, sewing at home.

She had no idea how to do that justice without sounding sentimental. And she must try not to look at Lydia, whose eyes could brim at a second's notice. As if she knew what was coming, Lydia was already blotting her eyeliner and even Constance looked tearful.

Finally, Claire finished and beckoned Margaret to the microphone. Now there was nothing to do but wing it. She extended the microphone six inches and took a deep breath.

ACKNOWLEDGEMENTS

My thanks to Robert Ashenburg, Miriam Ganze and Emma Smith for filling out my picture of Rochester and Syracuse. I benefitted from Gethin Edward's intimate knowledge of the Anglo-Catholic priesthood. Thank you, Marta Braun, for advice on the ways of graduate students and for making it possible for me to see *Murder of a Hatmaker*, Catherine Bernstein's documentary about her great-aunt Fanny Berger.

Marni Jackson read an early draft of this novel with her trademark combination of enthusiasm for what worked, solutions for what didn't, and all-round perspicacity.

Thanks to Lauren Warshal Cohen for some illuminating conversations about what it means to be a Jew.

My greatest intellectual debt is to Alexandra Palmer, whose three books—*Couture and Commerce: The Transatlantic Fashion Trade in the 1950s*; *Dior*; and *Christian Dior: History and Modernity, 1947–1957*—have been a master class in my understanding of haute couture and one of its greatest practitioners. "Christian Dior," her landmark 2017 exhibit at the Royal Ontario Museum, where she was the Senior Curator of Fashion, was the beginning of what became *Margaret's New Look*. I hope something of her learning and delight in Dior has informed my novel, but all mistakes are my own.

Although my skills do not extend beyond simple hems and button replacements, my two grandmothers and my mother were excellent seamstresses. Pearl Ashenburg, Katherine Siegl and Elsie Ashenburg introduced me to the absorbing world of fabrics and patterns and were profound influences on this novel.

With every book of mine published by Knopf Canada, I'm impressed all over again by the dedication and professionalism of the people who work there. John Sweet was a sympathetic and always conscientious copy editor. I didn't think Kelly Hill could surpass herself on the fourth book of mine she has designed, but she has, with a smart, elegant cover and wonderful illustrations. Thank you, Sharon Klein, for being the perfect publicist. And thank you, Martha Kanya-Forstner, for guiding the publishing of this novel through all the highways and byways a novel must travel.

As usual, my biggest thanks go to my agent, Samantha Haywood, and my editor, Lynn Henry. Samantha was her wise, honest, strategic and tireless self—thank you, Samantha. And Lynn Henry walks a tightrope of tact mixed with firmness, generosity mixed the clearest eye and, always, a determination to make the book the best it could be. Thank you, Lynn.

~

The recipe for Gabrielle Hamilton's "Sous-Chef Salad" is from *The New York Times*, July 24, 2021. And the poem ("This world of dew") that Margaret connects with the death of her father is by Kobayashi Issa (1763-1828), translated by Pico Iyer.

KATHERINE ASHENBURG is the author of six books and many magazine and newspaper articles. She has written for *The New York Times*, the *Times Literary Supplement, The Globe and Mail*, and *Toronto Life*, among other publications. Her previous books include the novels *Her Turn* and *Sofie & Cecilia*, and the nonfiction books *The Mourner's Dance: What We Do When People Die*, and *The Dirt on Clean: An Unsanitized History*, which has been published in many territories and languages. In former incarnations, she was a producer at CBC Radio, and Arts and Books editor at *The Globe and Mail*. She lives in Toronto, Canada.